LOOK SMART

WORK FOR IT
BOOK SIX

ALY STILES

WWW.SMARTYPANTSROMANCE.COM

COPYRIGHT

This book is a work of fiction. Names, characters, places, rants, facts, contrivances, and incidents are either the product of the author's questionable imagination or are used factitiously. Any resemblance to actual persons, living or dead or undead, events, locales is entirely coincidental if not somewhat disturbing/concerning.

Made in the United States of America

Print Edition
ISBN: 978-1-959097-11-2

NATE

"Dude, she's checking you out," my roommate says through a sip of his beer.

I resist the urge to look, one, because I have no idea who Marcos is talking about, two, because it wouldn't matter even if I did, and three... Actually, those two are probably good enough.

"Hey, you listening?" he asks.

"Yep," I say, staring at my phone. "Did you know cats can be allergic to humans? I guess that makes sense."

My other roommate Nash's sardonic amusement to my left earns him a mental high five. At least one person in my life isn't convinced that the cure for a nasty breakup is another doomed relationship. For real, that's like treating a bad burn with another burn. Wait, do they do that?

I type the question into the search field but miss the answer when my personal property is swiped from my hands by someone who claims to be my best friend.

"She's gorgeous," Marcos says.

"Who?"

"The woman checking you out."

"So?"

"So, you should talk to her."

"Why would I do that?"

"Because she's your soulmate," Nash cuts in dryly. "Look. She has a cell phone, and so do you. Oh, and you're both wearing shoes."

Marcos shoots him a glare that coincides nicely with my snort.

"You're not helping," Marcos says.

Nash shrugs innocently. "What? Proper footwear is the foundation of every successful relationship. Name one power couple that doesn't wear shoes."

Marcos narrows his eyes at him before focusing back on me. "Seriously, man. It's been four months since Myra dumped you. At least *look.*"

My stomach rolls at the reminder, but I'm careful to keep my expression neutral. Four months? He says that like four months is enough time to erase four years of being tethered to "The One." Too bad I was *her* one of many. In our epic fairytale, I was thinking about the M-word, while she was thinking about dating other guys.

But my friends can't know it still hurts. They can't know any of the confusing pain swirling around my secret abyss. I'm too exhausted for that conversation anyway. At this point just getting up in the morning is a cause for celebration. Have any Queen songs been converted to alarm tones?

I add that to my mental search list.

"We're at a resort bar," I say. "Even best case scenario with this person is what? A meaningless hookup? No thanks."

Marcos rolls his eyes. "We're here for an entire week."

"Which means *seven* meaningless hookups," Nash says, earning another glare from Marcos.

Thankfully, this is also the moment a drunk dude decides to re-enact the iconic ship-bow scene from *Titanic.* Unfortunately for him, the faux pirate ship in the corner of the Lost Lagoon Bar & Grille was not designed to be ridden in the height of romantic bliss. It was designed to make tourists say, "Oh, look at that half-pirate ship," so within seconds, Drunk Dude is crashing to the floor in a very unromantic flail.

Restaurant staff rush to the scene, and judging by their irritated expressions, this isn't the first time an inebriated amateur sailor has tried to ride a glorified wall-hanging. No one asked, but in my opinion, if the answer to the question, "How many potential lawsuits have been caused by this cheesy theme prop?" is more than one, that prop should be removed.

"And that, my friends, is why you drink responsibly," Eva quips as she approaches the table with Paige at her side. Eva Reedweather and Paige Andrews have become inseparable since Marcos' girlfriend joined business forces with Nash's. You would think besties pairing up with besties would be a good thing. I suppose it is for everyone except the perpetual fifth wheel (i.e. me).

I steal my phone back from Marcos and check the time. 9:30. I've been "social" for forty whole minutes. I'm just a regular rockstar tonight. (No offense to Nash who's an actual rockstar.)

"Where are you going?" Marcos asks when I push up from the table.

"I should head back to the room to prepare for tomorrow."

"Wait, are you presenting?" Paige asks with a disturbing amount of excitement for someone who's not even registered for this conference. I have no idea why she and Nash are even here. Neither of them work in the telecom industry.

"No," I say. "But I have an important person to track down."

"Nate's a bounty hunter," Nash whispers.

"Ooh, who are you hunting?" Eva asks, stuffing a fry in her mouth.

I indulge her only because she stole it from Marcos.

"Someone from your firm, actually."

"The Evolve Agency?" Paige jokes. "It's just Eva and I so far. Which of us do you need?"

"Not the firm you started," I say dryly. "Eva's other one."

"Reedweather Media?" Eva asks.

I nod. "Well, the parent company, Sandeke Telecom. The whole reason I'm here is to convince your Senior Director of Contingencies and Collateral Mitigation to use Eon Tech for all network and power systems needs."

"What the hell is a *Senior Director of Contingencies and Collateral Mitigation*?" Nash asks.

Great question. My boss' answer was, "Who cares? Get the account."

So here I am, three weeks into my lateral move to VP of Northeast Sales, nowhere near the Northeast. But hey, the annual gathering of the *TELECOM*munity at *Tele-Con* can only happen in four-star hotels in tropical states. It's an unwritten rule for any event that involves executives schmoozing other executives during company-paid luxury vacations. I thought it was fortuitous that my closest friends were also invited: Marcos representing SAT Systems, Eva representing Reedweather Media/Sandeke Telecom, Nash and Paige representing people who use telecom, I guess.

And me.

"We have a *Senior Director of Contingencies and Collateral Mitigation*?" Eva asks.

It's not a good sign when even a company executive doesn't know the person you're supposed to woo from their firm.

I shrug. "It's a new position, I think. That's why I'm being sent in. I couldn't even find the person on your website. We got a lead from the Sandeke Telecom Director of HR. She's supposedly in the same spin class as our CIO."

"Beverly?" Eva asks.

Marcos' face sours. He's not a fan of Beverly. Something about a spelling error? I don't know any details because the whole story makes him stabby.

"I guess? Not sure. My boss said this person is supposed to be at *Tele-Con* and I'm supposed to secure the account."

"After you figure out who and what that is," Nash says with his irritating mock-business face.

I join Marcos in glowering at our roommate.

"Apparently," I mutter.

"Remind me again why I don't want to be a businessperson?" he asks his girlfriend, who, for the record, is the epitome of a businessperson.

She returns a satisfying scowl, and I leave them to their bickering.

God, I'm tired.

"Okay, well, you kids have fun."

"You sure you can't stay for at least one more drink?" Marcos asks. "We have the whole week to be sober and boring."

"When will you get another chance to ride a real honest-to-goodness pirate ship?" Nash asks, waving toward the weird boatish thing. It's back on the wall, beckoning drunken seafarers from near and afar. Wait, is that a bandana-clad skeleton chained up at the back of it? Why would you sail the globe with a rotting corpse four feet away? And why did the parrot remain on its dead owner's shoulder instead of flying literally anywhere else? That's loyalty.

"Tempting, but my pirate days are behind me."

My playful tone feels realistic enough, and I'm relieved when it seems to fool them. I'm all out of fake energy. Just getting through the last eight hours of traveling has depleted the reserves. It's so hard to smile while your chest is caving in.

But it doesn't matter what's happening on the inside when you're supposed to be the life of the party. The fun one. The charming one. The vibrant, confident, stable one. The one who holds up the walls when they're collapsing and carries the load when others stumble.

I'm the one who has it all together.

I manage a reassuring smile before making my escape. My friends resume their conversations, and I weave through the tables to reach the safety of the lobby. A few seconds later I'm headed toward the elevators, trying to breathe through the suffocating ache in my chest.

Because I'm Nate Hanover, the perfect human in every way.

I'm also a total liar.

2—SUNDAY 9:36 PM

NATALIE

"It's him," Lanette whispers, slapping my arm.

"Ouch!" I rub the spot in protest, and she rolls her eyes. "It's who?"

"The guy from the bar!"

"What guy?"

She rolls her eyes again.

"Uh, the guy you stared at the *entire* time I was telling you about Tina's bachelorette party."

"Who's Tina?"

"Will you stop?" my coworker says.

At least she doesn't hit me this time.

I sigh and try to maintain an indifferent façade. You know, as if I didn't notice that the hot guy with the killer smile that made my entire body hum isn't walking toward us as we wait for the elevator.

"You have to talk to him," Lanette says.

"What? No," I hiss.

"Just say hi!"

"I can't! I've been drinking and you know what happens when I drink. Besides, what if he's in a relationship?"

"I didn't say propose to him. Just, *'Hello, can't help but notice you look like a fellow member of the TELECOMmunity.'*"

I huff a laugh at her horrible impression of me. Also,

"If you say *TELECOMmunity* one more time, I'm telling Theresa to send you home."

"Pretty sure our boss invented this year's catch-phrase."

Actually, she's probably right.

"Fine. But I'm not—"

"Heeey," Lanette hums with a smile that is so definitely not for me.

Crap.

"Hi," the guy says with a quick return smile.

But his gorgeous face immediately settles back into tired lines and the opposite of what I was admiring just minutes ago at the hotel bar. What happened to him? How do you go from celebrity grin to The Grim Reaper in two minutes flat?

"I'm Lanette. This is Natalie. Are you here for business or pleasure?"

Oh geez. Could she have been more creepy?

He looks confused by the continuation of this unnecessary conversation and offers another stiff smile. "Business. You?"

Lanette widens her eyes at me in a clear message. How is she missing the fact that this person is in no state to flirt? Or converse. Or do anything that involves people who aren't him.

"Also business," I say before she can make things awkward.

Well, more awkward.

He nods and focuses on the display above the elevator to commence the important task of watching the floors count down. His fist is clenched, his athletic body I *might* have noticed earlier now tense. Why do I think he's not marveling at the ability of a metal box to move vertically?

"Oh! I forgot my purse," Lanette lies.

She winks as she backs away as if I might have missed her clever ruse to give us privacy. I didn't and return a hard look as she mouths, "*You're welcome*."

Um, I don't remember thanking her for leaving me alone with some stranger who probably forgot I'm even standing here. You know, because numbers. Are moving. Sequentially.

A few rapid blinks of his pretty brown eyes has me wilting with concern, however. Something must be up. Then again, I'm a tad tipsy so my judgement might be *eh*. Ironically, that last margarita is probably also the reason I blurt,

"Hey, uh… you okay?"

His surprised gaze locks on me, and a rush of heat spreads through my body. Damn, he's gorgeous. Even the red rims around his eyes don't detract from the mysterious-hot-executive vibe. If anything, the exposure of raw pain makes him even more attractive. I'm so sick of pretense and the fake gloss of our world.

"I'm fine," he says.

"Okay, whew. Because you look like you just saw your kidnapped puppy listed on a black-market website for animal testing."

He chokes out a laugh. "That was disturbingly specific."

"And hopefully inaccurate."

"Very."

"Was I close?"

He squints in thought. "Well, I *do* have a computer, so I guess I'd be able to see something listed on a website. That part is plausible."

I grin, and his smile grows into the one that made me eye-stalk him from across a bar.

For the record, I don't do that. Ever. I don't have time to date. My life is about my career. Experiences, traveling, personal enrichment. My twenties are for putting everything in order and achieving goals, so I can enjoy the fruits for decades to come. Companionship is an unnecessary distraction and obstacle. It's one-night stands or no stands for me. I had already decided this career-making event was going to be no stands, because I have my eye on an executive position at The Panther Group by age thirty.

But then this guy smiled and… yeah.

Lanette just about choked on her nacho when she caught my reaction and realized I might be interested in someone. Probably why she made sure to ruin the unexpected development by setting up this clumsy introduction.

"A real computer, huh. What, are you a billionaire's son?"

He smirks. "Yeah, right."

"Millionaire?"

He shoots me a wry smile that makes my insides all tingly. Not good.

"A ward of the state, actually. Our group home had a boat, though."

Group home? I swallow the pinch in my chest. *Awesome job, Nat.*

"Was it a yacht?" I ask, recovering with a teasing smile.

He returns it. "A canoe with a hole, but it was great if you enjoy swimming four minutes after climbing into a canoe."

I'm about to say something and/or run away when two men approach. My crush glances at them, but his lack of response tells me he doesn't know them either—which makes it even weirder that one of the strangers claps him on the back.

"Waiting for the elevator, my boy?" the man asks.

His slicked-back salt-and-pepper hair is coifed to plastic-doll perfection. The younger guy with him has his blond hair styled in a similar manner, making him look like a Halloween version of the older one. They're also wearing nearly identical khakis, blazers, and polo shirts.

"Oh. Uh, yeah," my confused companion says. "You?"

"Yes, yes. Perhaps," the older man says. He crosses his arms and leans back on his heels. "You know, there was a time when riding an elevator was a privilege, not a right."

Okay...? Are we not still in that time?

"You're referring to 1973, sir?" his blond companion asks.

"I'm referring to the industrial revolution, son."

"Ah. That was the year you were poor, right?" the blond asks.

"No, son, that was something else. This is the birth of intercontinental commerce before it was *en vogue*, if you know what I mean." He adds a wink.

What exactly is happening right now?

I glance at my stranger-crush who looks just as confused.

"Oh, right. All the trains and shit," the blond one says.

The older man nods. "Among other things. Ferries."

"Horses."

"Mopeds."

"Trams."

"No, not trams. Wheelbarrows, though. They were doing wonderfully until the Great Wheat Harvest. *Collective Encroachment*, they called it."

Huh?

I can't help but notice that my enigmatic executive has taken at least two steps back.

"*Collective Encroachment.* Of course," the younger guy mumbles, typing something into his phone. Is he taking notes? I can't even follow this conversation, let alone think of a single reason to reference it in the future. "I was thinking Collective *Enhancement* but this makes way more sense if you factor in the crystals."

"Yes! Now you're getting it. A lot of young pups such as yourself make that mistake. Don't be fooled, my dear Chad. They'll try to tell you wheat is responsible for the gentrification of the geo-political severance of the pacific, but it wasn't."

"Ah." The younger man nods and types more stuff into his phone.

"They'll also try to tell you an imperial library can't be built in a day but they'd be wrong about that as well."

Who?! Who is telling people this stuff?!

The older man scratches his chin. "Hmm… on second thought."

He starts toward the emergency exit and waves his protégé behind him.

"Onwards and upwards, as they say," he calls back.

"With pleasure," his companion replies. He even adds a bow, which must be for no one because the other guy is already through the door.

They disappear into the stairwell, and thus ends the most confusing three minutes of my life.

When the elevator arrives a second later, my new-friend-slash-potential-witness follows me inside. I scour my brain for something to say as the doors close. I don't know what just happened, but I'm positive there's no logical follow-up. Even worse, this guy already looked on edge before the odd interruption. Certainly an encounter like that—

"Would you prefer I take a different elevator?" he asks. "I don't want to be guilty of *Collective Encroachment*."

I snort a laugh.

Yep, my attraction just doubled.

"If you don't mind," I say, then hold up my hand. "Unless, of course, you're a member of the wheat guild."

"Did you say *wheat*?" he replies, aghast. "You mean the malicious grain responsible for the gentrification of the geo-political severance of…"

His forehead creases in thought.

"The pacific," I say.

"Right. Yes, sorry. I got stuck on the crystals."

"Don't worry, I took notes if you need them."

He grins, and I push the button for the eighth floor.

"What floor?" I ask him.

"Eight," he says, his eyes flashing with humor.

Oh.

Damn.

"We're not in the same room, are we? Because that would be awkward," I say.

"I'm thinking we'd probably know that by now."

"True. You look like a guy who uses a lot of closet space."

He raises his brows, and I shrug.

"Do I? What do those guys look like?"

"I don't know… Put together?"

I thought that answer would be safe, but maybe not when he frowns. With another tight smile, he faces the door. Guess we're back to watching numbers do literally the only thing numbers can do.

Three.

Four.

Five.

Say something, Nat. You're about to part ways forever.

"You could come check out my closet if you want."

Not that!!

He fires what I count as his fifth confused look of the encounter, and I offer a conciliatory cringe.

"Sorry. That was *not* what it sounded like."

"What did it sound like?"

The elevator dings, and the door opens. Floor eight. Thank the heavens.

I step out with relief, then remember it's time for him to step out too.

Should have followed the wheat crystal debate up the stairs.

"Oh, uh. Well, I guess it sounded like I was inviting you back for sex."

What?!

He just about chokes on air, and I *OMG* myself for that one.

"I wasn't," I rush out. "That's my point. I was just… making conversation."

He hesitates, and I squirm beneath his curious gaze. He doesn't look upset, though. Or offended. Or even embarrassed. He looks… intrigued. By me? Most people aren't a fan of my no-nonsense approach to, well, everything. And when I'm drinking? All filters are off.

"I see. So in this 'making conversation scenario,' how would a person respond to a question like that?" he asks.

"Like what?"

"Like an invitation for sex that isn't."

I bite back a smile and shrug.

"However that person would want to respond, I suppose."

"Is it a nice closet?" he asks.

"Probably the same as yours."

"A little presumptuous, no? What if I have a suite? My closet would be very different."

"Okay, but now *you're* being presumptuous. What if I also have a suite?"

"Do you?"

"No. Do you?"

"No."

That breathtaking grin slips out, and suddenly I'm not sure I *was* just making conversation. My gaze drops to a dark button-down shirt stretched over a body that has seen plenty of action in a gym. His rolled-up sleeves reveal several tattoos that clash beautifully with the business-casual attire. Gosh, is there also a modeling convention going on at the resort? He could be the hot stock-photo dude in all those *"Look how cool it is to work here!"* photos on the Careers page of every company website.

My door looms ahead, which ushers in corresponding disappointment. Even worse, Cautious Brain is now berating me through the margarita mist.

You can't take a stranger back to your hotel room! This is the opening scene of every true crime show ever. You want your polaroid thumbtacked to a wall with a red string wrapped around it?!

Wait. Who uses the red string again? Is that a serial killer thing or more of a spy-conspiracy-theory thing? Do they still use polaroids for crime-solving? That seems inefficient.

"This is me," I lie, stopping at a random room.

Smart, Nat. Good work.

"Yeah?" he asks.

He leans against the wall on the other side of the door to face me. Brown eyes scan me with amusement and something else. Something that triggers all kinds of tiny bubbles in my stomach. Yep, I'm now a walking champagne flute. Fantastic. Why did he have to be smart and funny in addition to being achingly beautiful? Ugh. What an unfair combination in a stranger you can't have.

Well, *shouldn't* have. Because, I shouldn't, right?

Right. Because what you do *have is a big day tomorrow.*

The biggest.

"So, um, have a great night," I say.

He doesn't budge, and I start to panic. What if he *is* a creepy stalker? Aren't the worst ones charming and attractive? Or maybe he's considerate on top of everything else and is waiting for me to get safely into my room before going to his?

Or…

I mean…

He's not… actually interested in staying?

Not safe! Not safe!

Maybe, but I'm not getting a creepy vibe from him. I watched him with his friends all night and nothing about his demeanor screamed *FUTURE THUMB-TACKED POLAROID.*

"Okay, well, I won't keep you," he says, straightening from the wall.

The disappointment is real when he pulls a keycard from his pocket, but it's for the best. I've spent months preparing for this conference. It's bad enough I had one too many drinks tonight. The last thing I need is an even bigger mistake.

No! It's not! Come on. Break one simple rule. Just a small dose of "wild." You don't even risk the occasional rolling stop at a stop sign.

It's true. Stop means stop. But fine.

"Wait. Would you maybe want to see my closet after all?" I blurt out. "Not for sex. Just to hang out. Maybe a drink or two?"

The corner of his perfect mouth tips up in a smirk. "You want to hang out in your closet?"

"Sure. It might be a tight fit, but if we move the luggage stand, we could make it work."

His smile grows—and wow. Maybe I'm actually nailing this hookup thing.

"Sure. Why not?" he says. "It's been a while since I've spent time in a closet. My room or yours?"

He studies the door beside us that is very much *not* my door.

"Yours," I say.

He nods and slides his keycard into the slot.

Oh no.

"It's so weird that they put us in the same room, isn't it?" he says.

3—SUNDAY 9:39 PM

NATE

I can't explain it, so don't ask. Five minutes ago I craved solitude to shatter. Now, there's a stranger in my room. At my invitation. I don't even do this stuff when I'm not spiraling.

Because you were in a long-term, monogamous relationship.

Can we not go there for the next hour, please?

"You want something to drink?" I ask, moving toward the mini bar.

I sense her inspecting the space, which honestly makes me feel better about the whole situation. She's cautious and a little awkward about what's happening, which means she might be having second thoughts as well. We can be hesitant and uncomfortable together. Hell, we can even share some mutual regret tomorrow.

Because there's no doubt I will regret this, whatever it turns out to be. But I guess that's part of spiraling, right? The very definition, really. Bad choices lead to more bad choices which lead to more bad choices until, *bam*—you're chained up in the basement of some sadistic recluse in the wilderness of Saskatchewan or some shit like that. (And yes, it has to be Saskatchewan because no one would ever look for me there.)

"Vodka, if you have it," she says.

I grab a tiny bottle from the minibar and reach for a glass. Shit. I don't have ice.

"I don't need ice," she says, holding out her hand. "Or a glass."

Of course she doesn't.

Her gaze locks on me as I pass her the bottle. It's unsettling how she searches my face like she's looking for something. What does she see? The shiny façade everyone does or the truth I'm having such a hard time hiding tonight? It really is a terrible night for a meaningless hookup. Marcos is getting a demerit for encouraging this. Nash too because he's an ass.

"Cheers," she says, holding up her drink.

I twist the lid off mine. "Cheers."

We throw it back, and the burn feels better than I want it to.

"Wow, it's been ages since I've done shots," she says.

"Really?"

"Not since college." She scans the bar and plucks another bottle from the tray. "You mind?"

I shake my head, watching as she downs this one as well. The odd thing is she doesn't seem like the partying type. The sophisticated way she's dressed, combined with everything she's said and done up to this moment, make me think this is liquid courage more than anything. Courage for what?

And suddenly, the exhaustion returns. This was a mistake. I don't have the energy for a stranger, let alone a hookup. What was I thinking? I'm in no state to be in human contact right now. I'm also not an asshole, so I can't kick her out five seconds after inviting her in. I grab two water bottles from the mini fridge and hand her one.

"So what's wrong?" she asks, dropping to the edge of my bed.

I choke water down my throat. "I'm sorry?"

She waves over me. "The sad puppy vibe. What's it about?"

"Is this the kidnapped puppy on a black-market website or a different puppy?"

Her laugh kind of makes me not regret inviting her in.

She's beautiful, I'll give her that. And it's not even her looks that got my attention, although her silky blond hair would feel amazing in my fingers and her curvy body—whoa. It's her confidence I like most, though. Her direct approach makes me suspect I wouldn't get far with bullshit. She can't possibly know how much I need that right now. How it's the *only* thing I need—one person to see past my façade for two damn minutes to give me a chance to breathe. The fact that she's a stranger I will never see again bumps her perfection rating to a ten.

"You were Mr. Business Cover Model in the bar," she says, rolling the bottle in her hands. "And all of a sudden you're… I don't know. That's what we're trying to figure out."

"Mr. Business Cover Model? Is that something I should be getting paid for? That seems like something I should be getting paid for."

"I didn't say what kind of cover."

"Are there covers that don't warrant compensation to the model?"

She squints her light brown eyes in thought. "Probably. You'd donate your image to a charity magazine, right?"

"Depends. What's the charity that would want a Business Cover Model instead of whatever thing it's supporting?"

"You're missing the point," she grunts.

"Yes, very much so. That's why I'm asking for clarification."

Her eyes narrow playfully, and I can't stop another smile. I shouldn't be smiling. How is this woman getting me to smile so much?

"Are you being evasive on purpose or do you just suck at answering questions?" she asks.

I return an exaggerated shrug, and she releases a quick laugh.

The silence that follows should be awkward. A lot of things should be true of this situation that aren't for some reason. Even the way she drinks intrigues me, how her glossy lips graze the neck of the bottle while her eyes stay trained on me. Something moves in my chest—something I haven't felt in a long time.

Not since…

Never mind.

"Tell me something," she says.

"What kind of thing?"

"Anything. That's the point. Just say the first thing that pops into your mind."

"Have you ever felt like your life is happening to someone else?"

Wow. Okay, then.

She seems just as surprised by my sudden truth-bomb when her playful expression turns serious. I look away, kicking myself. I have no idea where that came from. I'll blame it on the warped history lesson we endured while waiting for the elevator.

"Once."

My guest leans back to brace her palms behind her, and I watch her sink into the plush comforter. Her dark blue pants contrast beautifully with the crisp, white fabric.

"Is that how you're feeling now?" she asks.

I draw in a deep breath.

"I don't know," I say quietly. "It's like the person everyone knows isn't who I am, but I've been that person for so long that I'm trapped. My life, my career, my entire identity is structured around a lie and…"

I rub a hand over my face. "Sorry. I didn't mean to dump on you. I know that's not why you came."

"It is, actually."

I meet her gaze, and she offers a weak smile.

"Truth is, I noticed you in the bar tonight," she says, studying me. "You light up a place. It's impossible not to notice you. Your smile is… magnetic."

I try to muster one now, but my lips barely move. Her attention rests on my mouth, then lifts to my eyes.

"But I never approached you because I wasn't interested in an evening of games and flirtation. As pretty as you are, I hate that stuff."

"Um, thanks?"

"Sorry. You know what I mean."

"It's fine. I wasn't interested either."

Her smirk helps me relax a little.

"Right, well, all of that changed when I saw you by the elevators. My point is, it was your smile that attracted me, but it was your frown that hooked me."

Wow.

She shrugs and takes another sip of water. "We spend too much time playing a role and not enough time figuring out who's behind the mask."

Damn. Who is this person? I'm accustomed to being the smartest person in the room, so this is a fun twist. Her perfect ten just became a twelve.

"What if there's nothing behind the mask?" I say, dropping beside her. "What if all we are is masks?"

She twists her head toward me, and I realize I sat much closer than I intended. Barely six inches separate our faces as we search each other. By the intensity in her gaze, she doesn't seem to mind. I know I don't.

"Doesn't matter for right now," she says, shifting even closer.

Her bare arm settles against mine, igniting long-dead embers. She smells like angels in a rose garden (assuming that's a good smell).

"The beauty of being strangers is that we can be whoever we want to be," she says, her gaze dropping to my mouth. "I never met the guy *everyone knows*, so tonight you can be the person no one does."

I so want to kiss her.

She beats me to it, and before I know what's happening, her warm, shiny lips are pressing against mine. She tastes even better than she smells, like sugar and lime, and I lean in to deepen the kiss. Her sexy hum vibrates through me as she grips the front of my shirt to drag me closer. I slide my palms up her neck and lock her mouth to mine.

Fire rips through me when our tongues meet. There's a desperation to our give and take, an urgency that sends sharp waves of heat through me. She swings her leg up to straddle me on the bed and tangles her fingers in my hair, tugging hard as we devour each other. It's been so long since I've felt like this. Months of no one after months of a lukewarm, dying attraction.

But this? I feel like I'm burning from the inside out. Like I can't get enough, and the way she claws at me tells me she feels the same.

I kiss down her neck, loving how she pulls my hair and writhes against me to some seductive rhythm in her head. Man, that feels good. Too good. All of this. So good it feels… wrong.

Her hips press into me, stirring old, forbidden sparks with each graze. Her lips find mine again as she starts unbuttoning my shirt with clumsy movements. I'm interested in removing her top as well, but not exactly sure where to start with that high-neck silk contraption she's got on. She shoves her palms up my chest and over my shoulders to peel off my shirt, still rocking against me in an agonizing cadence.

My shirt falls to the bed as she explores my body. It feels amazing to be touched, to be wanted, but strange at the same time. Her fingertips sink into my pecs, clawing and seeking and… yeah. This is weird. Hot, but weird.

"Hey, um…" As much as I want to do this—and believe me, my body is *craving* this—it doesn't feel right.

This isn't me, and I don't trust my judgment at the moment.

I gently take her wrist and lower it to her side. With a long sigh, she rests her forehead on my shoulder.

Our heavy breathing echoes around us in the silence, and I feel terrible for leading her on. Is she upset? Probably, but I don't know what to say. I thought I could do this. I *wanted* to—until I didn't.

But my tension eases a bit when she leans back with an apologetic expression of her own.

"Look, I really like you, whoever you are," she says. "And you're incredibly attractive, but this…"

"Feels wrong?" I finish for her with a laugh.

Her surprise melts into relief as she leans back further. She searches my eyes before finally relaxing.

"Okay, yeah. I'm so sorry. Full honesty? I didn't really want to have a fling this week. I have a lot going on and need to focus."

"There's nothing to be sorry about."

She untangles herself from my lap, and now I'm very relieved I didn't attempt an ill-fated extraction of her complicated top.

"You seemed hesitant as well," she says.

I let out a breath. "Yeah… sorry. I'm kind of coming off a bad break-up."

"Ah. So this is rebound sex?"

"Not even. It's… best friend pressure? Exploratory? I don't know."

"You're not a one-night-stand guy, are you?"

"Not really, no. I like my stands deep and serious," I say with a weak smile. "But I *am* a puppy guy."

"And a closet guy."

"And whatever-the-opposite-of-those-dudes-at-the-elevators are guy."

She snorts a laugh and falls to her back on the bed. With another heavy exhale, she grabs my hand and pulls me down beside her. We thread our fingers and lie on our backs for several seconds, staring at the ceiling like we can't decide if this is awkward or not.

I could laugh at the irony as we get lost in our thoughts. My body is still burning from that brief taste of her. There's no question certain parts of me wanted to go further. The way she touched me and then dissolved into that first kiss felt… authentic. It was captivating, charming, and just the right amount of clumsy to be real—like everything else has been since her unconventional approach at the elevators. How quickly awkward became intriguing. Go figure the second I commit to a terrible idea, it falls through in spectacular fashion.

On the plus side, I suppose it's better we crash and burn in the privacy of a hotel room than a physics defying pirate ship.

"You know, if I *was* going to hook up with some hot stranger for steamy conference sex, it would be you," she says finally.

I look over with a grin. "Yeah? Good. Because I'd pick you too."

She grins back at me and squeezes my hand. Something flashes in her eyes before she takes a deep breath. "So this may sound crazy, but do you think we could still hook up for a good conversation? You have no idea how much I need one of those."

"I have a pretty good idea," I say. "Honestly, I'm starting to think hot strangers are better for anonymous conversations than anonymous sex anyway. It's easier to share your body than your soul."

"Exactly. There are secrets that are only safe for someone you'll never see again."

I huff a dry laugh. "My entire life is a vault of those."

"I wouldn't mind a purge if you're up for it," she says.

"I'd love nothing more."

"Great." She straightens and pulls me up. "Should we make some coffee and share our deepest darkest secrets that we can't tell anyone else?"

"Careful what you wish for. Mine go pretty deep and extremely dark."

"My favorite kind. Wait until you hear mine."

4—MONDAY 7:01 AM

NATALIE

What's the protocol for a one-night stand that doesn't involve sex? It's not in my rulebook. Actually, none of this is.

That question parades through my head as I watch my fully dressed crush sleep beside me. I still don't know his name or anything superficial. Our one rule was that we couldn't share information you'd tell a stranger in an elevator. That meant no names, ages, occupations, or the state of the weather and/or sporting events. Basically, the things you'd know about a one-night stand that *did* involve sex.

My non-date's medium-length wavy brown hair, scruffy jaw, and long lashes are even more gorgeous now than they were last night. His open shirt is also sexier than when it was off as it frames his sculpted chest with the rise and fall of each breath. He was a business executive cover model last night. This morning he's… my private fantasy. Funny how a person's inside has such a heavy impact on their outside. Because every secret he shared, every additional glimpse he offered into that complex, fascinating mind just left me more hopelessly hooked.

Thank heavens I will never have to see him again. I hate to think what my rebellious heart would do if it had a chance to explore this person the way it wants to.

Instead, I brace through a rush of panic at the awkward confrontation about to come. Once he wakes up, we'll have to acknowledge what happened, and what happened isn't something I want to acknowledge. We bared our souls for hours, then fell asleep like middle schoolers at a slumber party. That's strange enough. Even worse, we now have an entire army of forbidden closet-skeletons dancing around the room, making this morning's sun way too bright. I need to escape before he wakes up and lures me into a bigger mistake with that criminal smile.

Except I can't stop staring.

What is wrong with you? You've seen hot guys before. Let it go. You have exactly one hour and fifty-two minutes to snap out of this irresponsible haze and return to the real world.

Right. The real world. For me, that means a 9 AM workshop called, *Making An Impact on the Saturated Consumer*—also known as, the workshop being sponsored by Sandeke Telecom, one of the biggest telecom companies in the country. They'll be leading four this week, and I've signed up for all of them. I don't even know what two of them are about. All I know is that I'm supposed to track down their Senior Director of Contingencies and Collateral Mitigation to sell them on The Panther Group's "unrivaled network systems backup technology and emergency service plan."

It's 7:07 when I check my phone, which means I'm already behind schedule if I'm going to meet Lanette for breakfast at eight.

Where's the workshop on, "How *not* to make an impact on a sleeping consumer"?

Step one: Don't roll off the mattress and shake the entire bed.

Crap.

"You leaving?" he asks in a groggy voice.

He blinks those pretty eyes at me, a deadly half-smile tipping up the right corner of his mouth. Have I mentioned he's cute?

"Yes. Our slumber party was fun, but nature calls," I quip.

By the sly grin on his face, I said something funny.

"You can use my bathroom if it's an emergency," he says.

"What?"

"*Nature calls* means you have to take a piss, right?"

Shoot. It does.

"Maybe that's what I meant," I huff.

"Okay." The humor in his eyes knows I didn't. "Offer stands."

"Thanks, but *duty* also calls."

"As it so often does," he replies, but his smile settles into something more serious when he shifts to his back and studies me.

His unbuttoned shirt falls open, exposing every line and groove of his chest and abdominals. Even his pants are a tad lower than they should be, hinting at a path to something I really, *really* want to explore. I'm pretty sure he wants to show it to me when his gaze drops to the straining fabric around my chest that also shifted from a night in someone else's bed. For the record, my body did not love being squished in this top for twenty-four hours. The website said size twelve, but there's no way that's true.

"Are you staring at my breasts?" I ask, narrowing my eyes.

"No," he lies, that grin returning. "Are you staring at my abs?"

"No," I also lie, forcing my gaze back to his face. But that's where that ridiculous smile is, and ugh. So much for my plan to escape before something like this conversation occurs.

"Seriously, though. Thank you for the chat last night," he says, looking quite serious. "I needed that. To be real, you know?"

Oh, I know. So much.

"Me too. And hey, maybe one day we'll meet up at another hotel for actual conference sex," I say.

He smirks and tucks his arm under his head in the sexiest adjustment of all time. For real, does the guy only move in cover model poses?

"Conference sex, huh. Is that different than regular sex?"

"Very different," I say, adjusting my clothes as I hover beside the bed.

"How so?"

"To start, there are rules that don't apply to regular one-night stands."

"Which are?"

"Does it matter?"

He shrugs. "Maybe. I'm here for a conference. I'd love to know the rules just in case the opportunity arises. Well, another one."

I know from his confession last night that he was in a serious, long-term relationship that hurt him deeply. Maybe he does need a refresher on how the *casual hookup* thing works. Based on my irritating crush on this guy, I probably need one too.

"Okay, fine. Rule number one: No cheating. Leaving your significant other at home doesn't give you a free pass to step out."

"Shouldn't that be a rule for regular sex as well?" he asks, tilting his head.

"Well, yes, but… Fine. Whatever. Rule number two." Let the record show that I'm ignoring his adorable smile right now.

Rule number two… uh-oh.

He raises his brows. "Does rule number two also apply to regular one-night stands?"

I shoot him a mock glare. "That's not the point."

His laugh draws a smile from me, and I take a quick mental inventory of the other rules. Yeah, maybe they all apply to regular one-night stands as well. No exchanging contact info, no talk of future encounters, no… wait! I've got one.

"Rule five is exclusive to conferences," I say with some measure of triumph.

"I'm intrigued," he says, swiping his phone from the nightstand.

"What are you doing?"

"Taking notes."

I smack him with a pillow, and he chuckles as he swats it away. Gah, there are so many rules I want to break with him right now.

Focus, Nat. This is exactly why the rules exist!

"Rule five, if you must know—no acknowledging the other person at conference events throughout the week. That means no flirty behaviors in public, especially in front of coworkers. There's no cutesy saving of seats at seminars or sitting together at meals and crap like that. You're not a pretend couple for the week."

He nods. "That one makes sense. I'll remember that."

"Oh! And another big one. No hooking up with anyone from your own firm, a customer, a vendor, or a rival firm. Conflict of interest and all that."

"Isn't that pretty much everyone at a conference? Isn't that *why* there's a conference?"

"That's not the point," I mutter.

The glint in his eyes makes me suspicious of his grave nod. "Well, I very much appreciate the guidance. This could have been an awkward week if I wasn't aware of the rules."

"You're welcome," I say in a smug tone. Also, now I'm very late.

I slip on my shoes and gather my belongings. "Hey, so, I really have to go. I'm supposed to meet someone for breakfast."

"Ah. Well, hopefully the person isn't a conference hookup. Rule number five, right?"

He lifts his hands to block my second shot with the pillow. His grin, though. I'm already jealous of whichever lucky conference attendee catches his eye. Pretty sure the rules were invented to protect people from impossible temptations like this guy.

"Good luck at your conference," I say, "Whatever it is."

"Same," he replies with a heated stare that makes me think he might be jealous of whichever conference attendee catches *my* eye. Yeah, pretty sure that won't happen after the standard set by this one. Who's going to be good enough to take back to my room knowing I turned *this* person down?

I'm adding "not sharing your soul" to the list of one-night stand *and* conference sex rules.

But you didn't even have sex.

Fine. Then I'm adding it to all the rules.

"Have a great life, Puppy Guy," I say.

"You too, Closet Gal."

I shake my head with a smile and force myself toward the exit. Why is it so hard to leave? What is going on with me? Just days ago I was gushing to my dad about how grateful I was to be single. My best friend Reece even gave me a lone monogrammed towel and one set of silver cutlery as a joke for my twenty-sixth birthday. I did not laugh. I *did* love the towel, though, because it was super soft and had this… never mind.

I feel my new friend's attention at my back the entire walk to the door. It burns through my silk blouse and pulls at my heart with magnetic force. He doesn't say anything, but he doesn't have to. Something incredible happened last night, and we're abandoning it. There's no question he's special, and if I had any time or interest in "special," I'd be turning around and demanding his name and number.

But Rule Number One in the Natalie McAllister Handbook for Survival is *No Attachments*. Not to a person, place, or thing. Attachments are anchors, and anchors, by design, hold you back. Life is too short to be weighed down by anything. That's why my rules are non-negotiable and strict. For twenty-six years, they've preserved my freedom to pursue my dreams without regrets.

And now, my rules are what give me the strength to yank open the door and convert one of the most captivating people I've met into another fond memory.

* * *

I lied to Lanette. Thankfully, lying doesn't go against any of my rules, although I try to do it as little as possible. But come on, even the most honest person has to fib on occasion. Are you really going to tell Great Aunt Esther that the porcelain leprechaun she just scored for you at her deceased neighbor's estate sale kind of freaks you out? Or your boss' boss that their new teambuilding initiative is total bullshit and exactly no one wants to spend their weekend freezing their ass off at a ropes course with coworkers they hate?

No. You smile and say you absolutely will put the leprechaun on your desk by the monitor where she so brilliantly suggested, and the only reason you hadn't already traipsed around twenty-foot highwires at the risk of certain death is because you were waiting for the opportunity to do it with Roy from Quality Control. You also tell Lanette that nothing came of your introduction to the cutie from the bar because he was married. You don't even know his name.

Wait. That part's not a lie. See? Rules work.

"Oh, crap. Don't turn around," Lanette hisses.

"What?"

"Asshole alert at seven o'clock."

I twist in my seat in the lecture room and nearly throw up my breakfast. Wait. That's… no. What?!

Also, in my defense, I never said the guy was an asshole. Lanette came to that unfortunate conclusion on her own, since she had checked for a ring first, and finding none, concluded he was available. This in turn led to her second conclusion that the only possible reason a married man would *not* wear a ring at a conference was because he intended to be an asshole. (I'm a hundred percent sure this bias results from personal experience.) I tried to point out that he immediately told me he was married, and therefore may have another reason for not wearing a ring, but she wouldn't have it.

I feel bad that my neutral lie morphed into an unfair lie, until she makes another observation.

"Oh shit. He's with Amit Patel and Colin Yardley from Eon Tech! That means…"

Hang on. I stare at the three men chatting like old friends. They aren't… no… can't be… Does my crush work for my biggest competitor?!

"He works for Eon Tech?" I whisper in horror.

Lanette lets out a low whistle. "Can you imagine if you'd actually hooked up with him? You would've been sleeping with the enemy. That's Karma for you."

Yes, I *can* imagine it… quite well.

Also, I'm pretty sure that's not how Karma works.

The woman in front of us waves to them, and my stomach drops. They're headed this way! Oh no. I'm already scanning the room for a new seat, but the three that were being saved by the waving person are the only multiples left.

"Shit, they're sitting right in front of us," Lanette whisper-shouts.

I do my best to keep my expression Lanette-level irritated and not the-building-is-on-fire panicked as they approach. My crush must not have noticed me until now, because he looks startled when our eyes meet.

Crap crap crap.

"Well, if it isn't The Cougar Twins," Colin says.

"Hilarious," Lanette returns. "You know, that's the one joke that gets funnier every time I hear it. Isn't he so hilarious, Nat?"

I nod because a question was asked, but I immediately forget what it was. My gaze is locked on Mr. Killer Smile, who is definitely *not* smiling at the moment.

"The Cougar Twins?" Amit asks, squinting at his companion.

"Oh, yes. See, we work for The Panther Group, but we're *also* women, and a cougar is another kind of predatory cat. See where this is going?" Lanette says. "Hilarious, right?"

My crush shifts his attention to his coworker with a frown.

"Really, dude?" he mumbles, and Colin shoots him an annoyed look.

"What? It's funny," Colin says. "Hey. Tell your boy to relax," he says to Amit, smacking his arm. "All you suits from New York are too uptight."

Amit and my crush exchange a look that can only be described as a virtual eye roll.

Wait, he's from the New York office? Hopefully, not Manhattan because that would mean we live in the same city which means…

Nothing! It means absolutely nothing because you will never see this person again!

Except right now. And for the next hour. And possibly many other times this week.

Ah!!

"Hey, Nate. Good to see you," the woman who was saving their seats hums. "How have you been?"

Nate? My crush has a name!

Hold on. *Nat and Nate? Really, Universe?*

I mentally remind myself to look up the definition of Karma because now I'm not sure.

Nate's smile looks stiff, and I swear he hesitates before shaking her hand. "Hey, Myra. Um, good to see you, too." There is nothing in his expression that says he's happy to be seeing anyone right now.

"You ever take that trip to Denver?"

Would that be the trip to Denver he was supposed to take with his ex but then she dumped him and… oh shit. He called her Myra. Is that *Myra,* the ex?!

What is happening right now?!

I scan our small circle for a quick inventory, and sure enough, everyone is glaring at someone else, except for the mystery woman. Well, and me. But if this *is* the woman who crushed my crush, then she will definitely be getting a glare once that's confirmed.

Nate looks like he's going to be sick when he's forced to take the seat beside her, and even from behind, I can sense the light and humor I so admired in him drain away. Lanette and Colin are still going at it over... something about the correct procedure for validating parking? Amit just looks pissed in general.

Yep, the right side of Rows 3 and 4 of The Lotus Lecture Hall is just a regular ole powder keg at the moment. The vibe degrades further when my boss, Theresa, enters the room and spots us rubbing elbows with our rivals. I try to visually explain we're not so much *rubbing* as *body-slamming* elbows, but I'm not confident in my message when her expression changes from unhappy to confused.

She's just started toward us when the lights go out.

A buzz of shocked murmurs spreads around the room. Did the power go out? Are we under attack? Is this a prank?

We jump in our seats at a loud trumpet blast. Two seconds later, the lights come back on to reveal… I have no idea.

I squint at the mascot-looking thing parading around the front of the room. It's clearly a human in a costume, but that's where any certainties end.

"What the heck is that?" Lanette whispers.

I shrug and lean forward, as if those extra four inches will explain why a giant headless mermaid is stalking back-and-forth to a Jarvis McKinnley song. Even Nate looks temporarily distracted from his private hell. There are very few things that could displace the torment of being stuck next to your ex, while seated in front of an almost-one-night stand who you just learned is a bitter rival, but *that*—whatever it is—has to be on the shortlist.

The Thing reaches for the laptop on the podium and swats at the keyboard with its arm-fin. I don't know what the purpose of an arm-fin is in the natural world, but it's definitely not to operate a computer. The fin swipes at it again, also failing to make meaningful contact.

"Can you hear me?" the headless mermaid shouts over the music blasting from the intercom.

"Not really."

"No."

"What did it say?"

"My daughter just got married to this song."

"Isn't Jarvis McKinnley dead?"

Dozens of responses pepper our host from around the room, but none are very helpful.

"What's happening right now?" Lanette asks me, eyes wide.

I share her concern. As well as her question. And just when I think this entire affair can't get more awkward, Nate turns in his seat and makes direct eye contact with me. By the way his gaze immediately darts away, I don't think he intended that. He was probably trying for a discreet second look, but too bad for him, I seem to be glued to his image whenever he's in visual range. Not even the flustered Mer-Presenter is dragging my attention away.

Where's the seminar on, *"You have a huge crush on your direct competitor. Now what?"*?

5—MONDAY 9:08 AM

NATE

My worst-case-scenario isn't even this. I knew Myra would probably be at the conference. Hell, the whole reason she dumped me (supposedly) was because of her promotion and subsequent transfer to the main office in Chicago. She didn't want to do the long-distance thing, but based on how quickly her social media feed filled up with some minor league baseball player, I'm pretty sure it was me she didn't want to do.

And now I find out the woman I spent the most amazing night of intimate soul-searching with also works for my main competitor. Oh, and her name is Nat, apparently. That feels like the universe just adding an *F-U* for fun.

As if all of that's not bad enough, there's a giant phallic tuna fish slapping at a laptop, while the grating music of Jarvis McKinnley crackles through an antiquated intercom.

If I woke up in the middle of the night with this scenario in my brain, I wouldn't have accepted it as a valid nightmare.

The fish manages to get the music turned off (small miracle number one), and then pulls off the peanut-shaped top half of its body (small miracle number two).

"Do I have your attention now?!" the newly exposed human head and torso shouts with a toothy grin.

The Mer-Man wears a sweat-stained polo shirt with his green, sequined tail-fin. If you went to a golf course at the bottom of the Atlantic Ocean, this is what you would see. Even worse, without the peanut head, he looks strangely familiar. There's no way I'd meet someone like this and not remember. Maybe I *am* in some weird dream. How do you wake yourself from a nightmare again?

"Hello, fellow members of the *TELECOM*munity. My name is Chad Smith, and I'm the Senior Director of Contingencies and Collateral Mitigation for Sandeke Telecom!"

Hold up.

No.

This can't be real. I'm definitely dreaming.

Except, the smack on the arm from Colin feels very awake.

"Wow. Congrats, man," he whispers. "It's not every day you get to wine-and-dine a mermaid."

His snide remark would normally get an irritated look from me, but all my emotional energy is currently invested in whatever the hell is going on in my fictional wormhole right now.

"We're so glad you joined us today to discuss, *Making An Impact on the Saturated Consumer.* As you can see, one way to grab attention is through the use of characters and costumes!"

A mist of uncomfortable chuckles lifts from around the room. Then we realize he's serious. I scan the rows of corporate executives whose expressions mirror what mine must look like. Literally, no one in this room would ever dress up as a mermaid to sell internet service.

Then he says the six words you never want to hear in a seminar.

"Let's start off with an exercise! Now, I know how much you like to huddle in your exclusive circles." He demonstrates a circle with his finger. "But this works best with people you don't know well, so row one, turn and face your counterpart in row two. Row three, turn to row four. Etcetera. Etcetera. Etcetera."

Did he just pronounce each dot in an ellipsis?

Never mind. My heart pounds too hard for grammatical puzzles when I realize who's sitting behind me in row four. The only thing worse would be if he'd said to pair up with the person beside you.

"Okay, now each pair will pair up with the neighboring pair. You four. And you four. And you four. And you four. And you four. And you four."

This can't be happening.

"Feel free to break off into private spaces around the room," Chad tells us. "And, begin!"

No one moves. Everyone looks confused.

Chad strikes a dramatic pose, then breaks into a grin. "Oh. Did I not give you clear instructions? Welcome to tip number two in attracting consumers!"

Wait, what was tip number one? Was it really, "Walk around dressed as an unidentifiable aquatic species?" Come to think of it, what is tip number two? I'm so freaking confused.

Our host clicks a button on his laptop—a much easier task without a fin, it turns out—and the words: LESSON NUMBER TWO BE TRANSPARENT are typed in nearly unreadable all-caps magenta font. Lesson one *should be*, "Don't use magenta font." Actually, no. That's lesson two. Lesson one would have to be related to the giant nut-head propped against the podium.

"Let's practice 'being transparent,'" he says. "Break up into your groups and share some truths with each other. The more shocking, the better. For example, have you ever had a pet wasp?" He over-grins and points to himself with both thumbs. "Other examples could include being kidnapped by the mafia, riding a miniature Ferris wheel, building a coffee table out of used lightbulbs and-or batteries…"

What is this person's life?

"*And… begin!*"

A few seconds pass while we convert those words into actionable instructions. Pretty sure most of us are waiting for a surprise *Lesson Three: None of this!*, but eventually, the dull murmur of reluctant conversation fills the room. Several groups do, in fact, rise from their seats and relocate to various corners of the space, including Colin, Amit, and the other TPG employee.

The quartet behind us leaves the room altogether, probably headed to the café for coffee. Twenty bucks says they don't return. If my entire career didn't depend on the goodwill of that enthusiastic Mer-Man, I'd be following them.

I squint at his face, his blond hair, that overly eager expression—and my stomach drops. Is that…?

Part of me can't believe our host could also be the guy from the elevators. Another part of me wouldn't accept a reality where it wasn't. This is my life now, right? Even the name Chad sounds vaguely familiar, but I have no brain-cells left for that investigation.

"Well, this is awkward," Myra says, breaking the silence.

My insides are rioting as she shifts in her chair to face me and the two people behind us.

"Awkward" doesn't begin to describe what this is.

"How so?" her partner asks. The poor guy has no idea what mess he's just inherited.

"Hi, I'm Myra Carroll with Eon Tech," she says.

The man shakes the hand she offers. "Blake Richter of Starr Industries."

"And you are…?" Myra directs at the woman I know so, so well and yet not at all.

"Natalie McAllister of TPG," she says, doing everything she can not to look at me.

"Whoa. Now I get the *awkward* vibe," the man teases. "Eon Tech and The Panther Group in close quarters? Should I be scared?"

You have no idea, dude.

Myra chuckles in a way that makes her seem sweet and conciliatory at the same time. This Blake guy is already smitten. No surprise there. Myra is brilliant, and also a genius with people. It's why she shot through the ranks even faster than I did. At twenty-nine, she's the youngest woman to hold an executive position at Eon Tech. At twenty-seven I'm just a below-average regional sales director who has no idea what I'm doing. I was so happy for her when she was promoted to Chief Commercial Officer and beckoned to the golden palace in Chicago—until she told me I wasn't going with her.

"Well, that's not even the worst of it," she says with a coy smile. "This is Nate Hanover, also from Eon Tech."

She cups her hands around her mouth and leans forward. "And the *awkward* part is that he's my ex."

Blake's playful smile is starting to look less playful.

"Maybe we should branch off and form our own group," he jokes to Nat. At least, I think he's joking.

She returns a tight smile, and I'm surprised when her cold gaze lands on Myra. Oh no, is she thinking about everything I confessed last night? She knows about the brutal breakup and the baseball player and the trip and oh god. This isn't happening.

Myra still has an oblivious polite smile plastered to her face.

"Let's just get this over with," I say. "I'll start. I've never been kidnapped by the mafia, ridden a miniature Ferris wheel, or built a coffee table out of used lightbulbs and-or batteries. I've also never had a pet wasp, although now I'm incredibly curious about how that works."

Natalie cracks a smile, triggering very unhelpful memories about what it was like to laugh and feel free with her for the first time in a long time. It made me want to do other things with her and regret *not* doing things she was willing to do earlier in the evening. Things I've been thinking about all morning, particularly in the shower and… grr.

"You'd have to line the cage with a screen, I presume," she says.

"I'm thinking a wasp might be an aquarium pet, right?" I say.

She furrows her brow. "Good point. What about toys? Maybe a plastic arm for it to sting?"

"Definitely," I agree. "Possibly even a tiny wicker chair for it to hide in while it waits for something to terrorize?"

We exchange knowing smiles, and our eyes connect for a second too long. Her gaze drifts over my face and down my body in the same way mine is doing to her. Her long blond hair is twisted up in a more severe style today, which happens to be a distracting turn-on in itself. I love the thought of pulling out that clip and watching those waves cascade over her shoulders. She's wearing a less complicated top as well. I could easily solve that one, should the need arise.

But the need won't *arise because she never wanted to see you again, remember? And even if she did, you're pretty much the opposite of what she wants with all of her rules.*

Plus, there's the whole works-for-The-Panther-Group thing—and in our extremely competitive world, it's a pretty big thing.

"Do you two know each other?" Myra asks.

I force my attention from Natalie's gorgeous smile to my ex's still-gorgeous frown.

"No, of course not. Why would you say that?" Natalie says, at the same time I blurt, "Sort of."

We exchange a quick glance, and I clear my throat.

"By reputation," I clarify. "All anyone talks about in the New York office is Natalie M… Mc…" Crap, what was her last name again?

"McAllister?" Myra finishes, raising a brow. Yep, she knows I'm lying. Of course she does. She knows me better than anyone. Well, used to.

I glance back at Natalie who weirdly might hold that crown now. There are things I revealed last night that even my closest friends Marcos and Nash don't know. I've convinced them I'm great. That everything is swell, and I'm still the rock-solid big brother who's been looking out for them for half our lives.

Natalie McAllister is the only person on this planet who knows I'm not.

Myra scans her with obvious disdain, and Natalie doesn't do much to disguise her opinion of Myra either. This is bad. This is *very* bad.

"Do you have any truths to share, Blake?" I ask.

The guy glances around the circle with a stiff smile. "Just one, really. I confess that I need to use the restroom. Will you excuse me?"

Tensions mount as we watch the only pin in this live grenade stalk toward the exit.

"So, Natalie, I hear TPG is working on a proprietary UPS that will *revolutionize* power backups. Supposedly, of course."

"Yes. And it's *proprietary*," Natalie says with a tight smile. "I hear Eon Tech has some space in its client list now that Brighthouse didn't renew their contract. How are you enjoying that extra breathing room?"

"It was perfect timing, actually, since Sandeke Telecom is shopping for a new provider. Isn't that right, Nate?" Myra asks in a smug tone. "Our all-star VP of Northeast Sales will be closing that account this week."

My internal groan might be a little loud when both women lock their stares on me.

"You're the VP of Northeast Sales?" Natalie asks with some measure of alarm.

I nod, now even more concerned.

"Small world," she says with an expression that makes my stomach collapse. "I'm TPG's Regional Director of Sales."

"Oh?" I force out. "Which region?" Can she hear the panic in my tone?

"The East Coast," she mumbles.

"Well, isn't that fun!" Myra says, clapping her hands. "Does this mean you'll be going head-to-head for the Sandeke account this week?"

That's exactly what this means, and she knows it.

"Well, then. I suppose that can count as a *shocking truth* for both of you." She grows serious and focuses on me. "Guess it's my turn. Nate, there's something I need to say."

I stiffen and shake my head. "Not now, Myra. Please."

Her expression fills with sadness. "It's not what you think," she says softly. "I swear I didn't intend to do this here, but seeing you again… I can't wait any longer. Maybe there's a reason Fate put us together like this. For the last month I've been wanting to call you but I was too afraid and didn't know how to say it."

I can't breathe as she leans forward and locks her gaze on mine.

"I made a mistake, baby. A huge one. I'm so sorry for how it all went down, but I'm still in love with you. I tried to move on and I can't. I'm not ready to give up on us."

W.

T.

F.

I have no words as I stare at her. Is she joking? This is cruel, even for her. But by the way her blue eyes bore into me and Natalie bristles behind me, she's being very serious. Also, I'm pretty sure this is the *worst* possible time and method of dropping that bombshell.

"I have to use the restroom as well," I mumble, pushing to my feet.

"Nate!" Myra calls after me as I rush toward the exit.

I almost make it to the door when I remember why I'm here. Shit!

I stall by the Mer-Golfer and force back the hurricane raging in my head.

"Hi. Just wanted to introduce myself. I'm Nate Hanover with Eon Tech. I'd love to meet up for a drink later if you have time."

Chad Smith grins as he shakes the hand I hold out.

"It's great to meet you, Nate. Based on the reactions in your group, it looks like there were some very effective truths being shared!"

"Extremely… effective. Great illustration," I lie.

"I'd love to hear about them."

"And I'd love to know more about… this." I wave over the peanut head.

He follows my gaze and softens with an adoring sigh. "Ah. It's really something, isn't it?"

We can agree on that, at least.

"It certainly is… something." I manage a quick smile. "I'm sorry to run, but I was on my way out for an urgent call. Catch you after the seminar?"

"Urgent? Ooh, sounds mysterious. You know I used to be a spy, right?"

I didn't, and I also don't know how to respond to that. I settle on, "okay."

"Here's my card." I hand him one of the several I keep on me for these types of situations. Well, seventy-two percent of this situation. I don't think anyone could be prepared for the other twenty-eight percent of whatever is happening right now.

"You got it, *Nathan Hanover, Vice President of Northeast Sales at Eon Tech, Incorporated, based in New York, New York*!" He finger guns me, which turns out to be a strange look on a man dressed as a fish.

"Great," I say, inching toward the door. "Talk soon."

Thankfully, not too soon. I have exactly thirty-six minutes to get my shit together.

* * *

Am I surprised our new friend Blake isn't in the bathroom when I arrive? No. I'm sure he's halfway to the airport after getting swept up in that drama. And he didn't even get to see the good part.

Myra's words echo through my head as I splash water over my face. There's no way she meant everything she said—except the part about not planning to tell me right then. That's probably true. I'm guessing it's not "Fate" that convinced her to confess, so much as the suspected interest of another woman. Hilarious, since Natalie is the last person I could date at this point. I've got a better future with Chad the Mer-Whatever than The Panther Group's Regional Director of Sales, East Coast.

The door creaks open, and I reach for a paper towel to dry my face. My hope of escaping unnoticed shatters when the person makes a beeline right for me.

"Natalie?" I ask, tensing.

"I'd ask if you were okay, but I'm pretty sure I know the answer to that."

I blow out a breath and finish wiping the paper towel over my face. I feel her attention as I toss it in the waste bin, but I don't know where to go from here. Where's a peanut-fish suit when you need one?

"I'm so sorry for dragging you into this. And for Myra." I shake my head. "None of what she said makes sense. Bet you're relieved you bailed when you did."

Except, she tilts her head in concern instead of smiling like I expect.

"It makes perfect sense," she says, studying me. "You're the complete package, *Nate Hanover*. Anyone who had you and gave you up is guaranteed to regret it at some point."

I stare back, confused, aroused, then back to confused because all of this is happening in a restroom while a life-changing meeting with a mermaid looms on my horizon. As usual, Natalie must read me like a freaking user manual when she grabs my arm and drags me into a stall.

She shuts the door and hovers close.

"Here. You need some privacy to sort out that complicated brain of yours," she says, running her fingers through my hair. It's an intimate gesture, but it feels right for some reason. Last night was a year's worth of insipid dates, and suddenly I'm not sure we broke apart as cleanly as we hoped.

I gaze into her eyes, realizing she's still playing with the ends of my hair.

"What are we going to do?" she sighs, stepping closer.

"About what?" I murmur.

"Everything. The Sandeke account?"

"What *can* we do? You have to land it, right?"

She nods, her other hand pushing up my chest. "You do too, right?"

I nod, and she exhales as her fingers curve around my neck. "So back to my original question. What do we do?"

"I'm a fan of this approach," I say, studying her soft, shiny lips.

Those lips spread into a smile I feel throughout my body. "Yeah? Enough to forgive a person for walking out on you this morning when she wanted to do something very different?"

"Maybe. What did she want to do?"

"This."

She pulls my head down in a hard kiss, and my palms clutch the sides of her face to guide her to me. Our tongues meet and search for each other like they've been waiting hours for this opportunity. Mine definitely has.

She moans when I press her into the door, our hips grazing each other in perfect timing to our kiss. She tugs at my shirt, loosening it from my dress pants and slips her hand underneath.

My skin burns from her touch as she drags streaks of fire over my abs. Warm hands curve around my sides to my lower back, where her fingertips dip beneath the waistband of my pants to force us together. Her head goes back against the metal door when I kiss down her neck and breathe in the intoxicating scent of her body spray.

"We shouldn't be doing this," she gasps out.

"Your rules?" I say against her collarbone.

She shoves her hands into my hair and tugs my mouth back to hers. Another deep, probing kiss silences us, until she finally pulls back slightly. Our heavy breaths share the same air with our lips just a centimeter apart.

"You work for Eon Tech," she whispers. Her grip tightens on my hair as the pain of that reality flickers in her eyes. "Our firms hate each other. If anyone found out…"

I close my eyes and rest my forehead against hers. She's right. Of course she's right. So many things could explode if it got out that we're hooking up.

I move to straighten, but she doesn't let go. If anything, her hold is more desperate as our gazes lock. We search each other for several tense seconds, our bodies in clear disagreement with our brains.

"We can't see each other again. At least, not like this," she says.

"I know. I promise to play fair this week. Everything you told me last night is in a vault and off-limits."

Her sad smile is begging to be kissed. "I trust you. And I'll play by the same rules, I promise. Just…"

She brushes her thumb over my lips as she searches my eyes again. "Be careful with Myra. After everything you said last night, I'm worried about how much she could hurt you. Again."

I nod and steal that last kiss I've been craving. She sighs into it and seems as reluctant to break apart as I am.

"We should go," she says softly.

"Yeah."

"It was nice meeting you, Nate Hanover."

"And you, Nat McAllister."

"Nate and Nat," she says against my lips.

"I like Nat and Nate better."

I file the image of her beautiful grin in the secure mental vault with everything else I can never have.

6—MONDAY 12:03 PM

NATALIE

I can't decide if fortune hates me or loves me by introducing the man of my dreams, only to make him the one person I can't have. Either way, Nate Hanover and his brilliant mind, beautiful soul, big heart, and gorgeous everything are off-limits in so many ways, there's no point in even listing them. I can't afford the distraction anyway, especially when fortune definitely loved me by granting a lunch date with Chad Smith and one of his colleagues (I think).

After introducing myself at the pointless seminar this morning, I invited him to lunch. He asked if he could bring a friend, which I thought was weird until this exact moment when I realize his "friend" is the other half of the odd elevator duo. I know almost nothing about wheat or mid-19th century transportation, so I really hope the topic doesn't veer too far from industrial power backups.

"Hello. Thank you so much for meeting with me," I say as they approach. At least they're not dressed identically like last night. Then again, once you've seen someone in a mermaid costume, it's hard to accept them in anything else. "Hi, I'm Natalie McAllister with TPG."

"Well, hello, Natalia! I'm Reed Reedweather the Third." He shakes my hand, then motions to the chair in front of him. I'm not sure what that means until he sits in it. Then I'm certain I don't know what that means.

I decide not to correct his pronunciation of my name as Chad takes the seat beside him. Reed Reedweather III is not the reason I'm here.

"Natalie was in our workshop this morning," Chad tells his friend.

"Is that so?" Reedweather says. "I would have attended, you see, but I didn't."

I wait for the rest, and realizing there is none, clear my throat.

"Well, we're sorry we missed you," I say. "Were you at a different seminar?"

"No."

He signals the server who comes to our table. "Trivello scotch neat and a frozen strawberry daiquiri for my friend here."

I'm about to protest when I realize he's talking about Chad.

"Actually," Chad says with a sly smile. "I'm feeling a bit naughty today. What Rosés do you have?"

"You'll find our beverage selections here, sir," our server says, plucking the wine list from the table and handing it to him.

"Ah! Excellent. I'll have this one."

He points at the menu.

The server leans forward to squint at the tiny print, and Chad holds it up so the poor man can read it.

"Thank you, sir. Would you like a glass or a bottle?"

"What do you think?" Chad asks Reedweather.

"Bottle," Reedweather says with a wink. "We're on vacation, right?"

Well... not really. Although my bestie Reece would disagree. He hasn't stopped whining about my "paid vacation" since I mentioned *Tele-Con*. He's just jealous because he's never been invited to a forklift operator convention.

"And for you?" the server asks me.

"Ice water, please," I say with a smile.

The server leaves to fill our drink orders, and I focus on my target.

"Thanks again for meeting with me. As the Senior Director of Contingencies and Collateral Mitigation, I'm assuming you handle Sandeke Telecom's UPS provider?"

"Oh, no. That would be Frederick," Chad says.

Crap. Really? I'm positive this is the person Theresa said I needed to talk to.

"Ah, okay. And is Frederick here this week as well?"

Reedweather and Chad laugh, but I can't tell if that's a yes-laugh or a no-laugh.

"No, my dear. Definitely not. Neither is Stacey," Reedweather informs me.

"Stacey handles your UPS needs as well? Are they in the same department?"

Chad shakes his head. "Frederick is at Sandeke Telecom. Stacey is at Reed-weather Media."

Right. Reedweather Media is the marketing subsidiary of Sandeke Telecom. I only prepared a pitch for a large telecom operation and data center, though, not a standard office building. I assumed both companies would use the same provider. This could get tricky.

"I see. So you're not familiar with the UPS?"

"Of course I am," Chad says. "I just don't sign off, ya know?"

"Ah."

"As am I. Very familiar," Reedweather says. "At home as well as the office. Everywhere, really."

So they're not the decisionmakers. Well, maybe I can get a jump on their scope to beef up my proposal for "Frederick" and "Stacey," whoever they are.

"Oh, well, great. If you don't mind me asking, what is it that you look for in a UPS provider?"

"Hmm…" Both men lean back as they consider my question. They even tap their chins in sync. I'd say it's creepy but… Nope, it's creepy.

"Reliability," Chad says.

"Yes, that's extremely important," Reedweather agrees.

Excellent. Here we go.

"Absolutely. What level of transfer time are you looking for? To what millisecond?"

"Well, hours I would think," Chad says. "Usually, around ten in the morning, right?" he asks Reedweather.

Hours?!

Reedweather nods. "Yes, but sometimes later. Later is okay as long as it's nothing important."

"Wow. Okay."

I don't know how to respond to that. I've never gotten an answer that was over 8 milliseconds. They don't mind if their entire system is down for *hours*? For a Telecom giant that's… unusual. For anyone, that's unusual.

"Well, we can definitely do better than, um, hours," I say, forcing a smile. "Anything else?"

"Attractiveness, I suppose," Reedweather says.

Huh?

"Friendliness would be good as well," Chad adds.

"Friendliness? How exactly…?" I don't know how to finish that sentence. "Are you referring to the tone of the service and alarm notifications?"

"Those are nice, sure," Chad says.

What in the world is an attractive, friendly power supply system?

"I suppose we could customize that," I say, making a mental note to talk to the design engineers. "What's your current—"

I'm cut off by the arrival of our drinks. After delivering the water and scotch, the server opens Chad's bottle of Rosé. He pours a tasting portion and hands it to Chad, who smiles and waves it away.

"More, please," he says.

The confused server looks at the glass, then at Chad's patient smile, then back at the glass. He adds another splash and tries to hand it back.

"No need to be shy. We're all friends here," Chad says, motioning toward the glass.

The server hesitates.

"He's referring to the wine," Reedweather explains to the employee. "He would like the one you're holding."

The server furrows his brow, clearly not sure what to do next. His brain gives up, and he hands the bottle and glass to Chad. The man then watches with a perplexed expression as Chad fills the glass to the brim.

"Can I get some ice and a straw for this?" Chad asks.

"Of course, sir," the server says, staring at his notepad like he has no idea what to write. "Are you prepared to order? May I offer any assistance with the menu?" There's a tinge of fear in that question.

"No, I believe we're ready," Reedweather says before I can speak.

I haven't even looked at the menu. Actually, none of us have.

"I'll have an eight-ounce filet, rare, no sides."

"Soup or salad?"

"I said no sides."

The server opens his mouth to respond, then thinks better of it.

"And for you?" he asks Chad.

"Your grilled cheese, how many slices of cheese?"

The man stares helplessly at his order pad again.

"Um, three?" he says finally. There's zero chance he didn't just make that up.

"Ah. Okay. And do you have provolone?"

"Yes?"

"Perfect. I'll take a grilled cheese, two slices of provolone, one of American. Grilled medium-well on one side and rare on the other. Oh, and can you be sure the sandwich is sliced diagonally?"

"Will that be two triangles or four triangles, sir?" he mumbles.

"Can you do three?"

Four adults are now trying to recall ninth-grade geometry.

"Two right triangles and an isosceles," I say to the server. "Assuming your bread is rectangular, of course."

I give him a tiny smirk, and a flicker of relieved humor flashes on his face.

"I'll check with the chef, sir," he says to Chad. "And for—"

"Oh! Wait. Is your American cheese white or orange?"

The man blinks at him for five long seconds. "White, I believe."

"Hmm… that won't work then. Can you change that to a slice of cheddar? You have cheddar, correct?"

"Yes."

"Ah, but cheddar can also be white or orange, can it not?" Reedweather says with a grave expression.

"Shit, you're right. Damn. Let me think for a minute."

"How about mozzarella? That's typically one color," I say. Anything to move this along.

"Brilliant!" Chad says. "Provolone and mozzarella are even in the same cheese family, I think."

"That's why they call them *cousins du fromage*," Reedweather says with an unintelligible accent.

Cheese cousins?

"Perfect. French cheese is my favorite," Chad says. "Let's do that. And can I add a cobb salad but hold any bacon, eggs, tomatoes, or cucumbers."

To his credit, the server is still trying to take this order. "Honey mustard dressing okay?"

"Oh right. No, hold that too. On a diet," he explains to Reedweather as he pats his belly.

"So… you want a side of lettuce," the server says dryly.

"Yes, but make sure it's Cobb salad lettuce, and not Caesar salad lettuce."

Our server does not make a note of this.

"And for you?" he asks me, now with blatant fear in his eyes. I try to give him the most reassuring look I can manage.

"What's the first thing on your menu?" I ask.

"Cheese plate," he replies with understandable hesitation.

I wince. "Second thing?"

"Pan-seared scallops in a lemon garlic sauce."

"Perfect. I'll have that." I meet his gaze. "And I'd like that with scallops, please."

He bites back a smile. "Pan-seared okay?"

"Depends. Is it a scallop-searing pan or just a regular pan?"

His lips twitch. "I believe it's been certified for scallop-searing, but I'll confirm with the manager. I'll get this right in for you."

We exchange another amused look before he leaves to *get that right in.* If he does, he deserves whatever the Lifetime Achievement Award for restaurant servers is.

I take a sip of water to center myself.

"Back to our previous discussion," I say.

"Yes, right. Anne," Chad says.

"Anne?" I ask.

He nods. "Our UPS person."

"I thought that was Frederick… and Stacey?"

Chad looks at me like I'm the clueless one in this conversation. Which is accurate. I have no idea what the hell is happening anymore.

"No. Frederick is our shipping manager," Chad says.

"Your shipping manager handles your…"

I stop.

No. It can't be. Please, be wrong.

"You know I'm talking about power backup equipment and not the ubiquitous package delivery service, right?"

By their confused expressions, they did not know this.

I do a mental faceplant as I take another sip of water to buy myself recovery time. This turns out to be mistake number I-don't-even-know, because in that split second, I lose Chad's attention to something to his right.

"Well, hello! What a pleasant surprise!" Chad cries.

Stuck against the back wall, I lean forward to see the action and my heart jumps in my chest. Nate? And he's with the other employees from Eon Tech— including *Myra.*

"Hey, Chad," he says.

His voice triggers a riot of fluttering throughout my body. Deep brown eyes lock on me, sending my own peeling away to focus on something less dangerous. For example, his torso that's deliciously framed by the fitted button-down with rolled-up sleeves I enjoyed this morning. Yeah, that's worse, actually. My eyes sink to a leather belt and gray slacks that must have been tailored directly to his body because *damn*.

The white tablecloth suddenly becomes very interesting to me.

"You have to join us!" Chad says.

Hang on. *What?!*

My gaze darts to Chad, then swings to Nate in disbelief. There are so many reasons Nate Hanover absolutely should *not* join us.

"Great idea," his colleague says with a subtle elbow in his side.

Of course they'd want him to crash this party. Who would turn down the opportunity to ruin your competitor's big sales pitch?

Nate's focus swings to me, and I see the conflict in his eyes. He has to choose between me and his job. We've already decided we're choosing jobs. I'll be pissed if he doesn't.

I pull my gaze away and take another sip of water. I'll be needing a refill soon at this pace.

"Nate would love to join you," Myra says, drawing my attention again. And by attention, I mean cold death stare.

He gives her a sharp look, and my heart hurts at the flash of pain on his face before he covers it with that disarming smile.

I still haven't figured out how to compete with that smile, by the way. Chad and Reedweather are already hooked. It's like they've totally forgotten I just guided them through the perilous lunch-ordering process.

"We already ordered, but I'm sure we can add another meal, my boy," Reedweather says, waving toward the space beside me in the booth.

Huh. Okay. Since I'm paying for lunch, that means I'm now buying for the person trying to steal my account from me. That expense report is gonna be fun.

Nate hesitates for another second, while his coworkers-slash-likely-bosses issue silent commands. His fist clenches and unclenches at his side.

"We'll catch you later," Amit says, clapping his shoulder.

Myra leans toward him and whispers something way too intimately for my taste. His expression clouds over as she talks, and he watches her with a troubled look while they walk away. Their retreat also leaves him with no socially acceptable choice but to slide in beside me. Great. Now we're practically sitting on top of each other.

"The *paella* here is excellent," Reedweather says, pronouncing *paella* with the same indecipherable accent as his "cheese cousin" trivia. I'm starting to think his mind only has two categories of speech: his and everyone else's.

"Really? At a steakhouse?" Nate asks. "Is that what you ordered?"

"No," Reedweather says.

"But you've tried it?" Nate asks.

"No. One can just tell these things."

We follow his pointed stare to the sign on the wall that says, Benton Brothers Steakhouse.

Nate's confused expression reflects my thoughts.

Oh, just wait, my friend.

Chad returns a grave nod. "You're referring to last summer," he says.

Reedweather smiles in approval. "Precisely, my boy. Nothing like a *good* paella and a *wicked* cigar, am I right?"

Chad grins, also agreeing with this.

Reedweather signals our server who was already approaching with an anxious expression.

"Your ice, sir," he says, placing a tall glass in front of Chad.

"Perfect," Chad says.

He dumps his wine into the cup of ice and swirls it around. Even Reedweather looks perplexed.

"My friend here will have the paella," Reedweather announces, waving at Nate.

"Oh, uh, I'm sorry, sir, but we don't have paella," our server says. The concern on his face is entirely understandable.

"No? Well! Do you have shellfish?"

"Yes."

"Rice?"

"Yes."

"Saffron?"

"Yes."

"Vegetables?"

"Yes."

"Chicken?"

"Yes."

"Well, then, see? You have paella!"

Hmm. Is that how cooking works?

"Sir, I—"

"Can I just have a Caesar salad, please?" Nate asks quickly.

The server visibly sighs with relief. "Of course. Dressing on the side?"

"That would be great."

I've never seen a person run so fast from a table.

My longing to follow him and get out of this situation fades at the sudden pressure against my thigh. Nate's leg is directly aligned with mine in the non-existent space between our bodies, causing the room temperature to spike. As if that's not bad enough, I get a slight whiff of his cologne that should be regulated on a man like him. How am I supposed to stay focused with the most tempting distraction of all time just a short touch away?

How short? Naughty Natalie asks.

Damn, she's bossy today, because suddenly my fingers are exploring the answer to that question beneath the table.

Nate flinches when my fingertips sink into the soft fabric of his dress pants.

Crap. I did *not* just do that.

I'm about to retract my hand when fresh tingles spread over my skin at the feel of his warm fingers on mine. He traces them absently, like he already has me memorized.

I try to imagine golfing Mer-Persons to tame the electric shock zapping every nerve he grazes, but it doesn't work. My hand drifts higher up his leg, which *really* doesn't help, and I sense his quick inhale when my palm slides to his inner thigh. I massage just enough to make my own body flush with desire. He shifts closer, practically inviting me to make this hidden scene R-Rated.

"This is Nathan Hanover of Eon Tech," Chad tells Reedweather. "We have a date tonight. Nathan, this is Reed Reedweather the Third of Reedweather Media."

"It's nice to meet you," my rival says. He clears his throat when it comes out hoarse. "And Nate is fine."

I pull in a sharp breath when my leg quivers from a retaliatory touch I fully condone. The thing with fires Nate starts is that they spread quickly. So quickly that my burning body squirms against his hand for more direct pressure.

"Nathaniel! You don't say," Reedweather chimes with a delighted grin. "We have a Natalia and a Nathaniel. How wonderful."

Oh god. My breath catches as his fingers graze the spot where I want them most. Except, it's not quite enough. Not... exactly... where...

I shift slightly and... *yes. So good.*

I fight to control my breathing as his thumb moves in small, tight circles.

"We were just discussing our favorite shipping methods," Chad says.

"Also, our favorite delivery times," Reedweather adds.

Time for revenge.

Nate gasps when my palm glides over the hardening bulge in those perfectly tailored pants.

Our companions return concerned expressions at his reaction, and he coughs when my hand makes another torturous pass.

"You okay, Nathaniel?" Reedweather asks.

"Yeah," he chokes out. "I just…"

Gosh, he feels amazing. I want so badly to strip him and enjoy every inch. Targeted and slow. All. The. Firm. Pressure. However and wherever I want it.

"I just love mailing stuff so much," he forces out.

"Of course you do, son," Reedweather says. "In what other country can you walk into a building and send something anywhere in the world?"

All of them, I think. Well, maybe not Antarctica. That's a continent, but is it also a—

My entire body goes rigid. *Ahh.* I bite my lip.

"I guess you love mailing stuff too?" Chad asks me.

I nod through a torturous rush, already so close it hurts when he stops. Damn, if this is what it's like when I'm trying *not* to succumb to his seduction, imagine what it will be when… When I *never* do because this can never happen. Well, not again.

Also, there's no way the others didn't notice my sudden flare-up of tension. Nate looks downright triumphant as he removes his hand and settles back into his seat. He has to know how much I'm aching for him right now.

"Are you okay, my dear?" Reedweather asks. "You're looking a little flushed."

"Please call me Nat. Also, I'm fine. Just…" Shit. I can't even think straight.

"The table behind us has strawberries. Is your allergy acting up?" Nate asks with a sympathetic look.

Warmth spreads through my chest. Not only did he come to my rescue, he remembered that small detail I shared last night? My closest friend Reece can't even remember and invites me to go strawberry picking with his girlfriend and him every June.

"Yes," I say, my voice calmer now. "It's probably that."

Our eyes lock, and his gaze softens with affection and a silent apology for what he just did. I should be mad at him, probably, except I kind of started it. And definitely loved it. And… gah! Now, I just want to hold his hand like a cheesy pretend couple and break all kinds of clauses in Rule Number Five.

"Oh dear. It's good you didn't order the strawberry daiquiri," Reedweather says to Chad.

"I know. I'm so sorry for almost killing you," Chad says to me.

I force a smile. "Oh. Um, yeah, no problem."

"I almost died once," Reedweather informs us. "Twice, actually, but the second time was pre-Omaha, so we don't count that."

He spreads his napkin on his lap and takes a sip from his glass.

Okay...?

"So tell us more about your special plugs," Chad says after a long swallow from his own drink.

"Special plugs?" Nate asks, looking at me.

"An industrial power backup system," I mutter.

As in, the thing we're trying to sell.

His return look is pretty clear as well: *The person we're supposed to convince to buy our product doesn't know what it is?*

I respond with a silent, *Yep.* I also add a silent, *that other thing was so hot but don't you dare try it again or I'm retaliating. Actually, I might anyway.*

I don't know how much of the last part he interpreted correctly, but his slight smile tells me he got enough.

"Actually, Chad, how about you tell us how you came to be the Senior Director of Contingencies and Collateral Mitigation?" Nate asks with what sounds like sincere interest. Geez, the guy is charming as hell. I'll have to up my game to compete with him for the rest of my career.

To be fair, I was wondering the same thing, so I'm glad he asked. I'm also hoping Chad's response will offer some insight on how to talk to him about "our special plugs."

"Do you want the long version or the short version?" Chad asks.

"Short would be totally fine," Nate says, making it seem as if he's doing *Chad* the favor. Normally, getting a potential customer talking is a good thing, but Nate must share my concern about giving this person's brain free rein.

And he didn't even witness the congressional hearing required to order a grilled cheese sandwich.

"Happy to," Chad says. "Well, I got promoted because of my success as an undercover potato."

Oh.

Nate's smile falters.

I didn't even know you *could* string two of those words together. Maybe we should have requested the long version.

"Really," Nate says finally, clearing his throat.

Chad nods dismissively and takes a sip of his iced wine. "Yep."

"You mean, you wore a potato costume like the mermaid one this morning?" Nate asks.

He shakes his head. "Not a mermaid, a Mer-Nut."

"I'm sorry?"

"A Mer-Nut. As in Sandeke Telecom's trademarked branding campaign for our Warp Speed Service."

"Mer-Nuts and the entire Kingdom of Macadamia are proprietary, you know," Reedweather says in a warning tone, as if Nate or I might be tempted to steal their idea. To do that, we'd have to understand what it is.

"Exactly," Chad says. "But to answer your previous question, no, not a costume." He scans the room with a wary squint before leaning forward. "Our biggest competitor, Brighthouse, stole our marketing idea, so I went in as an undercover potato to hack their server with this computer virus thing I made. It ruined the Range of War party website or whatever and cost them their relationship with Larinda Scott."

Interesting. So the long version is even more confusing than the short version. Good to know.

"It was quite the display of *Surreptitious Pantomime,*" Reedweather adds with an impressed nod.

"Wow. Thank you, sir," Chad beams.

I glance at Nate, expecting to find him as confused as I am, but his expression is more… Concerned? Irritated? I don't know, but he definitely doesn't look like someone who's enjoying anything about this story. Well, that makes two of us, I guess.

"So, how did the… undercover potato… lead to your promotion?" I ask, because I really, *really* don't want more details on whatever was just said. I'm already confused enough.

"Oh, well, yeah. So after we broke their company, Sandeke was afraid Brighthouse would try to attack us in return," Chad says.

"By sending in their own… undercover potato?" Maybe it's code for something?

By Chad and Reedweather's laugh, it's not.

"No, no. That would never work," Chad says. "We'd see it coming from a mile away."

"The potato?" I ask.

I'm so lost. Does this potato drive a car? Fly? Jog?

"And so, now my job is to figure out what Brighthouse will do to get back at us and thwart any nefarious activities. Hence the new role: *Senior Director of Contingencies and Collateral Mitigation.*"

"The job title was my idea," Reedweather brags.

I don't think anyone would challenge that claim.

"I see…"

So they attacked their competitor and are now bracing for a counter-attack by putting their entire future in the hands of the genius behind a headless mermaid and an undercover potato?

On the one hand, this is great news. A major corporation fearing an attack would be a goldmine for backup power systems and fully loaded emergency service contracts.

We quiet as our server approaches with our meals.

On the other hand, my ticket to the contract of a lifetime is now clasping his hands with glee at a weird-ass grilled cheese sandwich.

7—MONDAY 2:12 PM

NATE

Lunch was… intense. I still feel the sweet burn of Natalie's hand on me—heightened by the forbidden nature of everything surrounding that moment. I also feel a different kind of burn from learning that *Chad Smith* must be the dude Marcos and Nash have been whining about since our apartment's strange bond with Reedweather Media began.

As if that's not bad enough, it appears the guy is taking credit for the ransomware code *I* edited and gave to Nash for his strange spy thing this past May. Is Chad really telling people he *"went in as an undercover potato to hack their server and break their company"*? Because my understanding of his role in that whole debacle was… well, yes, the part about the undercover potato sounds plausible. Everything else, not so much.

So yes, I'm very familiar with the Brighthouse-Sandeke corporate espionage war, and found myself in yet another business wormhole while Chad was reciting his revisionist version of it. Thankfully, our food came at that moment to yank us back to reality for the duration of the meal—albeit a confusing meal where I watched Chad eat stringy breaded cheese triangles and a pile of shredded lettuce.

The whole thing is a lot to process, so I excused myself the second sales etiquette allowed, careful to avoid any further contact with Nat. I wasn't even supposed to be there, and now I have an impossible decision to make. If Chad truly is the "undercover potato ransomware guy," I have a huge advantage for winning that contract. All I have to do is tell him Marcos and Nash are my roommates and that I was the one who helped take down Brighthouse. It would be so easy—and make me feel like shit for using info I shouldn't even have.

I message Marcos and Nash during my escape from the sales lunch from hell. Hopefully, a roommate debriefing session will be enough to sort through this latest shitstorm.

For the record, it doesn't help chaotic mental states when coworkers practically tackle people the second they step out of restaurants.

"Tell us everything," Colin says, dragging me toward an alcove guarded by yet another fake pirate. Seriously, where do you even start if you're in the market for life-sized swashbuckler adornments?

My stomach is in knots at the familiar smell of Myra's perfume, and I try to focus on my other associates. All I want to do right now is hide in one of the glorious closets Nat so admires.

"Not much to tell," I say. "Natalie did a great job keeping things neutral and vague."

Their expressions sag, but I'm not sure what they were expecting by forcing me into that situation. Did they honestly think she was going to let me steal the account while she was sitting right there?

You could have.

I shake off the thought.

"Well, at least it prevented *her* from making a move," Amit says. "What's her angle? Anything we can use?"

They wait with expectant stares, and I have no idea what to say. It feels like I've been shoved into a vortex. Mentally, physically, emotionally—my entire existence is just an angry cloud pressing in at once. These last four months have already drained me. I have no idea how I'm supposed to get through the next four days.

"Not really," I say. "Like I said, she's good at what she does. She was careful."

"Damn," Amit mutters. "We need to figure out what TPG is peddling. At least get a ballpark number so we can come in close. They're always undercutting us."

"Right?! How do they keep their bids so low?" Colin hisses.

"Low overhead," I say. "They can be way more competitive, because they don't have to pad everything like we do."

Is there a slight edge in my tone? Hell yes, there is. Myra gives me a silent warning, so I know she heard it too, but I spent years fighting executives over their indulgent budgets as the VP of Finance. It's why I'm here doing a job I hate instead of the one I loved.

"Anyway, it doesn't matter," Colin continues. "If we can land Sandeke Telecom, the war is over."

"Exactly," Amit agrees. "That's why we have to get ruthless. This is our top priority this week. Not just for Nate, but for all of us, got it?"

Their eager nods are already gearing up for battle, and I want to throw up.

"I have an idea," Myra says. "How dirty do we want to get?"

"Filthy," Colin says to no one's surprise.

"But very legal," Amit clarifies. "What are you thinking?"

Myra releases a sly grin, and I already know I'm going to hate this.

"Natalie McAllister seemed very interested in Nate at the seminar this morning," she says.

I land a sharp look on her, my heart racing.

"Oh shit!" Colin says. A triumphant outburst from Colin is never a good omen. "Myra's right. Now that I think about it, Nat was totally checking you out."

"She seemed genuinely upset to learn you'd be her competition. You should use that," Myra says to me.

"*Use* that?" I retort. "Use *what*?"

"Yeah, you definitely need to work it," Colin says. "Show a little skin. Bat those pretty lashes. Shake that ass. You know, flaunt it if you got it!"

"What the hell are you talking about?" I ask, now annoyed on top of everything else.

"Flirt with her," Myra says after scowling at Colin. "Get her to fall for you and open up so you can get intel."

"Oh! Like a spy or whatever!" Colin says, way too excited by this terrible idea. To be fair, that's not uncommon for our junior VP of Midwest Sales.

"I'm not doing that."

"Why wouldn't you?" Amit says. "Colin's right. A little spying never hurt anyone."

"Because that's not *spying*. That's being a giant dick," I say in exasperation.

"Oh yeah. *Definitely* use that," Colin says.

We all scowl at him this time.

"Well, I don't see what choice you have," Myra says in a firm voice.

I glare at her, issuing a silent message of my own. Where's the woman who missed me so much and wanted to get back together? How much can you "love" someone if you're ordering them to pursue someone else? She still cares about me? Yeah right.

"You're already on thin ice, Nate," she continues, proving everything she said earlier was bullshit. Why she played that game in the seminar, I'm not sure. Jealousy? Or maybe just to mess with me because putting me through hell these last four months wasn't enough.

"You've already been kicked out of the finance department for refusing orders," she says. "This move into sales is your last chance. You do it again, I guarantee you'll be out of a job entirely."

I can't speak as I stare at her in disbelief. Did she really just air my dirty laundry in front of my new boss and coworker? I feel their shocked attention at the revelation. It was big news when I was transferred to sales. Everyone thought it was the pull of huge payouts from potential commissions that fueled my move. Only a select few knew the truth: That it wasn't my choice at all. It was a forced reassignment after I consistently refused to play budget games for the departments I oversaw as VP of Finance. *Everyone* plays that game, I was told, but I wouldn't.

So they got rid of me. Not officially, of course. On paper it was a "lateral move" to avoid any pushback or potential lawsuits, but everyone involved knows the real reason my office was transferred two floors down to sales a month ago. They couldn't fire me for being too ethical, but they sure as hell can get rid of me for "not doing my job" by losing a major contract.

Myra knows all of this. She would also know how much that transfer crushed me. All I ever wanted was a career in finance. Up until this moment, I envisioned her fighting for me behind closed doors while the rest of upper management mounted a joint attack. Maybe it was the other way around.

"Well, *how* you do it, is up to you," Amit says breaking the awkward silence. "But Myra is right. You have to land the Sandeke account by Friday night if you want any future at Eon Tech. I strongly suggest you play your spy card."

* * *

"Nate! Hold on," Myra calls from behind me as I stalk away from the public scolding.

What could she possibly want? She got her way, didn't she?

"Will you just…" She grabs my arm from behind when I absolutely do *not* hold on and pulls me toward a giant indoor palm tree. (I'm also extremely interested in the indoor tree store because it must be enormous.)

I'm about to snap at her when her expression fills with unexpected remorse.

"I'm sorry about what just happened," she says gently. "I know that was hard for you, but I had to do it."

Her fingers close around my bicep, and I yank my arm free.

"Really? You *had* to humiliate me, threaten me, and force me into an impossible situation?"

She shakes her head, eyes wide. "What? No! I had to rescue you. Like I always do. You're too good, Nate. Your heart is too big for the corporate beast. I've told you that since the day we met. So yes, I'm willing to be the bad guy in order to help you survive—also like always. I was in the meeting last week when this conference came up. Amit was told *not* to let you handle the Sandeke account. They don't trust you, but he insisted you deserved a chance." She leans close, and I try to breathe. "He has orders to override you if you fail, though. He's supposed to get Sandeke at any cost… including you."

My chest hurts. Everything does. I'm so lost and confused right now. It's all too much. I stare out the window to my left, watching guests mill around with giant smiles on their faces. That's what a resort is supposed to be, right? Life in general? You're supposed to walk around grinning and chasing dreams. Everyone around me seems to be doing it. I supposedly wrote the handbook on optimism. But there's no light in my world anymore. No color. No anything. I'm just so damn tired all the time, so done with everything and everyone I used to care about.

"Why would you tell me this stuff?" I ask finally. "You're one of *them* now. Why would you betray their confidence for some underling?"

"Some *underling*? Are you being serious?" I was, and so is she based on her expression. "I told you. I'm still in love with you. I think I always will be. I'm sorry for what happened, but—"

"No. Just, stop," I say, shaking my head. "I can't do this right now."

"Nate, please…"

She takes my hand, and our fingers instinctively thread like they have countless times before. Traitors. How weak are those little appendages? I want to pull away. I even try mentally, but that broken chip of my heart she stole is too strong right now.

She squeezes my hand and runs her thumb over mine. Her eyes search my face, begging me to let her in. When her gaze lands on my lips, it's like my body and mind have no idea what to do with this recognizable situation that shouldn't be happening.

Three months ago, I would have killed for this moment. Two months ago, I prayed for it. One month ago, I dreamt of it. Now? It physically hurts.

I extricate my fingers and step back.

"I have to go," I mumble.

"Don't. Just… let's go back to my room and talk. Please."

I shake my head and turn to leave.

"We can strategize about how to land the Sandeke account without breaking any of your ethical rules. Let me help you. Give me a chance to prove how much I still care about you."

I close my eyes and try to ignore my pounding pulse. Why is she doing this to me? She can't be telling the truth, right? That she really does love me?

Her palm presses into my back and pushes up in an intimate claim she rightfully had for almost half my adult life—then threw away for reasons I still don't understand.

I pull in a deep breath and storm toward the elevators.

* * *

"No freaking way! Nate Hanover?!"

I freeze when I hear my name.

A middle-aged man with short gray hair and a gym-obsessed build strides toward me sporting a giant grin that makes me positive we're not on the same page.

"It's me! Roger!" he says.

Who the heck is Roger?

"Oh, hey… Roger," I reply, mustering the friendliest smile I can manage. I also try for an expression that says, *Yes, I know exactly who you are and why we're having this conversation!*

Not sure how successful that one is.

"Wow! It's been, what, ages since the last time, no?"

Okay, well, that eliminates anyone I've encountered within this person's definition of ages.

"Yeah, I know. So long," I say, tensing when he clasps my shoulder with so, so much affection. Another clue: It's someone who likes me. That eliminates Ms. Juniper from downstairs who's convinced I stole a wreath off her door.

Excellent. So I know Roger isn't an eighty-year-old collector of dead pine branches. One down, seven billion humans to go.

Also, I *did* actually steal the wreath. (Just kidding. But if I had, I would've hung it on Marcos' door while he was out. Maybe even intertwined some LED lights and added a "I Heart Arbor Day" sign to it. Bonus points if I could frame Nash for the crime and start a bitter feud.)

"So how is that *garden hose* holding up?" Roger asks. The wink and weird way he says *garden hose* removes "garden hose" from the list of what that sentence is referencing.

"Oh, uh. You know," I say with a sly grin.

He snickers and smacks my arm again. "'Atta boy. Hey, you look amazing, dude. Still working out, right?"

I clear my throat. "Yeah, um—"

"I was just about to grab Erik and check out the pools. You want in?"

Erik… is… his…?

"Wow, thanks for the invite, but I'm on my way to meet up with some people. Tell Erik I said… hi."

He gives me a funny look. "You mean, *crab salad*, right?"

Huh?

"Oh, uh, ri—"

"Ha! Just messing with you. Crab salad, get it?"

I manage a stiff chuckle. "Yeah," I lie.

You would think an encounter that involved a garden hose, crab salad, and this person would stick in your mind for quite a while. This makes me even more concerned.

"Okay, well, look. Let's catch up soon. You here for the week?" he asks.

Shit. It's not like I can say no if there's a chance we'll cross paths again. A good chance, apparently, since at some point *ages ago* we were enjoying garden hoses and crab salad with someone named Erik.

"Yeah, but I'll be pretty busy. I'm here for a work thing."

He gives me another funny look. "Of course you are. Why else would you be here?"

I swallow hard at his offended look.

"I mean, of course you know that. I was just—"

He bursts out laughing. "Nah, I'm just messin' with ya. I'll text you later. Sound good?"

Wait, he has my number?

"Um, okay."

Before I can react, wide Roger arms are circling around me for a hug. "Good to see you, man. Seriously. And I'm glad you didn't shave your head."

How did I completely miss this event in my life?

He lets go, and I duck into the elevator as soon as the doors open. *Please* don't let him be going up.

The last thing I see as the door closes is Roger's conspiratorial grin as he holds up six fingers.

* * *

I take the elevator to the third floor which is where Nash and Paige are staying. In an interesting twist, Eva and Marcos are occupying separate rooms for this conference since, *technically,* they're competitors. Conflict of interest? Sure. Is anyone at Reedweather Media besides Eva smart enough to do that math? Probably not.

Paige and Eva are hanging out at the pools, so it's just the three of us when Nash waves me in.

"Everything okay? It sounded urgent," Marcos says, leaning against the desk.

Nash drops to the edge of the bed and pulls an acoustic guitar into his lap. Seriously, that thing is like his security blanket. He can't do anything without caressing it. Doesn't Paige get jealous?

"Everything's fine," I lie, forcing a smile. No way I'm telling them about the Myra drama. Definitely not the Natalie drama. Actually, best to just stick with this Chad dude. I have a feeling he'll be enough of a topic for one conversation anyway.

"I just learned that we have a mutual acquaintance, and I need some guidance," I say. "Tell me everything I need to know about Chad Smith."

A painful chord emits from Nash's guitar.

"Excuse me?" Marcos chokes out. "What could you possibly need with Chad?"

Shit. This isn't a good start. Not that I was expecting glowing reports after my official introduction to the legendary human puzzle.

"Well, apparently, *he's* the Senior Director of Contingencies and Collateral

Mitigation at Sandeke Telecom. He's the one I have to convince to sign on with Eon Tech."

Their expressions are a unique blend of confusion, humor, and horror. Yeah, this is not great.

"Um…" Nash goes silent and shakes his head. "Sorry, man, that's all I got."

My gaze swings to Marcos, who shrugs.

"Nash is right. 'Um' is pretty accurate."

Fantastic. How much more can my exhausted brain handle right now?

"How do I win him over?" I ask, now very nervous.

"Not sure you can," Marcos says.

"Unless you're a Mer-Nut," Nash mumbles, and Marcos snickers.

Oh. Right. The "proprietary" peanut fish.

"So, what exactly *is* a Mer-Nut?" I ask.

"You don't want to know," Marcos says.

I do, though, and try way too hard to remember the top half of that aquatic monstrosity. The giant tubal blob kind of looked like, well, something you wouldn't expect to see at a telecom conference—or any conference that didn't involve the adult film industry. But I guess it could have been an amorphous nut instead of a… other kind of nut. I want to say that would make way more sense, but I'm not sure it does.

"Come on. Help me out, here!" I say. "I have to land this account or I'm done at Eon. My—uh, *boss* just laid into me about it."

Shit, that was close. I don't want them to know Myra's here. They'll worry about me, which means they'll babysit me, which means I'll have to pretend even more than I already am.

Marcos sighs. "I know, man. Okay, look. I'll talk to him and put in a good word for you. Not sure why, but he likes me for some reason."

"But you work for their competitor," I say, forcing away thoughts of Natalie. Competitors can't be friends, right? Or… more than friends?

"Yeah. I don't think they've made that connection yet. I wish I still had any interest in the corporate espionage thing. It would be so easy it wouldn't even be fun."

"Maybe we shouldn't," I say, tapping my fingers on the dresser.

"Shouldn't what?" Marcos asks.

"Put in a word. I mean, is that too 'good ole boys' sleazy? I should win this account on my own, right?"

Marcos literally wrote the book on business ethics (well, the thesis paper) so certainly he'll back my hesitation to claim an advantage—because it's ethical, and not at all because it would trample over... other... sales reps... who might be... pursuing this... account.

By his expression, this is another misjudgment on my part.

"I mean, I wasn't planning on sleeping with him to get you the contract," he says, drawing a snort from Nash.

"If you're concerned, I could also put in a word to balance it out," Nash says.

"He *hates* me. Oh, and I also will not sleep with him to get you the contract."

"Okay, but..."

"Actually, why not just tell him you're the one who wrote the code for the ransomware virus?" Nash suggests.

"Great idea," Marcos says. "He'd love that."

I shake my head. "Can't."

"Why not?" Marcos asks.

"Because he's telling everyone *he* wrote the code that *broke their company*."

Nash is snickering again. No surprise.

Marcos is too. Also not a surprise.

"Just don't let yourself get kidnapped," Nash says. "He sucks at hostage negotiating."

"And presentations," Marcos adds.

"And marketing," Nash says.

"And probably senior directing contingencies and collateral mitigation."

Marcos and Nash exchange a grin I'm happy to ignore when my phone buzzes.

"No way," I mumble, staring at my screen. "Check it out." I flash the phone in their direction. "Just got a message from him."

"Ha! See? You don't even need us. You're already besties," Marcos says.

I open the text and stare at it in confusion.

Chad Smith: **Hey Nathan! Let's meet up at The Splash Bar instead of the Lost Lagoon for drinks tonight. Thanks for lunch.**

Well, Natalie paid for lunch, and where the hell is The Splash Bar?

"You seem perplexed," Marcos says.

I look up. "Yeah, um. Chad just changed our meeting spot for tonight. Either of you know where The Splash Bar is? Is it on site?"

Nash snorts a laugh. Uh-oh.

"I know where it is," he says. "Eva and Paige are there now."

Confused, I glance at my phone, then back at Nash. "I thought they were swimming or something."

"They are," Marcos says, clapping me on the shoulder. "You, my friend, just got invited on a pool date. That's the swim-up bar at the main resort pool. Better dig out that bathing suit."

8—MONDAY 8:11 PM

NATALIE

"Hey, look!" Lanette says, smacking my arm. "That's him, right?"

I follow her gaze, and sure enough, my sales challenge for the week is gripping the edge of the pool with one hand and holding what looks like a frozen cocktail in the other.

"Yeah, that's Chad Smith from Sandeke Telecom," I say.

Theresa shifts on her lounge chair and squints at the man who seems to be very confused about the role of the miniature umbrella in his drink. "You should go over and talk to him."

"Really? It's late. He probably just wants to chill," I say.

Mostly, *I* just want to chill.

The truth is, I'm still reeling from that lunch-date disaster. I should be furious that Eon Tech crashed my sales meeting, and instead, all I can think about is Nate. His warm, hard body. His beautiful smile. Intelligent brown eyes that offer a devastating glimpse into a complex soul I could explore for weeks and not get bored.

Ever since I spouted off the list of rules to him this morning, I've wanted to break every single one. Aggressively.

"Who cares? After what that jerk at Eon Tech did to you at lunch, you deserve another shot," Theresa says.

"He wasn't a jerk," I mumble. "He was actually very nice about it."

"About thwarting your pitch?" Lanette huffs. "Told you he was an asshole. First, the marriage thing, and now this."

"The marriage thing?" Theresa asks.

Uh-oh. I shoot Lanette a warning look—which she completely ignores.

"Yeah, so get this," she says, leaning in with disturbing glee. "Natalie almost hooked up with Eon Tech's VP of Northeast Sales on Sunday night. You know, the guy trying to steal the Sandeke account from her? How's that for a scandal?"

Theresa's glare at me closely mimics my glare at Lanette.

"I didn't know who he was," I say quickly. "We just chatted for a bit."

All night.

Intimately.

Soul-searchingly beautiful like nothing I've ever experienced and now I can't get him out of my head.

"Right, because he's *married*," Lanette spits out. "Like I said, an asshole."

"He's an asshole because he's married?" Theresa asks.

"Exactly! He shouldn't have been talking to Nat. I bet he knew who you were and it was all part of his diabolical plan to seduce you for information."

"*You're* the one who started the conversation to hook us up," I point out.

"Yes, because of his seductive powers!"

Theresa glances between us. "So, let me get this straight. This guy used his seductive powers to make Lanette start a conversation that would spark something with Natalie, and then immediately said he was married, thus ending said conversation?"

"Yes," I lie. Well, sort of. *Technically,* it's a lie, but in this fictional version of events, I have no doubt that's what he would have done. (Minus the first part which literally no one would have done.)

"So how does that make him an asshole?" Theresa asks Lanette, finally on my side of an argument.

"Well, because…" Lanette scrunches her nose to think. "He's playing hard to get!"

"By being honest about his availability?"

I'm just glad they don't need me for this stupid argument. My phone buzzes, and I glance down to find a text from Dad. **How goes it?** he wants to know. There aren't enough emojis in the world to address that question via text.

"Okay, fine," Lanette says. "But ruining Nat's chance at Sandeke makes him a jerk."

"Agreed," Theresa says.

I press my lips to stop the instinctive defense. I want to tell them it wasn't really his fault, that his superiors pressured him into it and he clearly didn't want to do that to me. Plus, he did nothing during that lunch to promote himself or "steal" anything. He was as much a victim of that whole affair as I was.

I just have to figure out how to say all of that in a tone that doesn't also say, *"I have a huge crush on this person and will fight you to the death if you continue to vilify him."*

"Good, so time for revenge," Lanette says.

Is she rubbing her hands maniacally? What *happened* to her at *Tele-Con* last year?

"Exactly." Theresa turns to me. "I know you don't like playing dirty, but in this case you need to think…"

My boss goes silent at the same time Lanette's eyes bulge. A surge of heat fires through me when I follow their gazes.

"Whoa," Lanette mumbles.

"Is that…?"

Lanette nods at Theresa's question, her focus still locked on my sales nemesis—along with pretty much everyone else in visual range. You don't have to be attracted to men to appreciate the artistic beauty of the human body walking toward us in low-hanging board shorts and nothing else.

Nate moves with a confident strut that has even my critical coworkers mesmerized.

"Still want me to crash the party?" I quip with impressive poise for someone whose insides are fizzing from head to toe. My brain is already spinning with alternate scenarios to this moment.

He releases a radiant grin when he sees me and approaches with casual confidence. When he ducks to kiss me where I sit, there's a collective sigh of disappointment that he's taken. He pulls me up and leads me somewhere hidden to talk and/or ravage each other.

Or we just do it here. I can be flexible on the logistics in this fantasy.

In reality, he doesn't even notice us. He scans the area, clearly searching for something, and abruptly changes course when his gaze lands on the bar.

"Of course he's here for Chad. Told you he was a cheat," Lanette says, now glowering, along with her gawking.

"How is meeting up with a potential client cheating?" I ask.

"Not relationship cheating," Lanette grunts. "Business cheating."

I squint at her but decide not to pursue this one. More urgent matters take priority, like my need to escape the pool deck before my coworkers decide—

"You need to go over there," Theresa says.

She has her manager face back on after that temporary glitch, and my tiny tummy bubbles turn sour.

"And interrupt them?"

"Yes! He did it to you. Go crash *their* party this time," Theresa says.

"But I—"

"This has to be fate. What goes around comes around," Lanette hisses at Nate. She doesn't seem to mind that there's no way he heard that victorious barb from thirty feet away through crowds of people.

"Go, before they get too far into the conversation," Theresa commands. "It looks like they're still just exchanging pleasantries. We'll keep watch."

"Ooh good idea. Like spies," Lanette says, shifting to the edge of her chair.

Pretty sure a good spy would *not* make an abrupt adjustment upon entering spy-mode. Again, good thing our target is thirty feet away behind crowds of people.

"Yes, this is perfect," Theresa says. "Lanette and I will monitor from here for any big picture intel while you go in for the kill."

"The kill?" I say, liking this less and less.

"His pitch," Theresa clarifies. "Kill his pitch."

"And his career!" Lanette adds.

I send her a sharp look.

"What? You don't think he'd do the same to you?"

I know he wouldn't. He already had a chance.

"Natalie, I'm serious. Go over there," Theresa says in a tone that makes it clear arguing will get me nowhere.

Can I afford to piss off my boss on day one of this weeklong team bonding expo?

With a heavy sigh, I force myself up and tug the coverup wrap tighter around my hips.

"This feels weird. I'm in a bathing suit."

"So are they," Theresa says. "You're at a pool. It would be weird *not* to be in a bathing suit."

"Plus, you look hot," Lanette adds.

I look hot? Not exactly the pep-talk you want before embarking on a career-making sales call.

"Go!" Theresa says, shooing me in the direction of the bar.

"And don't fall prey to those pretty abs!" Lanette calls after me.

I won't. He already hooked me with that pretty heart.

* * *

Nate sees me first.

I try to breathe through the rush of attraction at his shocked, hungry gaze. He's already in the water, facing Chad, who's babbling about something related to the inexcusable cost of ice sculptures. But I doubt Nate's comprehending anything as he scans me like he, too, wishes we had added more physical events to our epic night together. In other words, he's looking at me the way I just looked at him a few moments ago.

Ravenous.

Burning.

Desperate to be anywhere but here.

Because I *also* feel the rapt attention of my coworkers across the pool. A cold wave sweeps through me when I spot Colin and Myra nearby as well. Great. This telecom convention has become a full-on spy convention.

Chad stops speaking and turns to follow Nate's gaze. His eyes light up the same way they did when he spotted Nate at our lunch. Maybe this guy just likes being interrupted by things.

"Natalie!" he says, waving me toward them. "What a surprise! Are you here for a swim?"

"Yes," I say with a tight smile.

Just like everyone else at the pool, I bet.

"I love your bathing suit. Is it nylon?"

"Um…"

"Well, it's emerald green. That's all that matters," Chad says.

I bite my lip and force a nod. He's not wrong.

Nate's distracting eyes are shining with amusement, and I could laugh at Lanette's warning. How would you even notice his abs when his eyes are so beautiful?

"Can I offer you a drink?" Chad asks.

By Nate's reaction, it will be on *his* tab this time, so of course I say yes. Lanette and Theresa would be proud.

"Oh! Shit!" Chad cries, ejecting himself from the pool.

Nate and I watch in alarm as he leaps toward the side of the bar.

A rare pool shark?

Explosive diarrhea?

Debilitating fear of chlorine?

He shoves his entire drink—cup and all—through the opening of a wicker bin I'm pretty sure is for used resort towels. I decide not to tell him this since his face is already a mask of gloom.

"I'm so sorry, Natalie. I didn't know you would be here," he says, slipping back into the pool.

Is that why he launched from the water and trashed what was probably a twenty-dollar cocktail?

"That's okay. I didn't know you would be here either," I say.

He leans close and looks around like he's concerned about spies. He should be, actually.

"It was a *strawberry* margarita," he whispers, and Nate almost chokes.

Wow. Um. That's actually kind of sweet in a weird, overly dramatic way.

"You're not feeling tingly at all, are you?" he asks in an urgent tone. His eyes dart over my face as if searching for signs of my impending demise.

Well, I am feeling a tad quivery, but not because of strawberries.

It turns out Nate's almost-smile is just as tingle-inducing as his real one. This is going to be a problem. It was hard enough staying focused at a perfectly tame lunch meeting. How am I supposed to keep my mind on task with Nate barely clothed and positioned in a way that screams, *"wouldn't it be fun if this was an island getaway and you were pressed against my tempting body while we made out in this pool?"*

It would be fun. So, so fun, and while my hormones contemplate that forbidden fantasy, my brain is very aware of Chad's concerned expression and the probing gazes of at least four not-so-secret spies scattered around the pool deck.

"I think I'll be okay," I assure him. "As for a drink, whatever IPA is on draft would be great."

He nods and signals the bartender. "My friend, here, would like an IPA. And I'll have a frozen piña colada. Wait!" He turns to me. "You're not allergic to bananas, are you?"

"No…" I say slowly. Is it his piña colada or my IPA he's concerned about? Either way, I'm questioning my order.

Nate brings his cup to his lips, clearly blocking another smile.

I force my attention back to Chad.

"So, Chad. Tell us more about your security concerns," I say. "You mentioned earlier that you expected some kind of interference from your competitor."

Nate's surprised gaze catches mine, and I force down the ache in my chest. Normally, I live for the chase. I love the fire of competition and everything that goes with it. But right now, it feels wrong to launch into the script I've used countless times. Nate seems shocked I'm going for it, which means he wasn't planning to. But he also knows the stakes. He must understand that our jobs are our forever, and this fling is just…

A distraction.

A mistake.

His characteristic smile slips just enough for me to glimpse the alluring piece of himself that he hides so well, even his closest friends don't know it exists. Last night, that secret was an irresistible pull for me, but we were in a dreamworld then. We're back in reality. At a conference. Bitter rivals battling it out in what's essentially a cage match with our bosses looking on from the balcony above.

I've already decided that I won't be playing dirty, but I at least have to play. In a sense, this is the fairest scenario we could have—both of us privy to the same information with the same opportunity to engage.

"Yes, that's correct," Chad says, graciously accepting his new drink from the bartender. He shoves the straw in his mouth and chews on it while he thinks. I give that paper straw seven seconds before it's little more than a bonus garnish for his piña colada.

"You know how clowns are meant to make people laugh, but sometimes they kill them instead?" he asks.

Oh. Um.

Nate also looks one part confused and every part alarmed.

"Yes?" I say, not sure what other options I have.

Chad takes a hard suck on the collapsed straw. "That's Brighthouse. At first you think, 'Aw, look at that nice clown.' Next thing you know…" He slides his finger across his throat.

"So… you used to be… friendly with Brighthouse?" I ask when it's clear that was the end of the story.

"What? No," Chad huffs. "They're our competitor. I just said that."

"Right, but the clown—"

"The *murder* clown," Chad growls.

"Uh-huh. But it was a friendly clown first, right?"

Why am I still trying? It's that damn sales gene.

"No. It just makes you *think* it's friendly so you let it into your yard to make balloon animals or whatever, and then…" He slides his finger across his throat again.

"Ah. So Brighthouse *acted* friendly so they could…?"

Pretty sure it wasn't to make balloon animals. That's about all I'm certain of right now.

"It's the makeup," Nate says in a corroborating tone.

Chad's face lights up as he twists toward him. "Exactly! With the extra big lips and shit?"

Nate nods and holds up his glass for Chad to toast in agreement.

What is happening?

Nate's gaze slides to me, and he lifts his brows in challenge.

Ah, I get it. He also has no clue what Chad is talking about, but he's perfectly clear on how to play Chad. Well, two can play at that game. Or is it three? I scan the vast resort pool area. We might be at seven, actually.

"Don't forget the extra big shoes," I add.

I lift my cup and hold my breath, then release it in relief when Chad grins and taps my drink with his.

"Touché," he says.

I expect Nate to look annoyed that I got a point as well, but he just looks amused. It's a strange reaction for a rival. That's Nate, though. I can see him *helping* his competition before hurting them. How is he in sales? Other than his natural likeability and deadly smile, I haven't witnessed a single trait in the easy-going, considerate guy that would enjoy the cut-throat battleground of corporate sales. (Not to be confused with spurious clowns who cut throats.)

"Anyway, my point is, Brighthouse *thinks* they're so clever, but we have a huge advantage," Chad continues.

"What's that?" I ask.

He taps his head and smiles.

After a few seconds of silence, I force my expression to convey that I know what he means.

Nate looks like he does too, but I'm pretty sure he just has a good bluff face also. In fact, I know he must for him to hide his true self so well. As I study his casual expression, something twists in my stomach. It's incredible, really. If not for that conversation last night, I'd have no idea what was really going on in that complex brain of his. How has he carried that weight so long on his own?

My radar for his ex blares into action, and a quick scan finds her staring intently at us from her lounge beneath a cabana. Her expression is unreadable until her attention lands on Nate. There's definite longing in her slow perusal, a possessiveness that has me on edge, and I don't understand why. It's not like I plan on leaving this conference with more than a wild story to tell. I already made it clear to him I don't want more, and he still seems hung up on her, anyway. She's determined to get him back, so if anything, it's likely they'll end up reunited by Friday. In other words, that man is as far from "mine" as a person can be.

So why is my stomach swirling with jealousy?

"Oh, snap," Chad says, squinting into the distance.

We follow his gaze, but all I see is a public restroom dressed up like a tiki hut.

"They have bathrooms," he explains. "You mind?" he asks Nate, who immediately is holding Chad's drink. Good thing we're in shallow water or my competition would be drowning right now with a plastic cup in each hand.

Chad launches himself from the pool for the second time in this brief encounter and struts toward the faux island oasis.

"Guess we're taking a break," Nate says in a dry tone.

I return a smile, my heart beating faster now that we're alone. Well, not exactly *alone* if we count our thinly veiled surveillance.

"How are you?" I ask, searching his face.

He's about to respond, then quiets when he realizes my question was sincere, not polite.

His gaze flickers to Myra. "Not great, to be honest."

"Have you spoken to her since the seminar this morning?"

He doesn't look at me as he nods, and my insides clench again. *For no reason.* Because he's not mine and never will be and that's okay because that's how it's supposed to be. It's what I *want.* Right?

Right.

"It didn't go well, I guess?"

He shakes his head. "It's not just that. There's all this other shit, and I'm just so… Never mind. Let's forget it."

"Never mind? Really?" I say in mock irritation.

He returns a weak smile that tugs at me.

"I know. It's just… things are different now than they were last night in my room. I shouldn't have shared all that shit. I feel like the biggest loser."

"Nate…"

He shakes his head again. "It's fine. It's no one's fault, just… I don't want to talk about it anymore. I can't."

Everything in me wants to wrap my arms around him when his mask slips enough to reveal the pain beneath. He can't share it? He has to. I could see how it was crushing him last night. What's his plan, exactly? To live the rest of his life as someone else until he's not living at all?

"At least talk to your roommates about how you've been feeling. From everything you've said, you all legitimately care about each other."

"Yes, and that's exactly why I can't. They rely on me to be the strong one. I've always been the leader. The one taking care of them and looking out for them. I can't rip the rug out from under them by shattering their support system."

"Nate, that's not fair. You can't hold up the universe yourself for all of eternity. Friendship goes both ways. I'm sure they'd want to support you as much as you've always been there for them."

He shakes his head, his expression hardening. "You don't understand. It's… complicated. Our past is rocky and… Look, I know you're trying to help, but we swore last night was a one-off, right? We never expected to see each other again, so we definitely shouldn't be going for a repeat. That was your own rule."

I wince. He's not wrong. I did say that. It's a good rule. At least, it was until this person.

"And you were right because this thing is even more screwed up than we thought," he continues. "Apparently, I'm supposed to seduce you for information."

By his conflicted expression, he doesn't realize how rapid my pulse is pounding at the suggestion.

"Yeah? I'm supposed to seduce you, too," I say.

His startled look draws a smile from me.

"You're kidding," he mumbles.

"Nope." I make a subtle motion to the far end of the pool. "They sent me over here to interrupt your meeting with Chad and flirt with you to get intel."

"Same. What is wrong with our companies?"

I shrug. "Don't worry. I have no intention of playing along."

"I mean, a *little* playing would be okay, right?" he teases.

My body flushes with heat. He's not serious but… Maybe he should be.

"Hey, um." I meet his gaze, encouraged when I catch the return fire in his eyes. "I get the *no more intimate conversation* thing, but what if...?" My teeth sink into my lip as I cast a quick glance at our audience, then focus back on this walking temptation I can't get out of my head. "Maybe intimate touches could still be fair game? You know, in the interest of *spying*."

The intense flareup in his expression has me moving close enough to enjoy that distracting cologne. His back is to the edge of the pool as I close in. The water must be boiling around us at this point.

"I'm a yes to *spying* if you are," he says in a low voice.

"Good."

"Wait, we're doing this now?" he whispers when I take the drinks from his hands and place them on the concrete ledge.

"It's what they want, right?"

"Yeah, but..." He glances at Myra, and my Nate's-Ex Alarm screams in response.

"You're worried Myra will be upset?" I say with a sigh.

His troubled gaze lands back on me. "No. It was her idea. It was kind of an indirect order, actually."

What?!

As if I needed more reasons to dislike this woman. Geez, if Nate were mine, he'd be in a vault behind bulletproof glass. The claws would come out if another person so much as looked at him lustfully. And she *directed* him to pursue someone else?

Hell no.

Sparks fire through me when I touch his shoulder. I sense his quick inhale as I run my fingers over his warm, wet skin. He must feel it too. This volatile chemistry. The explosive heat.

Except, I totally miscalculated.

It seemed like a good idea a second ago. Our audience is silently begging us to do something we want to do. Why not use their gross game for our own benefit? Just a little touch to soothe the hunger.

But once my fingers landed on his skin, every other part of me wanted to participate. Even the most skilled seductress wouldn't be skilled enough to justify everything I want to do to him right now. My palm may have already gone too far with the way it fuses to his chest like it wants way more than information about competitive power backups.

Nate must sense my dilemma as well when he laughs like I just said something hilarious. I force my hand to sever the bond with his body, but I have no doubt my expression is having no such luck in taming itself.

I want him. Badly.

He leans in, his lips almost at my ear. "This isn't a good idea," he says, his voice rough and tortured. "I want you too much right now."

I close my eyes at the electric surge ripping through my veins. I know I shouldn't, but my right hand instinctively seeks his waist beneath the water. The others can't see that from their vantage points, right?

His breathing accelerates as my fingers glide along the waistband of his shorts. He feels so good, and they dip lower to sink into the apex of dense muscle.

"Natalie…" he warns.

"I know, I just…"

My defense stalls when I feel a firm grasp around my hip on the hidden side as well. His thumb moves along my pelvic bone, triggering bolt after bolt of electricity. The tips of his other fingers slip under the edge of my suit to graze my behind. My entire body is on fire, the need overwhelming as I fight the urge to shove him into the wall and devour him. His mouth, his neck, anything and everything. He'd feel amazing against me, hard and slick, the slight smell of chlorine mixing with the delicious scent of his lingering cologne. What would he taste like? I can't tell what he's drinking. Something with a slice of lime.

"We should stop," I say. "We're supposed to be seducing, not propositioning."

He smirks. "Yeah. I don't suppose we'd be able to pull off another bathroom stall rendezvous right now."

My blood pounds at the thought. I'd do anything to be pressed up against a metal partition with him. Instead, I should earn some kind of commemorative plaque for restraint when I force my fingers to release him and step back.

His expression drops, along with his hand as he lets go. "Sorry. That was inappropriate."

"No. It was hot and way too tempting," I say, capturing his fingers for a quick squeeze.

He meets my gaze, and I see the hunger in his eyes before he shifts and pulls away. I understand why when Chad saunters toward us.

Right. That.

Our associate slips back into the water with the grace of a drunken walrus. Mer-Man, my ass. This dude has no aquatic instincts.

"Now, where were we?" he asks, taking the cup Nate hands him. "Good, it's finally melted. Frozen drinks are so much easier to drink once they're melted."

He sucks on his collapsed straw, and Nate and I make a silent pact not to advise him of the existence of non-frozen cocktails.

We also silently agree that what just happened between us can't happen again.

9—TUESDAY 4:22 AM

NATE

How long do you stare at the ceiling before it's time to call it? That's a question I've considered a lot over the last few months. Usually, the answer is around two hours, sometimes three. Tonight, I don't know.

I rarely sleep anymore, and when I do it's a miracle if I stay unconscious for more than a couple of hours. Three to four AM seems to be the magic internal alarm clock, and I guess being at a high-end resort does nothing to reset it. Today it was 3:13, and as I study the textured ceiling, the crushing weight on my chest seems to grow with each passing second. It's amazing how the shroud of darkness amplifies the shadows instead of hiding them. Because everything that seems manageable during daylight hours becomes a fucking avalanche in the middle of the night.

Remember that time I accidentally cut off the guy in the blue Camry on Route 73 or accidently underpaid my portion of dinner for that birthday celebration at the Chinese restaurant? They don't, but I definitely feel terrible about it at 3:13 in the morning six years later. Forget about the barrage of catastrophic hyperbole regarding actual problems.

Unable to take any more, I reach over to turn on the lamp. Yellow light filters throughout the room, but the heavy silence still pounds in my ears. I press the heels of my palms against my eyes, fighting to calm the demons swirling in and around me.

I lost everything this summer. Myra, my career, my entire identity. I don't know who the hell I am anymore, where I'm going, or even what I want. While Marcos and Nash found their golden paths to fulfillment over the last few months, I'm spiraling further and further from any sustainable future. I won't be able to survive another month of this existence, let alone decades. Just the prospect of another hour is too much sometimes.

Like now.

Like every time I have to smile through the pain and pretend there isn't an invisible curtain cutting me off from the world around me. I feel it more and more now—the separation, the numbness that's making it impossible to breathe, and I just...

"Fuck," I exhale, scrubbing at my face.

I grab my phone from the nightstand and open the text app. My finger hovers over Marcos' name, my heart pounding in my chest. I don't have to tell him everything, just enough to take a full breath. If I could only breathe for a few minutes, maybe... He's been through enough shit to understand, right? We all have.

Hey. Can we meet up for breakfast? I type, then immediately delete it and toss my phone on the mattress beside me.

Meet for breakfast and do what? Tell one of the few people who care about me that I'm a total fraud? That I'm not even fucking real? Then what? He tells Nash and the next thing I know, I'm completely alone in this world. They've always been closer to each other than to me.

I lean forward and rest my head on my fists, shaking as I try to piece myself back together. I've survived so much worse than this. My story could be a movie on many levels. It makes no sense that I powered my way through a lifetime of trials, only to get knocked down in a four-star hotel on 800 thread-count sheets. I've *always* been the strong one. The brave one. The one who held us together and propelled the three of us from lost group home children to successful, thriving adults. So how did I become the weakest link? It's embarrassing. Pathetic.

Snap out of it! What is wrong with you?

I don't know, but it's getting harder and harder to pretend.

I pick up my phone to return it to the charger, but my gaze gets snagged on the group chat with Chad and Natalie.

Nate, I must sincerely apologize for complimenting Natalie on her swimsuit but not you. You looked fantastic as well. Will you be at the Agile

Synergy Seminar? I will. I looked up the word tiki. Also pina. Did you know it means pineapple not banana?

Yes, okay, and yes.

Chad had texted both of us this weird message after we parted ways tonight. Why he included Natalie is beyond me, unless it was to make sure she knew he apologized for a slight not a single person would have thought about ever. I had no idea how to respond, so I stuck with polite, safe pleasantries like Natalie did.

Polite and safe. The one thing Nat and I haven't been since the minute we started talking.

I open the chat and stare at her number. We never exchanged them. If not for Chad's text, I wouldn't even have it. She probably doesn't want to hear from me. In fact, based on her rules, I know she doesn't. With everything that's gone down in the last twenty-four hours, it's amazing she still wants to be physical with me.

I know I shouldn't do it even as I start typing but I can't stop myself for some reason. It's always like that with her. Shit just... comes out. Then again, who better to alienate than the person who's *supposed* to hate you?

Hey it's Nate, I type in a private message. **Can't sleep. You were right. I'm not good.**

And I press send.

* * *

The record for regretting an action was previously two minutes and six seconds. That was the day Marcos and Nash convinced me to get a surprise tattoo of their choosing. It took two minutes and six seconds to learn I will forever have an ice cream sandwich on my left shoulder. Thankfully, they also allowed me to disguise it in the wilderness motif I have going on my upper back, but close scrutiny can still make out two chocolate wafers nestled among moody wooded mountains and howling wolves.

The record is now nine seconds. That's the length of time it took me to press send and stare in horror at what I'd just done. I spent the next twenty minutes forcing myself not to spam her a text wall of retractions that would create a bigger disaster. Currently, I'm back to staring at the ceiling, enjoying yet another reason to hate myself. What was I thinking?

Lying in bed is getting me nowhere, though, so I push up and shuffle to the bathroom. It's almost five, anyway. The resort gym is open, and five isn't too early for the go-getters who have shit to do. I could easily hide there for a while and pretend I'm one of those.

Yep, don't mind me. Just gotta work those glutes before jumping into my jam-packed day of getting harassed by my ex, threatened by my boss, and humiliated in front of my competition, all while pursuing a guy who drinks wine from a straw and thinks bananas are the basic ingredient in everything.

With my head still crammed, I jump in the shower to rinse off and clear the stain of this night as much as possible. After brushing my teeth and throwing on a pair of gym shorts, I'm searching for a clean shirt when there's a soft knock at the door.

Shit. A manager, maybe? Was someone complaining about the loud water this early in the morning. It's not *that* early, right? Maybe there's an issue with my room? The reservation itself? That would be just my luck.

I check through the peephole and freeze.

Oh no.

Crap. *What have you done?!*

Natalie knocks again, and I lean my forehead against the door.

Everything in me wants to pretend I'm asleep, but what kind of asshole reaches out to someone, then ignores their response?

It's just, I don't think I can take any more blows right now. I didn't expect her to see my message so soon. I definitely didn't expect her to come to my room to… I have no idea. It can't be good, though.

I pull open the door with the brightest smile I can muster.

"Hey. Uh…" Yeah, I've got nothing.

Guess I don't need it when she pushes past me into the room. Okay, then.

I close the door and turn toward her, expecting a variety of reactions. Confusion at being disturbed by a virtual stranger at four in the morning. Anger for breaking several of her rules with that text. Irritation that, after our steamy encounter in the pool, I practically ran away to avoid further drama. Wait, that one could be anger as well. Come to think of it, so could the first. Yep, I'm putting anger on the shortlist of likely reactions.

What I don't anticipate are arms circling around my waist and pulling me in for a hug. I'm definitely not prepared for the soft brush of her hair and the soothing warmth of her body as she nestles against my chest. Stunned, I don't know what to do except fold my arms around her in return.

She doesn't say anything as we hold on, and I'm grateful for the silence. We don't need words for this moment, just the chance to exist in unison for a few precious seconds. It feels so good to be touched, connected in a way that isn't obligatory or self-serving. I close my eyes and breathe in stale hotel air that suddenly flows like a fresh alpine breeze.

I didn't even know I needed this, and now it feels essential.

After a minute or so, she lets go and takes my hand to lead me to the bed. She drops to the edge of the mattress and tugs until I lower myself beside her. Her fingers entwine with mine, and I manage a deep inhale as I focus on the wall in front of us.

"I'm glad you messaged me," she says, breaking the long silence.

She's glad? I don't know what to say, so I just squeeze her hand.

She leans her head on my shoulder, and we stare in silence for several more seconds.

"I'm still not sure why I did," I respond finally. "I'm sorry for breaking your rules."

"I'm starting to think a few of my rules need revision."

A smile flickers over my lips, and I see one on hers as well when I look over.

She straightens and faces me.

"The truth is, since the moment I told you I didn't want to see you again, all I've wanted to do was see you again."

Surprised, I search her eyes. "Really? I thought… I don't know. What about your life plan you were talking about Sunday night? No repeats, so there are no attachments."

She grunts. "Yes, well, it was a good *plan*, but you know what they say about plans."

"Don't assign them to Chad unless you're a mascot trainer?"

"Or a polo shirt designer."

"Or running a grilled cheese test panel."

She presses her teeth into her glossy lip to bite back a smile. It makes her look sexy and adorable at the same time, which is a tempting look on a woman as intelligent and accomplished as she is.

"What I meant was, what do most people who don't know Chad say about plans?" she says.

"They're made to be broken."

"Exactly. This conference may not be teaching me anything about telecom, but I'm learning quite a bit about the efficacy of my assumptions."

"I'm guessing you're not referring to Chad's suggestion to attract consumers by dressing up like a swimming penis."

She snorts a laugh. "No, I was not."

"In his defense, it *would* attract a lot of consumers. Probably all of them, actually."

She shakes her head with a grin. "My point is, having rules and a plan isn't a bad thing, but it won't stop life from blowing up in your face. Somehow, I think you can relate."

"You mean losing your partner, career, and future in the span of a few months?"

Her humor fades as she studies me. "Your career?"

Crap. That got dark quick. Another exciting talent I've developed.

With a heavy sigh, I pull my hand away and lean back on the bed for another staring contest with the ceiling. I have no idea how to tell this story. I've never tried. I'm terrified to hear it out loud.

"Nate?"

"Yeah, sorry. It's just…"

I swallow hard and gather the courage to continue. Maybe hearing it will help me finally make sense of it.

"I probably shouldn't tell you this since you're my competition," I begin hesitantly. "But…"

"But what?"

"I despise sales."

I feel her surprise as she reclines beside me. Our arms brush together, and our fingers instinctively find each other's again. How can something so new feel so natural?

"Wow. Was not expecting that," she says.

"Yeah, I know, but it's reality. There's literally no part about it I like except talking to people, and even that I hate when it's in the context of trying to push something on them."

I hold my breath, having no idea how she'll take my confession. Will she even understand? I've barely begun telling this horror story.

"Don't take this the wrong way," she says, a hint of amusement in her voice. "But I've been thinking the same thing about you since I learned you were my competition. You don't seem like someone who would enjoy this world."

"I'm not. It's kind of my worst nightmare, actually."

"So why do you do it?"

"It's complicated."

My stomach cramps with familiar anxiety. I want to tell her more, but I don't even know how. There are so many ways to answer that question, and most of them I don't understand well enough to express.

"What career *do* you want, if it's not in sales?"

"Finance," I say without hesitation. "It's what I studied in college and grad school. It's all I've ever wanted to do."

I smile at a memory and shift to my side to face her. "Marcos and I spent a couple of summers stripping, and you know our favorite part about it?"

"The thongs?"

I love that she doesn't seem fazed by the announcement. Most people have some kind of reaction—positive or negative—but as usual with Natalie, she just accepts what is.

I chuckle and shake my head. "Close, but no. It was building the business. We had everything running so smoothly, our professors would have been proud if our fun case study wouldn't have caused several strokes in the faculty lounge."

She releases a sly smile. "So you're saying your stripping business was a *well-oiled* machine?"

"So *well-oiled*," I say with a smirk. "My point is, I love numbers. Math, computer programming—anything that involves logic and order. I spent most of my life being dragged through chaos and uncertainty. I love the security of complex problems that have finite solutions."

Her fingers tighten around mine, so I know she heard the underlying pain in that confession. It's the truth, though. My entire life has been a variable. Being moved from one family member to the next, only to end up in foster care with strangers. Never knowing where I'd be sleeping tomorrow. If I'd be eating. Always aware that everything I knew could be torn apart at any moment.

"If you love finance so much, why not do that instead?" she asks.

"I... It's complicated," I repeat for what feels like the hundredth time.

Is it, though? So many things that were complicated just a few days ago, seem much simpler in her presence.

"Everything is with you," she says, tugging my hand. "Try me."

I blow out a breath and focus back on a small crack in the ceiling. It's worth a shot if hearing it out loud will help sort through the mess in my head.

"I've only been in sales for a few weeks. I was the VP of Finance prior to that, and I fucking loved my job."

She frowns when I look over, her brow creasing with concern.

"Who doesn't want to get paid for doing something they love?" I continue with a weak smile. "I honestly saw myself retiring from Eon. Maybe getting up to CFO one day, but even if I didn't, I would have been happy playing with number puzzles all day."

My jaw clenches at the next memory, and I return my focus to the ceiling. "The department heads didn't like me, though. They didn't like that I questioned their budgets and kept proposing alternatives that were more fiscally responsible. We fought all the time. I didn't mind it. I'm not afraid of confrontation if it's over something I believe in. The CFO loved me for it, until…"

I run a hand over my face and take a deep breath.

"Until?" Natalie encourages when I go silent.

Until everything fell apart.

"Myra and I were dating before I started at Eon. We disclosed our relationship during the interview process, so they knew from the beginning we were together. Since we were in different departments, they let it go. Everything was fine until she got promoted and dumped me."

"That must have been hard."

"Yeah, it wasn't great," I say quietly. "The emotional aspect was brutal, but I navigated it as best as I could from a professional standpoint. I thought I was in the clear until a month ago."

My fist tightens at my side. Old anger seeps into my veins, making the betrayal fresh and raw. I can still feel the nausea in my stomach when I got called into HR. The humiliation of packing up my desk, and the exhaustion from smiling through the introductions and announcements of a reassignment I didn't want.

"I refused to sign off on the marketing budget." I hear the resentment in my tone, so I know she does. "That action put me in direct conflict with Myra since it's her department. It had nothing to do with our breakup and everything to do with the obscene amount of money her VPs wanted for meals and entertainment. They requested a forty percent increase with no justification, at a time when we were making cuts across the board. I said I would only approve a ten percent increase, unless they could provide written rationalization for why they needed more. They were pissed, and even tried to go over my head."

"But the CFO sided with you?"

"She didn't weigh in on either side, but said it was my call, so they had to respect my decision. And so they got creative."

Natalie's hand tightens around mine.

"They campaigned hard with HR and upper management to frame my refusal as a personal vendetta against my ex. It worked, and they got me transferred out of accounting and into sales. Can't do much damage here, can I?" I mutter.

"Wow. That's awful. But isn't making her your boss an even bigger conflict of interest?"

"I'm pretty sure they don't care about that at this point. Plus, there's enough space on the org chart and physical states between us to justify it. I mean, it's kind of a brilliant F-U, no? Putting me in the department I fought with the most? It was the perfect retribution for them. Now my fate is in their hands instead of the other way around, and believe me, they're doing everything they can to take their revenge."

Natalie's face contorts with righteous anger.

"And Myra supported this?" she asks when I stop speaking.

Right. Now the nightmare begins.

"I always assumed she didn't," I say, absently picking at the comforter with my free hand. "She wasn't the one heading up the attacks, but after our conversation yesterday, I'm not so sure."

Natalie shifts and presses into my side. She drapes her arm over my chest, and I reach up to run my fingers across her skin as I think. There's more, the most dangerous confession of all, and I swallow it, not sure if I should say it. Actually, I'm positive I shouldn't say it, but it gnaws at me. Would I want to know if I were in her shoes?

Yes.

I take a deep breath.

"They pretty much told me if I don't land Sandeke this week, I'm getting fired. They've been looking for an excuse for a while. This is their golden ticket. I'm almost positive they're setting me up."

I sense her sharp inhale but don't look at her. I can't. I have no idea how she'll take that, but it seemed like something she should know.

"Nate, I… shit. I'm so sorry."

I squint at the ceiling, surprised to see more imperfections than I thought now that the first rays of sun filter into the room.

"I didn't tell you that to make you feel sorry for me," I say in a hard tone. "The opposite, really. I want you to understand what you're up against. This isn't your average competitive bid. You've been inserted into the middle of a civil war."

"I appreciate the heads up," she says. "I'll polish up my musket."

I force a slight twist of the lips, and she squeezes my hand.

"Can I ask you something?" she asks.

"Sure."

"Why don't you leave Eon? Find another job at a company that will value you instead of fight you?"

"I'm trying, believe me. But nothing has hit yet, and I can't afford to quit. Not just financially, but also career-wise. You know how it is. Your resume is way more marketable with a current position listed than a terminated one. I'm also stuck trying to explain why I want a career in finance when it looks like I want a career in sales."

"Crap, yeah. I'm guessing your superiors aren't lining up to give a professional reference either."

"No. They're too busy trying to make me quit so we don't have to fight over unemployment benefits."

She sighs and tightens her arm around me. "That's not right."

"It's... whatever," I mumble. "Anyway, sorry for dumping more secrets on you. I have no idea why that keeps happening when you're around."

She smiles and tugs a lock of my hair. "I like hearing your secrets."

"Well, they all boil down to one, basically. Four months ago my forever was fully mapped out, and now I have no clue what the hell I'm doing in any aspect of my life."

And there it is. Guess I was right. Hearing it out loud made it a lot clearer. Too bad this new clarity doesn't fix shit.

"Want to know one of *my* secrets?" she asks in a soft tone.

"What's that?" It can't be worse than any of mine.

A smile spreads over her lips as her eyes drift to mine. "I really like you, Nathan Hanover. The real you."

* * *

Two hours of deep conversation later, we've officially ushered in a second morning together. Not sure how this keeps happening, but it's kind of hilarious for two people who are trying so hard *not* to be a pretend couple.

Natalie is flipping through the TV channels when I shoot her a grin.

"What's so funny?" she asks, pausing on a home improvement show.

"We ordered room service for breakfast."

"So? We're both starving and we can't be seen together."

"I know. It's the only option that made sense, it's just..."

She bites her lip when I hesitate, and every part of me would love to be doing that on her behalf.

"We broke yet another of your conference hookup rules," I say. "We're sharing a meal."

She scrunches her nose. "I guess it's also another item on the list of things people do after having sex, even though we haven't had sex yet."

Whoa.

My body is immediately on high alert from one tiny word.

"Yet?" I ask.

She shrugs with a coy smile. "You haven't been thinking about it?"

My gaze runs over her slowly, my blood pumping hard. "I mean, yeah, but… you have been too?"

"All the time. I've wanted to jump you about twenty times in the last couple of hours."

Damn.

She scours me where I'm reclined on the bed with my arm tucked under my head.

"Do you know how sexy you look right now?" she asks.

I want to say something cheesy like, "not as sexy as you," but I forget how words work when she crawls toward me. My muscles coil for an immediate reaction, but I force them to behave as she closes the distance like a hungry predator. Kind of like a… panther. Great, and now Colin's offensive joke is skating through my head. I still want to punch him for it, maybe even more than when he first said it, but I have nothing but appreciation and respect for analogous cats when they're linked to Natalie McAllister.

The remote slips from her hand as her other palm slides up my bare chest. I never did get around to finding a shirt, a fact that she didn't seem to mind judging by the number of times I've caught her staring at me. To be fair, it was probably less than the number of times I've catalogued every detail of her appearance since she knocked on my door. She looks equal parts sexy and cute in an off-the-shoulder graphic tee and gray shorts.

Of course, what she's wearing means nothing when her hand traps the side of my face to guide my mouth to hers. Our lips fuse together with pent-up longing. Our tongues clash in deep, probing strokes. When her leg swings over my hips to straddle me, I forget all about *the quaint Victorian with the original outhouse that will be turned into a country-cottage-inspired landscape piece.*

Nat's fingers thread into my hair, gripping hard with each electric collision of our mouths. As our kiss deepens into desperation, she grinds against me to release wave after wave of restricted desire. I run my palms down her back and over her ass, enjoying every curve of her body. She feels amazing. She makes *me* feel amazing, and that's a thing I rarely feel anymore.

I slip my fingertips under the band of her shorts, loving the soft moan it triggers.

"This okay?" I ask.

"So okay. I want you to touch me. Anywhere and everywhere," she breathes against my lips before resuming the kiss.

Hell yes.

She gasps when I rub firm pressure over the soft fabric between her thighs. Her hips respond with aggressive thrusts against my hand, as if straining for more. Damn, this might be even better than having her hands on me.

Nope, I lied.

I'm a huge fan of her palm shoving down my stomach to breach the waistband of my shorts. She skims my growing erection. Once, twice, over and over with increasing pressure, until my fractured world fades into a distant mist. All the moments of restraint over the last couple of days, all the hunger to do exactly this, come rushing back in an explosive need—not for sex, but for her. An insatiable longing to connect with her on every level.

"You feel so good," she moans. "I want you so much."

"I want you too," I rasp against her neck.

She tastes incredible, feels like a forbidden fantasy in my hands. I slip my fingers beneath her panties, loving how she writhes and strokes me to the same rhythm in return.

"No, I mean, I want *everything*," she gasps. "All of you. Can we finally—"

She's cut off by a knock at the door, and our gazes snap to that interfering block of wood.

"Shit. You have to be kidding me," I grunt, collapsing into the sheets.

"Must be breakfast," she mumbles, looking as disappointed as I am. Her fingertips trail over my cheek as if tracing a memory. "I'd say we could skip food but…"

"Yeah," I say on an exhale. "It'll be a long morning. We should eat."

"And get ready for the seminar at nine. Agile Symmetry, right?"

"Synergy. Do you think Chad is teaching this one too?"

"We can only hope," she says dryly.

I chuckle as she rolls off me with a reluctance I feel in every cell of my body.

I already miss her warmth and the enticing floral scent of her shampoo.

Another knock has her on her feet, trudging toward the door.

"Coming," she calls out.

I'm still readjusting myself when she pulls it open to reveal exactly what we expected: a hotel employee carrying a tray of food. What we didn't expect was that employee to march into the room, place the tray on the dresser, and introduce herself as Verna.

"I see you ordered the breakfast combo platter. Excellent choice," she says with an approving nod better suited for a toddler demonstrating they know their shapes. "It's the perfect meal to replenish those calories after a *vigorous workout*." She winks and nudges Natalie's arm.

Huh, okay. Well, *that* just bumped up the age requirement for this conversation.

A slight flush spreads over Natalie's cheeks, and I can't tell if she wants to run away or punch the woman. Maybe both? I guess those reactions could go hand-in-hand.

"Oh, I love this show!" Verna says, dropping to the edge of the bed.

We stare at her, speechless, before exchanging a glance.

"You know, my cousin Frank has an old Victorian house that looks exactly like this one," she informs us. "Well, not exactly. His is a cape cod and doesn't have a porch, second story, or chimney. Oh, and no backyard or shrubbery."

So, basically her cousin Frank has the opposite of this house. Good to know.

"They replaced the shutters, though, and you'd never know they weren't original. They went to this barn auction in Louisville. You wouldn't believe the treasures they left!"

"Your cousin?" I ask.

"No, the people who owned the barn. They passed away in a boating accident. Or maybe it was malaria? I can never remember." She considers both scenarios before shaking her head. "Wait, no. Those were the other barn owners."

I couldn't name a single barn owner and this woman knows so many she can't keep them apart.

"The shutter barn owners retired to Panama City."

"In Florida?" Natalie asks. "My grandparents live there."

"No, Costa Rica. Or was it Colombia? One of those South African countries."

I'd bet my life that there are no former barn owners living in Panama City,

South Africa.

"You sure it wasn't in a South *American* country? Maybe, Panama?" I ask. Pretty sure Panama is actually *Central* America, but none of this is the hill I want to die on.

She shakes her head. "No, it was Panama *City*. As in, the city, not the country. Anyway, my point is, they're not dead but they had amazing antiques in their barn."

"That's great," Natalie says quickly. "So, um, we have to get ready for our busy day. Thanks so much for delivering our food."

"It's my pleasure! Are you here for a conference? There are several, you know. This place is always packed full of conferences. You'd be amazed how many things people can find a reason to meet about."

"Yes, we are." Natalie says, trying to encourage our guest toward the door. I would say her attempts are subtle but they're not.

"The main one this week is something with telephones. Or was it televisions? I don't know. Something technical-y."

"Telecom," Natalie says.

"Maybe?"

Definitely.

"Anyway, there's also a bachelorette, book, and cat convention."

Now, *that* sounds like a fun convention. Wonder if I can transfer.

"Not combined," she clarifies. "Three separate conventions."

Damn.

"A bachelorette convention?" Natalie asks. "Like a bridal convention?"

"No, no. Just an annual party week. The resort sections off two floors for the festivities. It's a whole thing. You should see *their* breakfast orders."

Verna lets out a low whistle and chuckles to herself, obviously enjoying her reminiscence about delivering those orders. I wonder if she makes herself at home in their rooms as well. It has to be more exciting than ours. Why is she still here?

She leans forward and scans the space to make sure we're alone. God, I wish we were. "Tomorrow is the main event. It's a huge hit every year. Strippers and everything."

"Strippers, huh," Natalie says in a crafty tone that really, really makes me regret telling her about that.

"I'd be happy to contact concierge for you if you're interested."

"Concierge would invite us to someone else's event?" Natalie asks with appropriate skepticism.

"Oh! No. I meant, interested in your own strippers."

Natalie appears way too intrigued by that idea. I give her a hard look as she lifts her brows in a very suggestive challenge.

"I think we're good," I say. "Thanks, though."

"Oh, well, are you sure? No offense, but telephones don't sound quite as fun."

She obviously hasn't delivered any food to Sandeke Telecom's Senior Director of Contingencies and Collateral Mitigation.

"We're sure," I say. "Thanks again. We really have to get moving. You know those demanding convention schedules."

"Do I ever! You should see what's involved with the book conventions! At first you think, oh books. So boring, right? But then you go in and whoa. All those banners." She fans herself with an expression eerily similar to her I-can-secure-strippers-for-you face.

Yep, Natalie looks like she wants to switch conventions as well.

"Right," I say with a stiff smile. "That sounds… educational. Look, we really need to eat that delicious meal you brought."

"Oh! Of course. I wouldn't dream of keeping you."

Her lack of movement makes me think she might be dreaming that a tiny bit, however. Is she stalling for a tip? Does she not know we already paid gratuity on the bill?

Natalie sends me a pleading look, and I clear my throat. "Well, I'm gonna go shower," I lie, pushing up from the bed.

This time it's Verna who looks flustered as she scans my half-naked body. Not surprisingly, it's with a familiar expression we've seen twice already. In her defense, she's not that far off. Marcos and I *may* have worked a couple of events at resorts back in the day. A lot of them, actually.

"Our showers are wonderful, are they not?" Her gaze is still locked on my torso, but at least she's on her feet again.

"So wonderful," I say.

"Yes. And um, plenty of complimentary bath products."

"So many. Thanks again!" Natalie says, this time walking toward the door and pulling it open.

Genius.

I breathe a sigh of relief when Verna follows.

"Good luck with your telephones," she says. "Have a fantastic stay, Mr. and

Mrs. Hanover!"

"Oh, we're not…" Natalie stops and changes her answer to a pleasant smile at my warning look. I really don't want to hear the long list of people Verna knows who are or are not married—especially if there are two floors of them somewhere in this hotel.

"Thanks for everything," I call back.

She grins and waves, then starts down the hall.

Natalie closes the door and leans against it with a long exhale. "Wow. She was… friendly. What are you doing?" she asks when I pick up my phone.

"Texting Marcos."

"About what?"

"A chance to make some extra cash tomorrow night."

Her eyes widen, then narrow when she sees I'm joking.

"Wait, are you disappointed?" I say with a laugh.

"No!" she says defensively. "Well, maybe. Is Marcos as hot as you?"

"Probably hotter."

She grunts and plucks the lid off the tray of food.

"Hang on, are you mad?" I ask.

"You realize that's all I'm going to be thinking about today, right?"

"What, Marcos and me reading romance novels in our antique barn?"

Thankfully, I have quick reflexes and manage to deflect the grape that comes flying at me.

"Was all of this part of your evil scheme to distract me from the Sandeke account?" she fires back.

"Yes. I've been planning this for eight years when we launched the bachelorette week to coincide with *Tele-Con* on the off-chance that one day I might end up needing a potential distraction for a competitor."

"I see. So you were a nefarious plotter even as a sixteen-year-old?"

"Nineteen-year-old. And *so* nefarious. You know my story."

"Well, unfortunately for your evil plan, I've also spent the last eight years preparing for this scenario, and I assure you, there will be retaliation. You should probably ask Chad for some training in contingencies and collateral mitigation for when that moment comes."

I grin through a stirring rush at her threat. The look in her eyes alone has me counting the seconds until this surprise offensive. Hell, I'd even submit to a tutoring session with Chad.

Maybe I'm more into this corporate spy thing than I thought.

10—TUESDAY 8:53 AM

NATALIE

"Missed you at breakfast," Lanette says when I drop to the seat beside her.

"What are you doing here?" I ask. "I thought you were doing the *Future of Intercontinental Subterranean Networking* seminar."

She shakes her head. "Theresa pulled some strings and got me into this one. She wanted to make sure you had backup for when shit goes down."

"What shit is going down?"

She shrugs and casts a dark look at the other side of the room where Nate is joining the Eon employees. It was a development I missed because I've been devoting every spare neuron I have to *not* looking in his direction.

In fact, I spent most of the morning trying not to look at Nate. I tried not to look at him while he was eating breakfast and being very witty and adorable. I tried not to look at him when we finished and agreed to part ways to get ready. I really tried not to look at him when he started undressing before I was completely out the door. (I *might* have looked a little at that one.) And now, my career depends on me not looking at him while he converses with the enemy and seems to be trying really hard not to look at me.

When he does, my entire body goes hot.

Our eyes connect for several seconds, and I detect a hint of a smile on his lips. Yes, lips that are so delicious and tempting and make it nearly impossible not to look. Well, until Myra literally pulls him away by tugging the sleeve of his shirt. He turns to her, and my blood chills when she fires a quick glare at me.

Shit. Is she sensing something happening between us? *Is* there something happening between us?

She whispers to Nate, who furrows his brow and shakes his head.

"So what did you learn last night?" Lanette asks. "You disappeared before we could debrief. Theresa was pissed."

I cringe and force an apologetic look. "Sorry, I had to call Reece and then crashed."

It's a lie. I just talked to my best friend a couple days ago, but after the turbulence of that pool meeting, I wasn't in the mental state to deal with any spy drama. Instead of filing an unofficial pretend report with my unofficial pretend handlers, I basically ran back to my room to escape. I felt bad for abandoning Nate like that, but I couldn't deal with being around him when every part of me was still tingling from that fleeting whisper of passion. (*Whisper of Passion…* Maybe I *am* at the wrong convention.)

Either way, it's getting harder and harder to pretend I'm not falling for the person I'm supposed to despise. My heart exploded when I received that text early this morning. The fact that he would reach out meant everything to me and was hotter than any steamy sext would have been.

But it's hard to reconcile the drowning man I hugged at five o'clock this morning with the confident executive currently chatting up his colleagues. Again, I'm floored by his ability to transform. He's like a chameleon. It's a shame he hates sales so much because he'd be awesome at it.

"I didn't learn anything useful," I say. "As you saw, Chad kept taking bathroom breaks when he wasn't trying to melt a frozen cocktail, and the little we did get out of him was unintelligible."

"So nothing about Sandeke's user requirements?"

"No. Just killer clowns."

"Excuse me?"

"That slit throats."

"Ew."

"But appear friendly at first."

She tilts her head, and I shrug.

"You now know what I know. Do with it what you will."

"Ugh. Well, it looked like you had a chance to flirt with the enemy, at least. Anything good there?"

My pulse races as I try to read her expression. *So* good, romance author Natalie croons.

"I tried to flirt a little, yeah."

Her grin would also do better in a romance novel convention than an impending seminar about an industry buzzword that can't possibly be an industry buzzword.

"From what we saw, you did more than try." Her brows lift quite suggestively. "Theresa was impressed. If we didn't know better, we'd say you were into him for real."

"Ha, whatever." I execute what I hope is a convincing eye roll. "He's not my type."

Which is true, because I don't have a type. Or… I thought I didn't.

Now I'm worried I might and that type is Nate Hanover. There's probably not a large pool of those out there, so this could be a problem.

I allow a passing glance at him and mentally break Rule Number Five so hard. Suddenly, my head is full-on saving a seat and holding his hand and being the cheesiest of cheesy pretend couples through this entire damn seminar.

Speaking of…

Oh no.

A man I recognize as Reed Reedweather III from lunch yesterday saunters toward the podium at a pace one might call, "the universe revolves around me so you shall enjoy the anticipation of waiting for my eventual presence." Behind him is my new BFF, Chad.

A quick, purely professional glance at Nate reveals he may be in a similar state of shock and dread. Hopefully, the next hour won't require any food ordering.

Our host is wearing what must be his tropical formal business attire, because the handkerchief peeking out from the pocket of his expensive, tailored suit jacket has a conch shell on it. Chad is dressed as a human for this class.

"Good morning, dearest of friends and fellow citizens of the esteemed *TELECOMmunity*," Reedweather says. "We are so imperiously thrilled and honored to guide you through the playful, yet dangerously complex, maze of *Agile Synergy*."

The murmur of conversation dies as we shift our collective attention to the front of the room. Mine does not appear to be the only confused expression in the audience. This might be the first lecture ever where the speaker lost their class during the introduction.

"I am Reed Reedweather the Third, founder and president of Reedweather Media, a subsidiary of Sandeke Telecom, three time recipient of the Premise

Award for Marketing Excellence, and proud sponsor of this year's *Tele-Con*. This is my cherished colleague, Chad Smith, whom some of you may remember from yesterday's seminar."

The guy prancing around in an X-rated mermaid suit? Yeah, we remember.

"Today I have the pleasure of immersing you in the deep waters of *Agile Synergy*. Chad?"

Chad jumps to attention and reaches around his colleague to push a button on the laptop.

Chad steps back.

"Agile Synergy" is typed in bold purple font above the question, "What comes to mind when you hear the words *Agile Synergy?*"

"Agile Synergy," Reedweather says in a grave, very important tone. "What comes to mind when you hear the words *Agile Synergy?*"

Chad raises his hand, and I assume this is a scripted exchange until Reedweather frowns.

"Anyone else have a thought?" he asks.

No one has thoughts.

"Yes, my boy," Reedweather says. His reluctant tone kind of makes me feel bad I didn't at least hazard a guess.

Coordination...

Flexibility...

Interaction...

Responsiveness...

"Bobsledding," Chad says.

Bobsledding...

No one even laughs because we're confused enough to believe that might be the correct answer.

But Reedweather shakes his head.

"No. Anyone else? *Agile Synergy.* What comes to mind?"

"Synergy," someone shouts.

"Better," Reedweather says.

I disagree. There are very few answers better than bobsledding.

Reedweather frantically motions around the room for more guesses.

"Agility!" another genius suggests.

"Closer. Anyone else?"

I resist the urge to shout *Agile Synergy.*

"Aggressive teamwork." This voice sends shivers through me, and I follow the sound to find Nate looking like he's both amused and intrigued by this discussion.

Reedweather appears stunned, before pointing at Nate with violent exuberance. "Precisely! How did you…?" He shakes off a thought. "Chad?"

Chad scoots into action to press the button. He's beaming at Nate when he steps back.

The words "Aggressive teamwork" dominate the screen, and I try not to grumble audibly.

"How did he know that?" Lanette hisses at my ear.

Bobsledding.

Just kidding.

"Let me tell you a story," Reedweather says with a wistful expression. "Chad?"

Chad jumps to attention, reaches around his colleague, pushes the button, and steps back.

I would say the thing we're looking at is the last thing I expect to see on the screen during a telecom lecture, but I'm not sure of anything anymore. A few days ago I would have ranked a cluster of multi-colored helium balloons pretty high, though.

"The scene before us is a pastoral meadow," Reedweather lies. It's balloons. "See the rich vista undulate with pulsing waves of voluptuous grasses and luscious wildflowers."

Huh, okay. I guess I'm all in on this R-Rated field as long as it doesn't involve wheat.

"Walk with me through the flora. Feel the gentle breeze rustling the fabric of your double-breasted dress coat and buckskin breeches. Is that a deer?"

We all know we're in a lecture room at a boring telecom conference listening to some dude's weird romance fantasy, and yet, we *still* follow his attention to the back of the room when he shadows his eyes with his hand like he's searching.

Not surprisingly, there is no deer, just a waste bin and framed print of an orchid because this is The Orchid Lecture Hall. Why am I disappointed?

We turn back to face our presenter who seems very invested in his nostalgic daydream. Twenty bucks says he ends up at the book convention as well next year.

"But alas! Look yonder as the charming summer sun transforms into angry storm clouds. Chad?"

Chad pushes his button.

And steps back.

Wait. What were the balloons on the last slide for?

"I'm so lost," Lanette whispers.

"Just go with it. It'll make sense soon," I lie.

After watching these two order lunch, I'm positive that's not true and this presentation has already peaked.

Confirming my theory is the current slide featuring a dog wearing a fake mustache.

"We have two choices, am I right?" Reedweather continues as if there isn't a smiling Labradoodle with a faux mustache behind him.

"One, we could run back to our carriage to escape the coming storm. Or two…?"

He poses this question to us. I guess he didn't learn from the first time he trusted us to answer one of his questions.

I resist the urge to shout, *"Run back to our carriage to escape the coming storm."*

"Build a shelter from the tall grasses," someone says.

"Dance," another person yells.

"Find a ditch!"

"Do nothing... Unless there's lightning, then lie flat."

"Hide under a tree."

"Not if there's lightning," the previous lightning expert says.

"There are no trees in a meadow," someone else points out.

"How do you know? Trees can be anywhere."

"Because by definition, a meadow is flat vegetation without trees."

That can't be true. At least three other people agree and are now looking up the definition of "meadow."

"Fly a kite with a key on it and try to invent electricity," a new voice says in a dry tone. I snort a laugh at that one, only to see it was Nate. Of course it was.

He shoots me a direct smile that reframes this entire conversation about lightning in a very personal, electric-buzz-inducing way.

"Is this field in Oklahoma? Can we find a tumbleweed?"

"Wait, is it a field or a meadow?"

"By definition they're the same thing," the former meadow expert informs us.

Five people are fact-checking that one.

"Oklahoma also has buffalo."

"And prairie dogs."

"That's a myth."

"No, it's a real state. My uncle lives there."

"I meant prairie dogs. They don't exist."

Okay, so maybe there are more than two choices in this scenario. And lots of other assorted misinformation.

Reedweather looks crestfallen to have his illustration so profoundly deconstructed. Bet he's regretting shooting down bobsledding so quickly.

He motions to Chad.

Who.

Pushes.

The.

Button.

Table tennis. *Competitive* table tennis judging by the blurred audience in the background and sweatbands on the foreheads of the players.

I'm definitely researching competitive table tennis later. At first thought, it seems like something I should know a lot about, but I quickly realize I don't. Are there leagues? Do they wear uniforms? Do they use a coach or a manager? What do the scoreboards look like? *Are* there scoreboards?

"Thank you for those… excellent… suggestions," Reedweather says. "Perhaps it's better to move on with today's exploration of *Agile Synergy*. Before we continue, we have a special activity."

Oddly enough, he now has everyone's rapt attention. Literally anything could happen next and we're on the edge of our seats.

"While the rest of us enjoy the deep entrails of this fascinating topic, may I have two volunteers for a special assignment?"

"It's a skit!" Chad cries.

Reedweather shoots him a sour look, and he shrinks back to button-pushing position.

"Yes, it's a skit. But a *special* skit," Reedweather tells us.

If he thought adding the word "special" to skit would change anyone's mind about volunteering, he was wrong.

Once again, Reedweather looks crestfallen.

After the most awkward twelve seconds of the conference, Chad rushes to his side and whispers something. There's nothing I like about the smile that creeps onto their faces when their gazes land on me… then Nate.

Oh no.

"Thank you, Chad, for suggesting a potentially illustrious, real-world demonstration of *Agile Synergy*. Natalia, Nathaniel, would you please join us at the front of the class?"

A chorus of oohs and snickers straight out of any middle school lunchroom echoes around us. It's not exactly a secret that Eon Tech and TPG don't get along. Then again, I'd rather be heckled for being paired with my mortal enemy than the fact that I'm crushing hard on that mortal enemy. Hopefully, no one (except maybe Myra) knows that part.

I can tell by the tension in Nate's body that he's not super excited about this either.

"Who better to illustrate today's topic than these two adversaries who have no hope of achieving *Agile Synergy*? Or do they? Lady, gentleman…"

I realize Reedweather is addressing Nate and me when his killer clown grin is inches from our faces. No wonder Chad has a contentious relationship with clowns.

"Chad will explain the mission."

Reedweather whispers this part like it would be devastating if anyone found out we were about to do something like make a skit.

"Follow me," Chad commands in a low voice, also convinced no one heard what was just announced forty-five seconds ago.

"While they're *on their mission*, let's review a patented Venn diagram that will revolutionize your understanding of this essential pillar of any successful organization. Chad—"

Our host stops himself, crestfallen.

The last thing we see before Chad leads us from the room is Reedweather glowering at the keyboard of his laptop, finger poised to push the button.

If only he knew which it was.

* * *

We weren't sure where Chad was taking us, but I should have guessed it would be a neighboring room with a sign that says, "Agile Synergy Workshop Lab Sponsored by Sandeek Telecom." Yes, Sandeke is spelled incorrectly, but so is the sign telling us, "They're are no food or beverages allowed beyond this point."

The "workshop lab" itself contains a few chairs, a folding table lined with a buffet of craft supplies, and a large plastic bin of… things. A quick scan of the contents reveals items that look alarmingly like costumes and props. So basically, an "Agile Synergy Workshop Lab" is a kindergarten classroom.

"Now, I know this will be a challenge since you two hate each other," Chad says in a grave tone.

"We don't hate—"

Chad holds up a hand to cut Nate off. "No need to pretend with me. Save the acting for the audience. The point of this exercise is to demonstrate how even the bitterest of bitter rivals can work together when using *Agile Synergy.*"

He passes a dramatic look between us. "Would you prefer I stay to mediate and call emergency services, if necessary?"

Emergency services? What exactly does Chad think we're going to do with the watercolor paint and glitter pens?

"I think we'll be okay," Nate says.

Chad rests a hand on each of our shoulders. "I don't mind. Truly. Your safety is my top priority."

Nate fights off a smile as he returns a reassuring nod. "Really. It's probably best we work out our differences on our own. Aggressive teamwork, right?"

Chad doesn't look convinced. "Yes but…" He leans close. "I could get in a lot of trouble for telling you this but it's not just about *aggressive teamwork.* It's also about *suppleness.*"

Suppleness?

"I see. That makes sense," Nate says, somehow with a straight face.

I can't even look at him as Chad nods somberly.

"Exactly. Hence my concern."

His concern for what, exactly? Still not sure about that.

"These types of things escalate quickly is all I'm saying." Chad gives us a warning look like there's no way Nate and I will be able to handle working together in an aggressive, supple way. He couldn't be more wrong about that. There's nothing I'd love more than to get aggressively supple with my smoking hot competitor right now.

Just not with Chad in the room.

"Wouldn't it be more fun for you to be surprised by what we come up with?" I ask.

It definitely would be for us.

"Hmm. Maybe, but—"

"We have your number," Nate says. "What about a code word if things get out of control?"

Chad ignites with excitement I haven't seen since his grilled cheese was delivered in three perfect triangles.

"Great idea. How about…"

Please say bobsledding.

"Crescent moon?"

Damn.

Nate nods with a stern look that says *Crescent moon* is pretty much the only code word that makes sense for this scenario. *Is* it a code word? That's more of a word and an adjective, right?

We sigh with relief when Chad does.

"Okay. Crescent moon, it is," Chad says. "Just… You signed the waiver, right?"

"Waiver?" Nate asks, then shrinks when I fire a sharp look at him.

"The waiver!" Chad repeats.

Nate manages to make his face look less confused as he nods. "Oh, right. The waiver. Yes. It's signed. And, um, dated."

Chad relaxes. "And you, Natalie?"

"Yep. Sure did." I wouldn't even know where to *start* looking for a waiver about skit-writing, but the last thing we need is a reason to follow Chad around the resort.

"Okay, then." He straightens and gives us a solemn look like we're about to go off to sea, not sift through a plastic tub of yard sale junk.

"Godspeed," he says, also much more in line with seafaring than skit-making.

Once he's gone, Nate closes the door and lets out a breath. "Thank god. I was worried he was going to insist on participating in this."

"Yeah, um…" I nudge the bin with my shoe. "What exactly *is* this? He never gave us instructions."

Nate shrugs and joins me to stare into the bin. "No idea, but we're definitely using this." He pulls out an object I can only describe as a giant fake lollipop.

"It would fit the theme of the slides. Is there a mustache or dog in there?" I ask.

He smirks and fishes through the contents. "Not that I can see. There's this, though."

I almost choke at the fur-lined handcuffs dangling in his hand. "Okay, either someone doesn't know what those are typically used for, or this bin belongs to a different convention."

My pulse pounds a little harder as I study the cuffs. I've never been much for sex play, but suddenly, the thought of being chained to a bed with Nate hovering over me has my body hot and wired. *He'd slip them around my wrists, kiss down my neck, straighten abruptly to rip his shirt over his head.*

Yeah, I want him. A lot.

"Nate." My voice is breathless, and his eyes flash with heat when they land on me. I know we're in public. I know it's dangerous. Anyone could walk in at any moment, but…

We launch in unison, colliding in a furious grasp for the other. I grip his hair as he walks me back into the wall. Our mouths meld together in a fight for the same air, for relief from a hunger that is always so overpowering when we're together.

He groans as he shoves against me, and I adjust to deepen the kiss and feel him with more of my body. My hands travel down his back, latching onto his belt to drag him into me for hit after hit of mounting friction. I'm on fire, every part of me aching for more.

I gasp when his mouth moves to my neck, his tongue exploring my skin as his hands skim my breasts, first over my silk shirt, then unbuttoning a few to slip inside. His fingers graze my skin, and I arch into his touch. I want more, need it, and I'm practically whimpering at the steady surge of sparks ripping through me. I've never felt this way before. This deep desire to lose myself in a person. It makes no sense that I'm willing to break all my rules for someone I met two days ago, but here I am, risking everything for something that doesn't feel like a risk at all. It's terrifying and exhilarating and—

I catch movement outside the long, thin windows lining the door. Shit, that could have been anyone! What are we doing?!

I pull back, gasping from the fire still clawing at every recess of my body. My heart, soul, every limb clenches in protest at my brain's betrayal, but we need to pause. People don't fall in love this quickly, and they certainly don't risk their hard-fought careers for something as petty as a crush. Anyone could have walked in on us just now. If this is going to continue, we need to be more careful. My brain clearly doesn't function properly in his presence.

Nate searches my eyes with concern, maybe a hint of fear, and I reach up to brush my thumb over his cheek to reassure him. This entire situation is so messed up. I have no idea how to talk about it. How do you tell someone you want them *too* much?

I feel like I'm falling in love with you, but that's absurd, so I have no idea what this is or what's happening here. And it's making me reckless.

"Are you okay? What's wrong?" he asks. "Did I—"

"No! No, it's not you, it's me," I say, then kick myself when he flinches.

He drops his hold, and I grab his hand.

"Wait! I don't mean that in the cliché way," I rush out.

I squeeze his fingers to keep him from leaving.

"The opposite, actually. I really like you, Nate. As in *really* like you, but think about what we're doing. We *just* met and we're already acting like that pretend conference couple we were joking about. Worse than that. We're being irresponsible about it."

He doesn't respond, just blinks his deep brown eyes to veil the hurricane I know is raging behind them. What am I trying to say? I don't even know, and maybe that's the problem. It's all happening too fast, disrupting too much of my equilibrium to process. Just a few days ago I was telling my father how much I valued my rules. They've protected me, pushed me, saved me time and again, so how can I just throw them away for something as fleeting as a feeling? If anyone had walked in on us, I could have lost everything I've worked so hard for. All for a person I just met.

"It's fine," he says, pulling away.

My chest hurts as he crosses to the table to pretend to examine the supplies. Except, I'm pretty sure he's not interested in the bag of assorted pompoms locked in his absent stare.

"Nate, I mean it," I say, joining him. "You're... I'm loving getting to know you. You seem amazing, a once in a lifetime kind of person. You're so smart, and kind, and genuine, and just beautiful inside and out. But this whole thing... We're both responsible people, and we're making poor choices. Anyone could have seen us just now. And you're great, but no one is that perfect, so obviously my head isn't in a rational place. My judgment must be off."

His expression darkens.

Crap. *Again, Nat? Where did you learn human interaction skills?!*

"Wait, that didn't come out right. What I mean is—"

"Like I said, I get it. Believe me."

I reach across the table, but he shrugs out of my hold.

"It's fine, Natalie. It's better that we don't pursue… whatever this was. It couldn't have worked anyway."

He moves toward the door, and my heart screams at me to throw myself in front of it.

Don't let him leave!

"Nate, please. Let's figure this out. At the very least, we still have to work together."

"Actually, that's the thing. We're not *supposed* to be working together. It's fine. Really. You're not doing anything wrong, just putting things back to the way they should be."

I shake my head, my throat clogging with so many words, so many pleas and protests but I can't make sense of them enough to use any. In fact, it's almost guaranteed my terrible relationship skills will make it worse.

"I'll text Chad to let him know I had to run out," he says, pulling open the door. "Good luck with everything."

And then he's gone.

What just happened? What have I done?

I have a feeling Chad and Reedweather aren't going to like our skit on *Agile Synergy*.

* * *

I have no idea what to do after Nate leaves. I didn't want to do this pointless skit *with* him, let alone without him. Maybe I can make up a story about a gas leak in the "workshop lab" that resulted in a forced evacuation. Insect infestation? The Adult Film Convention suddenly realized *their* workshop lab has way too many telecom props and maybe their bin of furry handcuffs is down the hall?

Worst case, I could smuggle in a forbidden food or beverage and get escorted to whatever resort jail holds the rebels who disobey temporary paper signs.

I don't get a chance for any of those options when the door cracks open and Chad pokes his head in.

"Natalie! Thank god," he says, slipping into the room.

He closes the door and looks around. I don't even know what he's searching for this time. I'm starting to think he's just in permanent spy mode and assumes everyone else is as well. I'm also starting to think I've grossly underestimated the number of spies milling around in and among us.

"I got Nathan's text," he says. "I'm so sorry to hear about his post office box. I hate when that happens."

He shakes his head.

"Right, yeah. The, uh, post office box. It was… so urgent."

"Well, the good news is, I'm here now. He asked if I could take his place. He said you're very capable and skilled and have some excellent ideas."

He did? So, even when he was upset he was kind?

I really have to get out of this room so I can find him.

Chad scans the table, his expression pinching with irritation. "You didn't start the poster."

"Poster? I thought we were doing a skit."

"Yes. A skit with a poster."

"Oh. Um, what's supposed to go on the poster?"

"That's the point of the skit," he says in a "duh" tone as he grabs a box of markers.

"Right. How can I help?"

"See if you can find a pair of sunglasses in the bin. Not the regular ones. The ginormous ones people wear when they're drunk. Also, a squeezy starfish."

He returns to his poster-making like that sentence should make total sense to me. I stare into the bin, concerned about my odds of success. Maybe he'll let me work on the poster instead. I ran for student council in high school. I know my way around glitter.

"I have a lot of experience with poster-making," I say, joining him on the other side of the table. "I'd love to help."

I glance down at his project and immediately change my mind.

The words "AGILE SYNERGY" are scratched in huge capital letters that take up the entire surface. He's tracing the green lettering with blue to enhance it even more. So… the "skit about Agile Synergy" is making a poster that says Agile Synergy?

And giant sunglasses.

And a starfish. Maybe.

I pull out my phone to send another quick text to Nate.

"You know, I've been thinking. You both are so nice," Chad says as he sketches yellow lines around the blue ones. "I don't want to have to choose between you and Nathan. Maybe I could buy those special batteries from both of you. We can put some of his batteries in some buildings and some of yours in the others. We have like a gazillion buildings. Plenty of rooms for batteries."

Now he's adding an orange layer.

"Yeah, um, that's…"

What's a polite word for ludicrous?

"Probably not a good solution," I say. "That's not really how backup systems work."

"You know what I think?" he says, again in that low whisper that tells me there are at least as many invisible spies as visible ones in our world.

"About *Agile Synergy*?"

"No! Collateral mitigation."

"Oh. What's that?" I pull a marker from the box. "How about red next?"

"Great idea. Nate was right about you. I think Brighthouse isn't going to retaliate."

"Why do you think that?"

"Let's call it *Acquired Intuition*." He adds a conspiratorial grin.

"Ah, okay."

"You know what that is?"

Does it require starfish, mustached dogs, or table tennis?

I could lie, but I'm fairly certain it will be exposed immediately.

"No," I say.

He winks. "Stick with me and you will. That's a scout's honor. You ever do the Scouts?"

"No," I say, assuming he's referring to what I think he's referring to—which, to be fair, isn't a safe assumption.

"Okay, done!" he cries.

He straightens abruptly and tosses the red marker on the table.

"You ready to do this?"

Before I can see the final version, he snatches the poster and positions it upright to show me his masterpiece in all its exultant glory.

AGILE SYNERGY

With a line underneath.

11—TUESDAY 9:26 AM

NATE

I'm not mad at her. I'm mad at myself. At my soft, stupid heart that keeps trusting, keeps hoping, and keeps getting crushed again and again. Of course the only possible explanation for why someone would be interested in me is a lapse in judgment.

Natalie's words cut into me over and over as I storm through the passageways of the resort, searching for any place to hide. I don't want to go back to my room because she might try to find me there. She'll want to "fix" this and probably feels terrible for hurting me, but the last thing I need right now are more painful explanations and trite platitudes. More people using words to convey the opposite of what their actions are saying. I thought there couldn't be anything worse than your girlfriend dumping you because you were too supportive, but then I got rejected for being "too perfect." No, I'm not *too* anything, except gullible.

I let Natalie in, let her see the real me, and she bolted. That's what really happened.

My phone is buzzing in my pocket, and I don't have to look at the display to know who it is and what they're saying. But she doesn't need to apologize. She didn't do anything wrong. In fact, I don't even disagree with anything she said and should be grateful one of us had enough sense to put an end to the ridiculous (and dangerous) fantasy. She's right. We were playing with matches in the middle of an explosives warehouse. What did I think was going to happen? I should be grateful it wasn't worse.

I'm already on the verge of a breakdown when a hand latches onto my arm and yanks me around. Myra's eyes are hot and angry as they bore into me, and I jerk my arm away.

"What are you doing?" she snaps.

We're not in a heavily populated area, but we're not exactly in an isolated vault, either. Maybe I should care about witnesses, but right now, I could give two fucks. Honestly, what do I have to lose? I've already lost anything worth having.

"I don't know what you're talking about," I say.

"I followed you out of the lecture hall in case you needed help with that difficult situation, but it appeared you had everything *very well under control.*"

"You think we *wanted* to work on that stupid skit? What was I supposed to do?"

"You know that's not what I'm talking about. I saw you with her in the workshop lab. You two were a step away from having sex on the craft table."

Okay. One, can we stop calling it a "workshop lab"? That's not a thing. And two, there is something inherently wrong with the phrase "having sex on the craft table."

But instead of either of those corrections, I settle on a return glare of my own.

"*You're* the one who told me to throw myself at her."

"I said *flirt* with her. Not sleep with her!"

"What do you care who I do and do not sleep with, anyway?" I fire back. "You dumped me, remember? I took you out to dinner to celebrate your promotion and ended up paying for my own breakup! What the hell do you want from me, Myra?"

Her anger softens into something else the longer we face off. Maybe it should calm me, but all it does is explode long-dead embers of resentment. I'm seething when she reaches out to touch me, and I duck away, staring at her in disbelief.

She frowns and hugs her arms around herself instead.

"I told you already," she says quietly. "I want you—"

"No! You don't want me. You fucking *had* me, Myra. You had me and you threw me away. What you *want* is what someone else *might* have. I can't handle this anymore. This push and pull. We're coworkers now, nothing more, okay?"

I turn and start away.

"She's the enemy," Myra says, and I freeze. "Not only could it ruin your career if this gets out, she's playing you. That's all this is. She's using you, Nate. It's the only explanation."

I can't move as her words pollute the air around us. What she said hurts, but it's what she didn't say that crushes me.

"It's the only explanation..."

Because you're not good enough for someone to actually care about you for real. It's inconceivable another human would want you enough to risk everything.

"You're too naïve, Nate. Too good. Sandeke is a multibillion dollar company representing a multimillion dollar contract. Don't you get what people are willing to do for that kind of payoff? You're an easy target, baby."

I wince, but don't turn around. I can't. I don't want to see her gentle expression that's supposed to soothe the violence of her words. As if a sad smile can erase months of tears.

I'm an easy target. Maybe. I'm also done. With Myra. With Natalie. With this whole freaking job I hate that hates me even more.

Your ray of sunshine, people.

Your precious optimist.

Your poster child for why sometimes it really is better to quit while you're ahead. Who knew I'd peak at twenty-seven?

"Nate, please..."

"Stay away from me, Myra," I say in an even tone. "I'm serious. Stay. Away."

Everyone can just stay the hell away.

* * *

They must track my phone. It's the only explanation for how my roommates always seem to find me, even when I have no interest in being found. I've managed to hide for a couple of hours, but I guess it was inevitable our paths would cross eventually. I've gone numb to the barrage of texts all morning and stopped looking at the display when another one comes in. I'll deal with them at some point, but for now, this turkey sandwich is about all my brain can handle.

I call on every ounce of energy I have left to muster a smile as Marcos and Nash approach.

"There you are," Marcos says, pounding me on the back before he drops to the extra chair at the café table.

Nash grabs a seat from the neighboring table and swings it around to straddle it backwards.

"How'd the seminar go?" Marcos asks. "Wait, was this the *Agile Synergy* one?" he asks with a smirk.

I force a weak smile and shrug. "Yeah. It was amazing. So much synergy happening in that lecture room."

Nash snickers and steals one of my chips. "Please tell me it was run by Reed-weather."

"With the assistance of Chad," I say. "How was yours?" I ask Marcos before things go too far down that path.

"Boring as hell, but Martin and I have been talking about expanding into more extreme environments, so he wanted me to see what's going on in the world of weather-resistant technology."

"Wow, what a treat. And to think I had to sleep in and hang at the pool all morning," Nash says.

"I have an idea. Why don't you shut up and go work on your album or whatever it is you do?" Marcos mumbles.

Nash shrugs with a grin. "I was. In the pool. I came up with new lyrics for the 'Losing You' chorus. I'll share if you promise not to."

Marcos shakes his head and focuses back on me. When his smile fades, my fingers grip the edge of the chair.

"You okay?" he asks, tilting his head. Even Nash's perpetual smirk sinks into concern.

"Fine, why?"

"Because you don't look fine," Marcos says. "Something happen? Wait… shit. Myra isn't here, is she?"

Great. How do I answer that?

"Yeah. But it's no big deal."

Nash grunts and fidgets with the salt shaker on the table. Marcos doesn't look like he's buying my deflection even a little.

"She wrecked you, dude. It's a big deal. Have you talked to her yet?"

"A… few times," I force out.

Don't they have things to do? Well, Nash doesn't, but certainly Marcos must. Where are Eva and Paige when you need them?

"And?" Marcos asks.

"And what?" I reply.

"How did it go?"

"Fine."

"Nate, come on, man. There's no way it went fine. What aren't you telling us?"

"Pretty sure you've given me plenty of lectures about being 'fine,'" Nash adds. "You know how I feel about hypocrites."

He's joking, but he doesn't realize he's staring at the President of the League of Hypocrites. Well, assuming they'd have a president. Would it just be a person pretending to be the president? What would the membership process look like? Those conventions would be even more confusing than this one.

"Can't a guy just be fine? Is it so hard to believe I'm over it?"

"Yes," they say together, then look at each other, then scowl at each other, then look back at me.

That was weird.

"Okay, well, I don't know what to tell you. I'm over it. End of story."

My phone buzzes on the table, and we all stare at the display in unison.

Oh shit.

Natalie: **Please talk to me. I'm so sorry for what I said. It's not what I meant.**

"Hang on. Who's Natalie?" Marcos asks.

I shrug and swipe my phone off the table. "No one."

"She's clearly *someone*," Marcos says.

"Really. It's nothing. Just a work thing."

"A work thing that requires groveling?"

"She wasn't groveling. She just…"

I don't know. I'm too tired for this.

"Stop being stubborn. What is going on? Who is this person and what happened that she thinks she needs to apologize?"

"Nothing! She's just some salesperson from TPG that I clashed with at the seminar this morning."

Uh-oh.

"TPG?" Marcos says, lifting a brow. "As in The Panther Group? As in Eon Tech's main competition?"

I shrug again, but I'm pretty sure that's not going to work at this point.

It doesn't.

"Dude, what the hell?" Marcos cries.

"It's nothing! Just… I'm handling it."

"You're *handling* it? Handling *what*?"

My shoulders tense in preparation for another shrug. At what point is shrugging considered an acceptable workout for arm day?

"Nate, talk to us. You've been weird for the last few weeks. Ever since your transfer. We didn't say anything because we figured you were still adjusting, but enough is enough. Is this about Myra?"

"No," I lie.

Is it a lie? I don't even know what "it's" about. Myra? Natalie? Me, and the shell of what I was, what I *should* be?

"I actually have to go," I say, pushing up from the chair. "You want the rest?" I ask Nash who ate most of the chips, anyway.

He slides the plate toward himself as Marcos continues boring his stare into me.

"Nate," Marcos says, less kind and more stern now. "Sit down and tell us what the hell is going on."

"Nothing is going on. It's just the pressure of this Sandeke thing, and now I've learned TPG is going after them too. *Natalie* is their sales rep and we've been competing for Chad's attention all week, that's it."

Marcos looks skeptical. For the record, there's no way he'd be accepted into The League of Hypocrites. "And your competition is texting you apologies?"

"Apparently. She's a nice person."

Maybe. I'm not sure anymore. I'm still having trouble believing she was playing me this whole time like Myra said, but what do I know? I didn't think Myra was going to dump me until I was sitting alone in a Michelin Star restaurant, staring at her untouched forty-dollar salad. I still don't understand what could make lettuce worth forty dollars.

"Seriously, I have to go. I'm supposed to meet up with Colin to see what I missed at the Agile Synergy seminar."

I walk away before they can stop me again, happy to dodge the bullet for now. I know they mean well, but I wouldn't be able to explain this twisted situation even if I wanted to—which I don't.

It's not until I'm well out of view that I realize how badly I just screwed up.

My roommates are too intelligent and insightful to miss the fact that I just confirmed their theory by admitting I lied about attending the seminar this morning.

* * *

It's a good thing my meeting with Colin was fabricated. I wouldn't have made it.

"Roger" must track my phone as well, because heading right for me is a wide, expectant grin that tells me I'm about to be terribly confused. Is there anyone who *doesn't* know where I am at all times?

Besides Natalie.

"Nate! My man! Where you been, dude? You didn't respond to my messages. We have to plan."

Roger slings his arm around my shoulders and squeezes.

"Yeah, sorry. I've been busy." I shrug out of his hold as politely as possible.

How close *are* we?

Hang on.

"Plan what?" I ask, searching his wide, alarm-inducing grin.

"For tomorrow night!"

"Tomorrow night?"

He narrows his eyes. "I've been messaging you all morning. I know you have your telephone shit or whatever this week, but certainly you can take a break from the boring stuff for one night of fun."

One night of fun. In a non-existential-meltdown state, that phrase would concern me and be a hard *hell no*. When everything is blowing up in your face before you can even process the last shitstorm? "One night of fun" sounds pretty damn necessary.

"Yeah, sorry for not responding. Like I said, lots of… telecom stuff today."

He slaps my back, his smile returning. "No worries, my man. I already told the guys you were in. Just meet us at six in room P4 tomorrow."

I absolutely should not do that.

"Sure," I say with a tight smile.

"Fan-fucking-tastic! Good to see you again. Really. Missed you, dude."

He smacks my shoulder. Why does he keep hitting me? Is that a clue?

"Yeah, uh, you too."

Maybe?

"Oh, and don't worry about your outfit. We got you covered… or not. Ha ha!"

He salutes and takes off like he's in a hurry to track down someone else to confuse.

Room P4 at six for *one night of fun* with Roger and *the guys*. Outfit covered.

Yes, this is such a great idea.

12—TUESDAY 4:37 PM

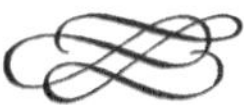

NATALIE

I've texted Nate multiple times now, even knocked on his door, but got nothing. I don't blame him. I'm bruised from kicking myself so many times for my bumbling attempt to explain my heart. I'm not good at this—relationships, feelings, any of it—so I'm not surprised I screwed it up so royally. But that doesn't ease the pain over what happened. How can it hurt so much to lose something you didn't even have?

Ever since that word vomit spilled out of my mouth, my brain has been subjecting me to a constant replay of our time together since we met. I've been searching for anything in those stolen moments that didn't seem authentic, any sliver of rotten I can cling to in order to justify this gnawing ache in my gut.

But every time I try, I come up with the same image: Nate flattened on his bed, staring at the ceiling while he shed a piece of his soul. I feel the warmth of his fingers in mine, the swell of my heart with each second of trust we shared.

And I just told this lost, hurting person he was an error in judgment.

"What is wrong with you?" I mutter to myself.

That's not what I meant, of course. Well, it was, but not that *he* was the error, just the way we were handling it. But I didn't say that and realized too late how it must have sounded to his brain that's already spiraling and convincing him he's useless and unwanted.

My chest ached for him Sunday night and this morning while I listened to all the lies his depression was telling him. He didn't call it that, and neither did I, but it's not hard to sense what's going on in his head is more than some hurt feelings over a breakup. That man is entrenched in a deep well that's drowning him. He probably needs professional help, but it's not like it was my place to suggest that as a total stranger. My goal that first night was to get him to share all this information with his roommates who *would* be able to get him the help and support he needs. Besides, after what just happened in the workshop lab, I can only imagine how terribly I would have butchered a sensitive conversation like that.

Back in my room, I text Reece to see if he can talk. When he doesn't respond, I try my dad, who answers my video chat on the second ring.

"Twice in one week. Wow," he says.

The weight pressing down immediately lifts at his soft hazel eyes and warm smile. On paper Reece is my best friend, but really, it's my father. We'd always been close, but after my mother passed away ten years ago, we became each other's rocks. I almost lost him to grief, and he's lifted me up and pushed me forward more times than I can count.

Not sure how he's going to feel about this active volcano, though.

"Yeah, it's your lucky day."

"It always is when you call. How's the conference? You kicking ass?"

I force a weak smile. "Kind of. It's been… eventful."

The amusement dies on his face as he studies me through the screen. "Eventful. That sounds like a euphemism if I ever heard one. What does 'eventful' mean in non-sparkly terms?"

I sigh and drop to the edge of the bed. "It's… Ugh, I don't even know how to explain it."

I groan and scoot back to rest against the headboard of the bed.

"Start with words and we'll go from there."

I roll my eyes at his bad joke, but I kind of appreciate it. He always knows how to put me at ease.

"Okay. Now, don't freak out, but I sort of met someone."

His eyes widen. His jaw drops. He's freaking out.

"I know it's weird," I continue before he can say anything. "I'm still reeling from it all. That's kind of the problem, actually."

"Wow," he says, blowing out a breath. "That was the third last thing I was expecting to hear."

"*Third* last? What were one and two?"

"You got a snake tattoo and Pluto is a planet again, respectively."

I laugh. "You're so weird. Wait, is Pluto not a planet? When did that happen?"

"It was the year you discovered boys. You were distracted. Speaking of which, a few days ago you were *so relieved to be single*."

I cringe and bite my lip. "Yeah, um. I said that but… Look, I know it's odd, just hear me out before the lectures."

"Whoa, hold the fort," he says, turning serious. "First off, I supported your self-imposed detachment because I support *you*, Natalie. I will always support you, whether you choose a man, a woman, no one, two men, three women, two men and a woman, a—"

"Okay, I get it. Geez," I mumble.

He chuckles. "My point is, I will always support what you want for your life, but that doesn't mean I will always agree with your decisions and think they're wise."

"Wait, are you saying you wanted me to date more?"

"More? Sweetie, you don't date at all. Which is fine!" he says quickly. "But I'm worried you aren't being as honest and fair to yourself as you pretend to be. Are you staying away from relationships because you want to or because you're scared?"

My jaw clenches as I stare at him. I don't even know what to say. I always thought he understood my reluctance. Hell, I thought he encouraged it. After watching how he imploded from losing Mom, of course he wouldn't want his daughter to go through that kind of pain. I recognize Nate's symptoms so well because I've lived with the destructive pull of mental illness in my house for years. Dad fought hard to dig out of the abyss and manage it, but I know he still struggles. He's still on and off meds, in and out of therapy. He still has mornings he can't get out of bed. Sleepless nights. Endless days. Mom's death didn't cause his illness but it certainly helped hurl it out of control.

"I'm sorry for pushing us off course," he says. "You called for a reason. Tell me about this person you met. I'm intrigued."

I swallow hard, my insides churning again. I was already rocked by the whole thing with Nate, and now I have to reframe everything I thought I understood about my father's support? I called thinking I'd have to justify my ridiculous crush before we could discuss it, not the other way around.

"His name is Nate," I begin, not sure where else to start. There probably is no other place to start. "We met Sunday night at the elevators and spent the entire night together… talking."

"Talking?" he asks, squinting at me. "Is that the new slang for… well, you know?"

Is he serious?

A smile threatens my lips. "No, Dad. Talking still means talking."

"Like, with actual words ejecting from mouths?"

"Ew. Now you're making it slang. Yes, with actual words."

"Got it. Sorry. Continue."

I try to read his reaction, but he gives nothing away as he settles back into his *Compassionate Dad* face. It helps a lot, how he just listens instead of "fixes" like so many people try to do. Sometimes that's the only "fix" I need.

"It was… amazing. I've never experienced anything like it. We thought we were never going to see each other again, so there was no reason to hold back. We didn't exchange names or information, so there was no threat of anything we shared coming back to haunt us. We opened our souls and poured them out. And Dad, his soul is so incredibly beautiful."

Emotion lodges in my throat. What if this morning was the last time I got to glimpse it? What if I never get to show him more pieces of mine?

Even Dad's expression has sagged in reaction to my own. He must see the pain in my face.

"And now you're regretting letting him go?" he guesses.

My eyes burn as I shake my head. "No. It's worse than that. It turns out, he's a VP of Sales for Eon Tech. He's my direct competition for that Sandeke Telecom account I was telling you about."

"Shit," Dad mumbles. "So basically, you're Romeo and Juliet."

"Sure, if Juliet ruined everything by telling Romeo he was a lapse in judgment during one of their secret rendezvouses."

"Oh." Dad presses his lips together. "Was he?"

"Was he, what?"

"A lapse in judgment."

"No! Dad, I can't get him out of my head. I know it doesn't make sense, but I've never felt this way about a person. It's like every piece he reveals about himself draws me in more. Making out in the skit workshop lab was the lapse in judgment, not *him*."

"Um, sorry, not to go off topic again, but what exactly is *a skit workshop lab*?"

"You don't want to know."

"I kind of do. It sounds pretty fun if people have secret rendezvouses there. So you *are* doing the other kind of talking with this guy?"

"Dad!"

"Sorry. Continue."

"Anyway, my point is, I messed up. I know it's probably impossible to have a real relationship, but I want to at least have the chance to explain and tell him how I feel. Even if nothing comes of it, I want him to know how special and important he is, but he won't answer my texts."

"He might just be busy."

"No, pretty sure he's upset. He stormed out after I said what I did. He was really hurt."

Dad is silent for a few seconds as he thinks, and I wait for his *Compassionate Dad* face to become his *Are You Ready for Some Truth?* face. I typically don't enjoy that one as much.

"You say you're hung up on this person because your souls connected and you know him so well, even though you've just met, correct?"

Why do I feel like I'm about to shout "Objection, your honor! Leading the witness!"?

"Yes…" I say slowly, narrowing my eyes in suspicion.

"If that's true and that's the justification for your intense feelings, you should know how he will respond and it will be in a way you respect and accept. Trust your gut, Nat. If this guy is everything you say he is, he will prove to be that person. If he doesn't, then he's not what you think and you can let him go. Either way, you will have your answer about what's next. But be patient. Even the saints need time to process pain. You've done all you can by reaching out. Now, you wait to see who he really is."

Wow.

"Objection, your honor?" a tiny speck of my brain squeaks. But the rest is being short-circuited, yet again, by one of the wisest, most understanding people I know.

He's right. If I really am falling in love with Nate, it's not with a person who wouldn't forgive or would leave a relationship he valued in a tattered state over a misunderstanding. If he feels even remotely the same about me, he will read my messages and give me a chance to explain.

And if he's not what I thought, well, all is not lost. At least, I won't have to feel guilty about winning the Sandeke Telecom contract and getting that promotion.

* * *

I feel better after my conversation with Dad. He's right. We put so much pressure on ourselves for other people's actions. Sure, we have a duty to be kind and do our best, but we all make mistakes and even when we don't, we can't control other people's thoughts and hearts. Maybe I could have expressed my concerns in a better way, but it's on Nate not to blow it out of proportion. I have a feeling if he wasn't already spiraling, we wouldn't even be having this issue. That whole exchange was definitely the perfect storm of bias-induced melodrama.

My phone *dings* with a text, and I glance down with a racing heart.

Please be Nate.

It's not. I open the message from an unknown number, expecting another one of those annoying spam texts. I'm shocked to see my name.

Unknown: **Hi Natalie. Sorry to bother you. We got your number from Chad Smith. This is Marcos Oliveira and I'm also here at Tele-Con. I believe you know my roommate Nate. Would you be willing to meet at The Lost Lagoon around 6 to talk? We're worried about him.**

Marcos. I know Marcos. Nash is the other one, I think. Well, I don't *know* them, but feel like I do from what Nate's said. I also know Marcos is the Director of Operations at SAT Systems, another account on TPG's wishlist, but I'm going to guess the likelihood of landing *that* one is less than successfully taking shelter in a tumbleweed during an Oklahoman lightning storm. In related news, we never learned the correct answer to the question of what to do in that scenario, so hopefully none of us ends up in an undulating field wearing double-breasted dress coats and buckskin breeches.

All of this is to say, I trust this text is legitimate and I'm eager to meet with Nate's roommates if it means a chance to help him survive his own personal lightning storm.

* * *

I don't remember what Marcos and Nash look like since my eyes didn't drift from Nate that first night, but I know Marcos is a ridiculously good-looking executive and Nash is an angsty, heavily tattooed musician. It's not hard to figure out which table is theirs, since there's only one that contains both of those.

"Natalie?" the business one says, rising when I approach.

Wow. Yep. "Ridiculously good-looking executive" would be the description on his unofficial profile page. The other guy isn't painful to look at either. Geez. Suddenly, there's so much I want to know regarding Marcos and Nate's well-organized stripping business.

"Yes, hi. Are you Marcos? Nash?"

"You know my name?" Nash asks as I take the empty seat.

"Nate's mentioned you, yeah."

They exchange a concerned look I can't interpret.

"You want anything?" Marcos asks.

"Maybe in a little bit," I say. My stomach is in no state to eat right now. "Thanks for messaging me. I'm worried about him too."

I sense their wary evaluations, and I don't blame them. I have no idea what they know about me, but most of it probably isn't good. As far as I know, they called me here to yell at me and accuse me of heaven knows what. I came anyway if it also meant making sure Nate leaves this resort with the support he needs.

"If you got my number from Chad, you must know I work for TPG," I say. Might as well take the direct approach. There's no point in playing games.

"Yeah. Chad shouldn't have given us your number," Marcos says with a cringe. "Sorry for taking advantage of his… Chadness."

I smirk. "I get it. It's fine. Like I said, I'm glad you contacted me. I won't betray Nate's confidence and tell you anything specific that he told me, but your instinct is right if you're concerned about him."

They exchange another look, and I settle into my chair, prepared for battle.

"Hey, so, don't take this personally, but can you explain to us why his biggest rival gives a shit about his health?" Nash asks.

"Because he's amazing, and I think I'm falling in love with him."

Whoa.

Their poker faces slip as they stare at me like I just said what I said. Instinctively, I prepare to take it back, but realize I don't want to take it back. It's the truth. It's absurd and implausible and doesn't just break *my* rules, but pretty much *everyone's* rules, but it's the truth.

I wait with a calm expression while they process that bombshell.

"Um, okay…?" Marcos says finally. "So you knew Nate before this conference?"

"Nope."

"Right." Marcos stares into his beer glass.

I sigh and lean forward. "Truth? Nate and I met Sunday night. We didn't know who the other person was. We spent an incredible night together thinking it was a one-time thing, but then the next day we learned we were enemies. Except we're not, and even after we found out we were competing for the same contract, our bond has only strengthened every minute we've spent together."

Well, until the last minute.

"That's why he wouldn't let us talk to Chad," Nash says, and Marcos mutters a curse.

"Talk to Chad?" I ask.

Their gazes land on me, and I see the conflict there. They don't want to betray him any more than I do. It's going to be a tricky exercise trying to join forces to help him without hurting him.

"We probably shouldn't tell you this, but you need to understand the kind of person he is," Marcos says. "Nate could have locked down that contract the second he learned Chad was the decision-maker. All three of us have strong ties to Reedweather Media. In fact, Nate was the secret weapon behind Chad's precious spy mission he brags about all the time."

"Wait, the undercover potato thing?" I ask.

Nash snorts a laugh. "The *undercover potato thing?* God, I hope that's how history remembers that event."

Marcos is fighting back a smile as well. "The part Nate probably didn't tell you is that he was the one who wrote the ransomware code that made *the undercover potato* a success."

I vaguely remember from lunch something about ransomware that "broke the company." But didn't Chad claim *he* was the one?

"In Chad's version, he wrote the code," I say.

Marcos shakes his head. "Yeah, right. Chad couldn't write the code for his phone's lock screen. That was all Nate, but Chad doesn't know that. Nate could have told him, but he didn't. He had the winning ticket to that contract and left it on the table. We practically begged him to let us talk to Chad on his behalf and put in a good word, but he wouldn't let us do that, either."

"Now we know why," Nash grunts.

Hold on. He had all those advantages, all those aces to play, and he didn't play any of them?

"Why would he give all that up?" I ask, confused.

"You. Obviously," Nash says with some bitterness. I guess I can't blame him. They still don't have any reason to trust me or believe anything I'm telling them.

"Wow," I breathe out, leaning back in my chair.

"Yeah," Marcos says. "Nate is one of the kindest, most genuine people you will meet. You know the term, wouldn't hurt a fly? He wouldn't even hurt his enemy. Clearly," he says, waving at me.

I'm not sure what to say as I consider this development. Combined with everything else I've learned about him and his situation, it's almost too much to handle. Even worse, would I have done the same if the roles were reversed? If I had a guaranteed win, would I have passed up a huge advantage to even the odds for my competition?

So he's everything I thought and more. What am I willing to do for him?

"He's in a really dark place," I say quietly. "I know he's acting like he's not, but he is. I don't know if we'll still be talking at the end of this week, but no matter what happens, please do everything you can to help him. He's carrying a lot more than he's letting on. I'm really scared for him."

I search their eyes and notice they have softened significantly since the start of this conversation.

"We will," Marcos says. "He put himself through hell and back multiple times on our behalf. We promise you, we will do the same for him."

I feel like I can breathe again as I return a sincere smile. These guys are so fortunate to have each other. Nate told me a little about their difficult past and how it drove them together. It hurt to hear him describing the pain of his childhood, but it's also encouraging to see the good that can come out of something so hard.

"Hey, one more question," I say. "Agile Synergy. Is what you said also the reason Nate knew the definition? He'd been exposed to it before?"

"You mean, Reedweather's ode to 'aggressive teamwork'? Was there a Venn diagram?" Marcos asks with a snicker.

I nod, and I can tell Nash is on the verge of a laugh.

"*Agile Synergy* has been a running joke in our apartment since Reedweather rolled out that bullshit while I still worked there months ago. Yeah, he knew what it meant. And yeah, he could have owned that seminar and Reedweather's heart if he wanted to. Good for you, he didn't want to."

I manage a stiff smile.

Good for me.

I don't think anything will be good for me until I can talk to him again.

13—TUESDAY 9:02 PM

NATE

It's been a long day. All of them are long, but today was particularly brutal. I had too many people to hide from, and as the hours dragged on, my resolve to do so dwindled with it. Marcos and Nate have been blasting me with messages. I finally appeased them by promising to meet for breakfast in the morning.

I should try to sleep, but my mind is racing, and forefront in my thoughts is Natalie. I know her heart. Despite what she said in the lab, there's no way she meant it the way it sounded. I was just so hurt already, so insecure and on edge with a brain that's expecting to be injured. It takes almost nothing to knock me down anymore. I was always the one to hold others up and fight their battles, and now I can't even touch the surface of my own.

I overreacted. I know it. I knew it as it was happening. That's the new me, though. The patient big brother has become an irritable old man sitting on his porch screaming at the dogwalkers who let their pet skim a blade of forbidden grass as they go by. I could add my shit attitude to the ever-expanding list of things I hate about myself now, but it's so long there's no point.

I do owe it to Natalie not to be a dick, though. So yes, it's twelve hours late, but I finally pull out my phone and read through the long string of texts pouring her heart out.

Thanks for saying all of that, I type back. **Sorry for overreacting. Come over if you want to talk.**

There's a knock at my door a minute later.

I fight a smile as I pull it open, my heart thawing a bit when she rushes inside and slides her arms around my waist.

I reach over her to shut the door, then return her embrace, standing in silence while we wait for the moment to decide what's next. Heaven knows I'm too exhausted to make that call.

"I didn't mean *you* were the mistake," she says into my shirt. "I meant how we were handling it was dangerous, that's all. God, Nate. You could never be a mistake. You are such a gift."

Her arms constrict around me, and I close my eyes to absorb the balm of her words. I don't know if that's true, but I believe she believes it.

"You're the gift," I say quietly, resting my cheek against her hair. "I'm sorry for how I reacted. You deserved better."

"Yes. I deserve everything, which is why I deserve you," she whispers.

My chest hurts as we hold each other, and I try to make sense of what's happening. This entire week has been a whirlwind of emotions. I'm worn down just from the effort of *feeling*.

She pulls back and searches my face in the dim light. She looks about to say something, but leads me further into the room instead. This time it's to the head of the bed, not the foot.

"I'm tired, so I know you are," she says. "We've had a really long day."

Confused, I stare at her as she tugs the comforter on the left side of the king bed and slips beneath the sheets.

"Um…" I'm not sure what else to say. What's going on, exactly?

"What's going on, exactly?" I ask.

"I'm sleeping."

"Here?"

"I slept here Sunday night."

"Yeah, but, not on purpose."

"Speak for yourself."

Wow.

Her smile is so beautiful coming from beneath my sheets. What defense do I have against that?

I slide in on the other side and turn to face her.

"So now what?" I ask.

"Now, we turn off the light and talk until we fall asleep."

"So… another one-night stand?"

"Third in a row. That has to be a record," she says.

"Pretty sure it's a new category once there's more than one night in a one-night stand."

"Yeah? So what category are we in now?"

"Let's see, hooking up with your hated rival three nights in a row for intimate conversation and no sex? *Is* there a category for that?"

She shrugs. "I'm sure Reedweather would be able to come up with a pretentious term for it."

I huff a laugh. "*Ascetic Intimacy*."

"Ascetic?" she says, raising her brows.

"Are you impressed?"

"A little. How about *Temperate Affection*?"

"Aw, do you have temperate feelings for me?" I ask.

"So temperate," she says, inching closer.

She releases my hand so she can trace my jaw instead. It's strange how quickly everything can shift from wrong to right when I'm with her. How her touch and compassionate gaze help soothe the thorns tearing at my soul.

"Hey, Nate? I have to tell you something." She takes a deep breath and searches my eyes. "I met with your roommates today. They reached out because they're worried about you, and so am I."

I'm silent for a moment, mesmerized by the concern on her face. Why does she care about me so much? I still don't get it.

"I know," I say finally.

Her relief is visible. "You do?"

"Yeah, they told me. They said they contacted you."

"Because they love you," she says, spreading her palm over my cheek. "I truly believe they will not only be able to handle 'the real you,' but they will love him as much as I..."

She winces and removes her hand. "Crap. I didn't... I mean... Gah, sorry... Let's just..." She covers her face and shifts to her back.

Huh. Interesting.

"You think they'll love the real me as much as you love... mailing things?" I say.

She glances over, a slow smile spreading over her lips. I return it and brush her hand until our fingers lace together. We stare at the ceiling, enjoying the soporific whir of the air conditioner. I could fall asleep like this. I probably *will* fall asleep like this. It would be a welcome change from most nights.

"You missed a great skit," she says, reaching over to flip the switch on the reading lamp. Strange how the sudden darkness doesn't feel nearly as dark as the light just an hour ago.

"Yeah? Can you reenact it for me tomorrow?"

"No, I don't have posterboard."

"You need posterboard for a skit?"

"The posterboard *is* the skit. You write *Agile Synergy* on it and hold it, while Chad reads the definition of Agile Synergy to the audience."

I squint through the dark, trying to picture it. "What makes that a skit?"

"The squeezy starfish."

"I'm sorry?"

"And tracing the letters in four different colors with a bonus underline."

"Any glitter?"

"No. The use of glitter would have required a fifty-dollar surcharge to the room rental due to cleanup liabilities, so we weren't allowed to use it."

"Then why was it there?"

"That is the question. Now you're thinking like a true Agile Synergist." She pats my cheek with mock approval.

"I don't get it."

"None of us did. Maybe that was also part of the skit? Anyway, I'm so sorry about your post office box emergency. Glad to see you're okay."

"My what?"

"Chad said you had to run out because you had a post office box emergency?"

I laugh and shake my head. No idea what to do with that one.

"Okay, well, I didn't say anything about a post office box emergency. What would that even be?"

Her thumb moves over mine, and I love that she's thinking about this as hard as I am.

"You didn't pay your rental fee on time and there's a large package that arrived for you but nowhere to put the little locker key to access it?" she suggests.

"If I didn't pay my rental fee, would they keep the package for me? Wouldn't they send it back?"

"Maybe it didn't have a return address."

"Who would send a large package without a return address?"

"Hmm… A drug cartel?"

"Ah. Yeah. I *did* hear the cartels are moving away from drugs and trying to corner the market on scented candles and affordable home décor."

Natalie laughs and shifts to face me. "Hey, Nate?"

"Yeah?"

"What are we going to do about the Sandeke contract? I don't want to hurt you."

My humor fades as I make out a few details of her concerned, beautiful face in the dark. With a sigh, I draw her in, and she settles against my chest. I wrap my arms around her, appreciating the security of her warmth against me.

"I don't know," I say quietly. "I don't want to hurt you, either."

"I wish…" She doesn't finish the thought with words, but I feel the rest in the way her hold tightens around me. She buries her face in my chest, her hot breath branding my skin with a fantasy I want so badly to be reality.

She wishes things were different. She wishes either of us were anyone else. She wishes this was real and had any hope of lasting beyond this week of being a make-believe couple. Basically, she wishes everything I've been wishing since I found out who she was and that I couldn't have her.

"I'm in eight-thirteen," she says in a sleepy voice. "Maybe we can spend tomorrow night in my room."

* * *

Something feels different when my alarm goes off at seven. The feeling is warm and substantial, like the heat of another body. I rub my eyes and can't stop a smile as Natalie stirs beside me.

Her arm is draped over mine, her hair spread on the pillow, begging to be gathered in my fingers. I suppress the urge and force myself to wait patiently while she adjusts and decides how she feels about our current position. Sure, this sleepover was her idea, but I know from experience that things look drastically different in the bright morning sun than they do in the bold midnight haze. Genius becomes embarrassment. Bravery becomes shame. Big ideas become huge regrets.

What will this morning be for her? Will she be happy or horrified to find herself in my bed… again?

I breathe easier when she tilts a groggy smile in my direction.

"Morning," she croaks.

"Morning. You sleep okay?"

"Yeah. You?"

137

"Better than I have in a while."

Her eyes soften as she stares at me, and something moves in my chest when she adjusts to snuggle closer. She slides her arm around my stomach, and I wrap her in an instinctive embrace. Her lids drift close, and I wish we could stay like this all day. I'd love nothing more than to spend lazy hours absently running my fingers through her hair, while she draws invisible murals over my skin. It would be so easy to get lost in the peace of just existing with this person.

Too bad we live in a world where alarms don't just wake us up, but govern our entire day.

"I have to meet Marcos and Nash for breakfast," I say, and a wave of dread pollutes the peaceful oasis. I survived yesterday's confrontation, but there's no way they're going to let me off the hook so easily today. Breakfast was an easy promise to make when tomorrow seemed like a distant mirage.

"You okay?" Natalie asks, angling her head to see my face.

The instinctive lie creeps onto my tongue, and I stop myself.

"Not really," I confess. "I'm nervous. I don't know what to say to them."

"Just tell them everything you've told me."

I pull in a long inhale. "I wish it was that easy."

She gives me a tight squeeze before relaxing back to a casual position against my side. "Do you want me to join you?"

"You'd do that?"

"Of course."

"You don't have to meet your own people?"

"I'll see them at the *Think Big, Think Successful* seminar."

"You're going to that too?"

"It's another Sandeke lecture, so yeah."

Right. I wonder who will be running this one and wasting another hour of our lives. So far this week, I've learned golf shirts coordinate with tailfins and meteorology isn't a universally accepted science.

Natalie's fingertips run over the grooves in my stomach, and I lose myself in the soothing cadence of her touch.

Up. Down. Across.

Up Down. Across.

"You're the same person, Nate," she says in a thoughtful tone.

Confused, I glance over to find her captivating brown irises shining back at me.

"You're the same person," she repeats with more authority. "All the things you think are 'wrong with you now' aren't, and in many ways, have nothing to do with you. They're external. Myra leaving, losing your job, this current messed up situation that's culminated in one giant shitstorm—it's all other people, other things. Even the mental fog you've been living in for the last few months doesn't change who you are down deep. In the center of that evolving vortex is an amazing guy who is intelligent, kind, funny, driven, resilient, and principled. That person is beautiful inside and out and nothing this world throws at you can change that if you don't let it."

She runs her palm up my cheek to tip my face toward her.

"Circumstances don't define who you are. How you handle them does. Whether you're the CFO of the world's biggest corporation or doing taxes in a local strip mall, you're a person I admire, a person I'd want in my life."

I don't know what to say as I absorb her words. She's all of those things too. She's more than that, and I not only *would* want her in my life, a sliver of panic erupts in my stomach at the cavity she'll leave when she's gone.

"Your path may be unclear," she continues in the melodic voice I'm craving more and more. "But you are the same person now that you were four months ago. You know what that means?"

"What?" I ask quietly.

"It means that strong, beautiful person will find his way again."

* * *

Verna isn't prepared for the sight that greets her when she delivers this morning's breakfast. I was really hoping someone (anyone) else would deliver our room service today.

"You took my advice," she says in an approving tone as she scans Marcos and Nash with disturbing interest. There's no way she's coming to the right conclusion about what's happening here.

"I'm sorry?" Marcos says, helping her unload the cart.

In order to include Natalie, we had to hold our breakfast date in the only safe place we could be together. While she made a quick run to her room to freshen up, I told Marcos and Nash to join us in mine. They agreed, but not without several irritating cracks about Romeo and Juliet, followed by an intense argument about which of them was Mercutio and which was Benvolio. I still don't know where we landed on that.

"Are you here for the week or just the day?" Verna asks Marcos.

Her eager expression clearly has a preference, and that preference is "locked up in her shed for all of eternity."

Crap.

"The week," he says with a polite smile.

"Wonderful. You too?" she asks Nash, who nods.

He immediately abandons the conversation in favor of sorting through the food.

She winks at Natalie and me. "It must have been a fun night if it lasted 'til morning. I didn't even know that was an option."

"They're friends," I say. "Not… strippers."

Marcos' eyes widen, while Nash smirks. Uh-oh.

"Speak for yourself," my smart-ass roommate says. "This place is a goldmine," he tells Verna, who gazes at him with stars in her eyes. "I'm making a fortune this week."

"I imagine so. You are probably involved in today's festivities?"

"Of course," he says, stuffing a slice of toast in his mouth. "I'm headlining," he lies. Ass. He doesn't even know what she's talking about.

"Really? Well!" she exclaims. "What's your act?"

"My act?" he garbles through his mouthful of food.

"Yes. Your theme. Let me guess, sexy rockstar?"

"So sexy," he says, taking another bite. "I wear nothing but my guitar for the entire last song."

Her eyes grow three sizes as Marcos looks ready to throw something at him. Ironically, Nash is the only man in this room who *doesn't* have stripper on his resume.

Natalie is stifling a laugh, so she'll be no help with our annoying roommate.

"He's kidding," I say, giving him a hard look. "Sorry about him. Anyway, thanks, Verna. We really appreciate you delivering our breakfast."

"So you're not strippers?" she asks, looking very disappointed.

"*They* are," Nash says, waving at Marcos and me.

We glare at him, and he shrugs.

"Were," Marcos corrects, and I transfer my dark look to him. "What? It's true."

Great. Now, all three of us are naked in Verna's head. I have no doubt that if she wasn't already assigned to whatever "festivities" are taking place today, she will do everything she can to make that happen—even if she's not sure which of us will be taking our clothes off at this point.

"Thanks again, Verna," I mumble, directing her to the door.

"You're a lucky girl," she whispers to Natalie, who chokes on the coffee she was drinking.

"I am," she forces out. "The luckiest."

Verna nods and takes her leave with one last, very extended, perusal of us. We have no hope of getting anyone else to deliver our food this week.

"Hey, do you think it's too late to get in the lineup for that stripper festival?" Nash asks once we're alone. "Marcos, you can play bass with Nate on cajon?"

Marcos is closer so he smacks him on our behalf.

* * *

Nash's stripper band idea becomes way more enticing once the topic of conversation shifts to me and my messed up life. I'd learn to play cajon naked if it meant avoiding the probing stares of my friends.

"Talk," Marcos says. "Tell us what's going on."

I push the pile of hashbrowns around my plate. Where do I even start?

"Start with Myra."

Grr.

"Fine, but there's not much to tell. She's the CCO so of course she's here. So are Amit and Colin. Apparently, their job is to babysit me and make sure I don't screw up the Sandeke account."

Their gazes lock on Natalie who shifts uncomfortably.

"Yes, she and the TPG team are also trying to land the Sandeke account."

"Damn Capulets," Nash mutters.

Natalie cracks a smile.

"Huh. Well, that's… complicated," Marcos says.

"Yeah," I say, dropping my fork on the plate and pushing it away.

"So what's the plan?" Marcos asks. "How are you going to resolve the fact that you're fighting for the same contract?"

"There is no plan," I say with a shrug.

"You don't know how you're handling this?"

"Nope."

"So how do you operate?"

"We're winging it. So far we've managed."

"Yeah, but…"

Marcos' strategic mind is probably imploding at that revelation. I don't think he even grocery shops without a clear action plan.

"You'll need to decide soon. You get that, right? It's already Wednesday and by Friday one of you will have that contract and one of you won't."

"Yep. That's correct," I say.

Marcos stares at me, then visibly shudders. "Okay, fine. Moving on. So Myra. You talked to her?"

I take a deep breath and force a nod. "Yes."

"And?"

"Don't lie to us," Nash says. "We know there had to be drama."

Drama? That's one word for soul-wrenching confessions that blindside you then kick you in the gut over and over again.

"She says she, um…"

Shit.

"Just tell them," Natalie says, taking my hand.

I lace my fingers with hers and brace myself. "She says she's still in love with me and wants me back. She also told me to flirt with Natalie for intel and that if I don't land this account I'll be fired."

Silence.

Yep. This is my life now. I could say sentences like that all day.

"That… is fucked up," Nash says.

I shrug, and Marcos studies me with a pensive expression.

"So this?" he asks, waving between Natalie and me.

"Is real," she says.

A strange warmth spreads through me when she squeezes my hand.

Marcos grunts and massages his temples. "So let me get this straight. He's pretending to flirt with you, but *actually* flirting with you. And you're pretending that it's working but it's *actually* working?"

"Close," Natalie says in a casual tone. "I'm supposed to flirt with him too. So, really, we're both pretending to be flirting with each other, while *actually* flirting with each other."

I didn't think this scenario could sound worse than it did in my head, but I was wrong.

"Yep. Pretty sure the only difference between angsty artists and business-people is where they display their drama," Nash quips.

He's got a point, actually.

"And the firing thing?" Marcos asks. "Do you think that's legit or just a bluff?"

"It's legit," I say. I decide not to tell him how I know that, because then I'd have to tell them everything else.

Marcos releases a breath and shakes his head. "Damn. This is some heavy shit, my friend. No wonder you've been off this week. Why didn't you tell us what was going on?"

I shrug and try to ignore Natalie's imploring look. I know what she's thinking. Marcos unknowingly gave me an out from the real conversation, and she's pleading with me not to take it.

Yes, I've been "off" this week. I've been off for months. In fact, I'm pretty sure this "off" is my new "on." I'm drowning and see no way out. Every day feels like another hopeless step on the trudge toward nothing. The darkness is closing in and cutting me off and sometimes I feel like I'm suffocating.

That's what she wants me to say.

Instead…

"Yeah. It's been a rough few days, but we've all been busy. I didn't want to bother you. There's not much we can do to fix it, anyway."

"Are you kidding? It's been the three of us against the world forever," Marcos says. "We're a fucking army when we need to be. A brain trust for survival."

"We're figuring this out," Nash says, steeling into battle mode.

Marcos also braces for war, and suddenly, we're back at Bellevue. Out in the yard, ducking behind the half wall of decaying bricks no one knows why it's there. Billy Stanton and his posse of mindless sheep pace threateningly in front of us, thinking they're about to laugh their way through a slaughter.

What they don't know is that Marcos, Nash, and I are invincible when we come together as a unit. It's impossible to fail when the others refuse to let one quit. No fear, no surrender. That was the motto that fueled our resilience and drove us into adulthood. Nothing has changed in the ten years since, except the bullies we face.

At least, that's what my friends think. What they don't know is that one of us has quit. One of us is afraid. One of us is ready to surrender.

I can't look at Natalie as Marcos leans forward and prepares to devote his brilliant, strategic mind to my dilemma. Nash settles back to observe and share the profound insights he hoards in that perceptive brain he hides so well.

I pretend solving this one problem will fix anything.

"Let's start with Myra and work our way from there," Marcos says.

14—WEDNESDAY 9:55 AM

NATALIE

Lanette and Theresa don't look happy to see me as I slide into the seat between them. I expected as much and queue up the script I've been rehearsing for this scenario.

If I'm a spy who's supposed to be gaining intel from my competitor, but it's my own side I'm lying to, does that make me a double agent? What does it make me if I don't use the information to benefit either side and have no interest in any of this spy crap?

Irritable.

"We really needed you to come to breakfast this morning," Theresa hisses.

"Why? We're meeting for lunch, right?"

"*That's* why," she says, waving toward Nate and the Eon Tech crew. "We needed to discuss what to do about that *before* this seminar, not after."

"What is there to discuss?"

"That's what we needed to figure out," Lanette says. "You haven't told us anything. What happened with the skit-writing session? He never came back for the skit, so something must have gone down. Then you and Chad show up? What happened with your one-on-one with Chad?"

"It wasn't really a skit," I say.

They narrow their eyes at me, not impressed by my insight.

"Not the point," Theresa says. "You had direct access to Nate *and* Chad yesterday. What happened with each of them?"

Whew. Saved by the presenter.

My coworkers glare at me like I purposely showed up right before the session so we wouldn't have time for this conversation. They are correct.

"Good morning, everyone," an authoritative man says in a rigid tone. Everyone goes silent like the God of Telecom itself is running this seminar on *Thinking Big, Thinking Successful.* Three words in, and this person has already garnered more respect than the last two Sandeke presenters combined.

"I'm Denver Sandeke. It's a pleasure to be here."

Ah. Apparently, this class *is* being run by a telecom deity. This guy is the golden crown every salesperson and executive in this room wants to be wearing by the end of the week.

Ew. Maybe I could have phrased that better.

"*This* is why we needed to plan," Theresa whisper-barks.

I'm not sure how we would have planned for this scenario when we didn't know this would be the scenario.

"*Egotistical,*" Sandeke clips out. He passes his hard stare over us. "*Arrogant. Obstinate. Inflexible, callous, condescending.* All of these words have a negative connotation and all of these words have been used to describe *me.*"

He comes around from behind the podium to pace in front of us.

"If you want to *Think Successful,* you need to *Think Big,* and I don't just mean big ideas. I mean, big egos and big personalities who know what they want and get things done. The corporate battleground is no place for coddling and a soft heart. Weak people do not do great things. It's kill or be killed, predator and prey. Which are you?"

His penetrating gaze seems to bore into each of us, and a chill runs down my spine as I study his cold features. Everything he's saying, the look in his eyes as he says it, has me squirming uncomfortably in my chair. His words are worse than controversial, they're downright dangerous in the way they convey just enough truth to validate the lies. He's right, snakes like him do get ahead in life —because they don't care who they crush on the route to their goal.

My gaze drifts to Nate, who's expression is unreadable, his eyes glued to the powerful, icy man before us. What's he thinking about all of this? Funny how one of the things I admire most about him is the fact that he's *none* of what Denver Sandeke just told us he's supposed to be. I hope he realizes Sandeke is the one doing it wrong, not him.

"It's come to my attention that there are two firms in this room who can provide the perfect demonstration of what I'm talking about."

My heart seizes in my chest. Theresa tenses beside me, and I know we're about to get hit… hard. My fears are confirmed when Sandeke's frosty gaze lands on us, then swings to the Eon employees.

"TPG and Eon Tech both want something from me. Isn't that right?"

He pauses to give us time to shiver through his relaxed threat.

"What is it that you want?" he muses. "Enlighten us."

"To provide a comprehensive power backup system and emergency service contract," Myra calls out in a direct tone that draws an approving smile from Sandeke.

Crap. A point for Eon Tech.

"Yes. You've both been chasing our Senior Director of Contingencies and Collateral Mitigation all week, haven't you?" he says, waving at Chad.

The younger man beams back, oblivious to the hostile atmosphere his boss is intentionally building. Reedweather sits beside him looking like he's watching viral cat videos.

"Natalie McAllister and Nathan Hanover, you are the representatives of this competition, correct?"

He centers his attention on me and Nate, respectively.

"That's correct. Our customizable, proprietary system would be an excellent fit for Sandeke Telecom's divergent needs across the spectrum of the organization," I say. "Other systems may be cheaper, but won't provide the flexibility a large campus like Sandeke Telecom would need."

I'm the recipient of his impressed brow-lift this time. Another point distributed, this one to us. I sense Theresa and Lanette's mental high-five.

My heart is racing with excitement, but plummets when I also sense Nate's attention. My triumph deflates further at how easily I got swept into Sandeke's dirty game. Nate didn't even play, and I threw my best hand.

"Well, we shall see, won't we?" he says, scanning the audience. "For a real life demonstration of what it takes to be successful in this industry, join us in The Lily Lecture Hall Friday morning at ten."

He focuses back on us, and my blood goes cold.

"Each of you will have an opportunity to present your pitches directly to my colleagues and me in a public forum. We will also award the contract at that time. Best of luck to you both."

* * *

There's a chicken quesadilla in front of me that I doubt I'll be able to eat. I couldn't even get through the two tortilla chips I attempted.

Lanette and Theresa chatter about something, laptop open and already collecting notes for the showdown.

"I have a two o'clock with Barry and a taskforce he's putting together to help us," Theresa says. "Lanette, you research Eon Tech to find anything we can use to take them down. Nat, you know what you have to do."

"No, what do I have to do?" I say with a surly tone.

Her look says she knows I know what she's talking about.

My return look says I know she knows I know but I don't like it.

"You don't think that boy is doing the exact same thing with his team right now?" she says. "I guarantee you, they're strategizing about how to use you to take us down."

They probably are, but Nate isn't. I know in my heart he doesn't want to fight this war any more than I do.

"Double your efforts on him," she says. "Whatever it takes."

I glare at her, furious. "I will help with research and refining our pitch, but I'm not going to trade myself for information. How can you even ask me that?"

She straightens in surprise. "I'm not suggesting you *trade* yourself. I'm just saying, continue your friendship with their VP of Sales. We've been watching you play him all week, and you're doing a fantastic job. He seems to have warmed up to you in a real way. Where's this crisis of conscience coming from all of a sudden?"

I'm a horrible person. Okay, I'm not, but I feel like one. Especially, when I lower my gaze, too afraid to come clean.

"Just continue being nice to him and make him think you're friends," she says in a softer tone. "I'm not asking you to do anything *more* than what you're doing, just do more of what you're already doing."

"You should have seen how many times he looked at you during the seminar," Lanette says. "He's definitely close to serving up some valuable info. You sure he hasn't given you anything we can use? Not even a tiny piece?"

"Not yet," I say.

Ugh. I hate everything about this.

"Can't we just focus on our pitch and beat them on merit? Why do we have to play dirty?"

"I don't understand why you're chickening out all of a sudden," Theresa says. "The whole point of Sandeke's seminar is that business is war. He *wants* us to play dirty. Eat or be eaten. With us or against us. Your boy Nate has been playing hardball, so why shouldn't you? It's not personal. It's business."

Nate has been doing the opposite of her accusations, and what Denver Sandeke said is bullshit. Just because that's the way things are, doesn't mean that's the way they should be.

Also, that was an obscene number of clichés for one speech.

Too bad I can't bring myself to say any of that no matter how much I know it's the right thing to do. It's amazing how quickly things can change. Up until this week, I had a completely different view of my career. I loved sales. I loved the conflict and challenge of "eating before being eaten." I would have had no problem stomping over Nate to get what I wanted because Nate would have been an idea, not a person. He's the rival, the enemy.

And then we stayed up all night talking without prejudice. We saw beyond the warped lens we use on others when we convert them to theories instead of nuanced human beings. In one night, the illusion shattered without us knowing it. My "enemy" became a very real, hurting person, and now that I know the truth behind the label, I don't know how to put the label back on.

Labels obscure the truth, not clarify it.

My phone buzzes, and a flutter of anticipation shoots through me at the name. I glance at my coworkers, relieved they're wrapped up in their villainous planning and didn't see the display.

Nate: **Can we talk?**

I suck in a breath, already tense with longing to be close to him. I haven't had a chance to kiss him today since I wouldn't let him near my mouth before I brushed my teeth and his roommates were present every second after that.

Can we talk?

That has to be about Sandeke's borderline sadistic challenge, right? He must want to figure out how to navigate this as much as I do. Knowing everything I do about him, that whole session must have been a punch in the gut for him. It was for me, and now I have this strange need to be near him.

In fact, as I sit here staring at his name, I'm struck by the power he has to make my world a little brighter even when he's not here. Just knowing he's somewhere thinking about me and being his kind, ethical self helps ease the sting of the negativity around me. It makes me crave his gentle, witty presence. His beautiful laugh and his effortless ability to pull one from me. His deep, intelligent gaze, and the strange way his eyes manage to project strength in the midst of alluring vulnerability.

Yes, I want to do more than kiss him. I want to experience him, to explore every part of him inside and out. I don't want a one-night stand with this person—I want everything.

The irony is not lost on me that I'm desperate to make love to the person I'm supposed to hate.

* * *

Nate agreed to meet me in *my* room this time.

I pace with embarrassing anticipation as I wait for his knock. I told him two o'clock, because Theresa and Lanette will be occupied with the "taskforce" tele-conference at that time. It seemed like I should have been on that call as well, but she didn't want me to waste any time on something "that could easily be condensed to an email once they formulate their strategy."

I was annoyed that I got assigned to flirting while they ran the war room, so it feels fair that I'm betraying her by doing exactly what she wants me to be doing.

I jump at the knock and hurry to answer it. Nate waits outside looking as gorgeous and troubled as always.

"Hey. Come in," I say, stepping back so he can enter.

He gives me a tight smile and obeys.

Once the door closes, an awkward second passes as we stare into each other's eyes. Does he want to do to me what I want to do to him?

Slowly unbutton his shirt. Slip it over his shoulders. Run my hands over his warm, solid chest, up his neck. Frame his face for a deep, hungry kiss.

"Just thought you should know, I'm no longer the competition. I'm off the team," he says, dropping his gaze again.

"What?!" I cry.

He shrugs and moves into the room.

"The stakes are too high now," he says in a flat tone as he perches on the end of the bed.

I study his mannerisms for clues about his state.

He leans forward and runs his fingers through his hair. When he remains hunched over and locks his elbows on his knees, I have my answer. He's a mess.

"Nate…" I say, my heart hurting as I watch him break right in front of me.

He doesn't say anything, just shakes his head. And then I see the glisten in his eyes.

"Hey," I whisper, rushing to his side.

I wrap my arms around him and pull tight. He doesn't respond or even make a sound as he returns my embrace. I know how hard he's fighting his emotions right now. He wants to be strong, and strong people don't cry in the face of awful, unfair situations. But he's wrong. Strong people aren't afraid to use whatever emotion they have to fight back when they're faced with hardships.

"I'm so sorry this is happening to you."

He pulls back, and I wince at the pain on his face. Shit, this isn't just about the Sandeke account, is it? There's more.

"What happened?"

He averts his gaze and shifts to face forward again. "We called corporate to discuss our strategy. They, uh…"

He stops, looking shellshocked as he studies the wall. "They said they'd mail me any personal items still at the office. I'll see if I can stay with Marcos for the rest of the week."

"Oh my god."

I can't breathe as I stare at him in disbelief.

He doesn't look at me, no doubt lost in that dark place in his head. I only glimpsed it during our time together, and I know he won't let anyone near it now. My concern for him escalates into fear.

"It's whatever," he mumbles, digging at the carpet with his shoe. "I knew it was coming. It's not like it's a surprise."

"Yeah, but…"

They didn't have to do it in the most brutal, humiliating way possible. Who fires someone while they're away at a conference?

I want to ask about Myra. What role did she play? How did she react? How is he processing her involvement in this entire mess?

But when he finally looks at me again, I forget everything except the lost, broken man in front of me.

"I'm nobody now," he says, eyes heavy with a touch of bewilderment. "Literally, *nothing*. I don't even…"

He scrubs at his face, and suddenly it's not just compassion but rage running through me. How *dare* they?! How dare those heartless, greedy monsters crush this beautiful person because he refuses to be one of them? How dare we define the path to success only one way and discard other voices that don't fit the mold?

You fit the mold. You forced your entire life into the mold.

Correction: I *was* the mold, because if this is the standard and the way things are "supposed" to be, then we need a new standard.

"No," I snap.

Nate looks over in surprise, and I don't try to hide my anger. "That's bullshit. You aren't *nobody.* What you *are* is someone who's too good for this cesspool. What you *are* is the kind of person who is going to do amazing things by doing them *better.*"

"Natalie, I—"

"No, you listen," I bark, pointing at him. "You are beautiful and flawed and perfect and messed up and all the things humans are. What you're not, is *nothing.* A weak person caves to the status quo, not fights against it. Don't you see? You are the opposite of nothing. You are too much. You are so much, your executives couldn't handle you so they had to get rid of you."

His eyes sift over my face, filled with a mosaic of all the things I love about him.

So confused.

So stunning.

So perfectly imperfect like all of us.

I can't take the distance anymore. It's been too many hours of suffering through his close presence but not close enough. I stand in front of where he sits on the bed and tilt his head up to read his expression.

His eyes are red-rimmed, but there are no tears. He just looks tired and resigned, and maybe a little hungry when his focus sinks to my mouth. I know I'm starving.

"I want to kiss you," I say quietly.

"You still want me?" he asks in genuine confusion. "Even though—"

"Don't you dare finish that sentence."

His lips are everything I've been craving as I straddle him and force him back on the bed. His fingers slide into my hair, gripping hard as he kisses me back with an aggression that makes me burn. His tongue presses into my mouth, drawing a whimper when he takes control of the kiss.

How can he think he's weak? His strength of character is one of the hottest things about him.

My body scrapes along his, seeking friction to soothe an ache that only grows with each slow stroke. We move in a synchronized wave, building heat and electricity with every timed collision. This must be the sexy, undulating meadow that Reedweather was talking about.

I separate enough to unbutton his shirt, loving how my new position puts me in direct contact with the hardening bulge in his pants. My fingers fumble with the rest of the buttons, already anticipating their reassignment to work on his belt.

Once his shirt is free, he twists to shrug out of it, and I grip his undershirt to rip it up his chest and over his head. My breath catches when I pause to study him. He's so freaking gorgeous with his messy hair and the wild look in his eyes, so mesmerizing that I straighten to take him in. He props up on his elbows, staring up at me as I hover above him, still straddling his hips. His biceps swell from supporting his weight, his chest and abs damn near perfection as they work in unison to maintain his position—trapped beneath me, exactly where I want him, where I've imagined him so many times this week.

"You okay?" he asks.

"So okay."

I smile, surprised that the blistering urgency from a second ago has been replaced by a tender need to explore him with slow, deep precision instead.

I pull off my top, watching his eyes ignite as he takes me in like I'm doing to him. He doesn't even have to say anything to make me feel beautiful. His expression screams his appreciation.

"How could anyone ever be satisfied by a one-night stand with you?" he asks, running his gaze up my body to my face. "One night could never be enough."

His focus rests on my eyes, and I know he means more than the physical. My exploding heart fires scorching embers to every recess of my being.

I don't have the words to respond, so I lean down to kiss him instead. His hand slips back into my hair to guide our mouths and deepen the connection. His tortured groan when I grind against him is enough to ignite those scattered embers into a furious blaze.

"Please tell me you have a condom," I murmur against his lips.

"No," he says, then flips us around and presses into me for a painful temptation I've just learned I can't have.

"No?" I repeat, almost whining.

"Even if I did, we're in *your* room, remember?" he says through a smile I can taste. So delicious.

I frame his face to hold him to me, driving our mouths and tongues to do what our bodies can't. But it only fuels the craving instead of satisfies it.

A moan escapes me, a wordless plea for more. "Don't guys keep them in their wallets or something?"

"Not guys at a telecom conference who have no reason to think they'll need one."

I pull back and grip both sides of his face to center it on me.

"It never occurred to you during the many times we've come close and discussed it that you might need one at this particular telecom conference?"

His smile is too shy to be devious and too devious to be sheepish. "It occurred to me, but never when I was in a physical and mental state to act on it."

"Ugh, fine. What about your roommates?"

"What about them?"

"Don't they have some you can have?"

"*Some*, wow. This is getting more intense by the second."

I glare at him, and his cute smile spreads into a dangerous grin.

"You know what I mean."

"Okay, well, I just told them this morning I'm even in a position to possibly need a condom, and you were standing right there. How exactly did you want that conversation to go down?"

My body warms from the thought, and I'm not even sure *which* thought.

"Fine. Then what about on your way to my room just now?"

"Ah," he says with a nod. "Right. Most people's first reaction after getting fired is to buy condoms."

"Fair point," I mumble. "Guess we only have one option." He fights a smile, and I narrow my eyes. "Now what?"

"Are you sure that's your stance? Don't you remember what happened last time someone assumed there was 'only one option' to do something?"

I snort a laugh. "Fine. There are probably sixty-eight options, but I'm referring to the one that makes the most sense and is scientifically plausible."

I tug the buckle on his belt and slide open the button. Funny how quickly my hand is able to shut him up.

"What were the options you were thinking, Mr. Hanover?" I tease, running my palm back and forth over his erection. I knew he'd feel amazing. I'm not sure which of us is enjoying this more.

His breathing intensifies with each stroke of my hand, his eyes hot and trained on me. He inhales sharply when I wrap my fingers around him. My thumb skims over the tip, drawing a distinct shudder.

Maybe there's something to be said for patience, because I own him in this moment. He's mine to touch and explore and experience, and I'm dying for him to do the same to me. Plus, I love being right, and I'm pretty sure he's okay with my temporary solution to our dilemma.

That is, until his heated gaze flashes with humor.

"Another option would be to go back to school for a theoretical physics degree and build a time machine that will take me to Monday morning when I learn who you are. I quit my job right then and march off to the hotel's sundries shop to stock up for what will be a much better three days than what we've gotten so far."

"Really," I say with a skeptical look. "*That's* what you would do with your time machine?"

"Well, it's not the *only* thing I'd do, just the one thing that pertains to the present conversation. You still look skeptical."

"I am. There's no way you're walking out on Monday's seminar to buy condoms."

He laughs. "No? Why not?"

"You'd never miss a second chance to see Chad in his mermaid suit."

* * *

It's a testament to Nate's skill that he can erase all memories of a man in a mermaid nut costume with nothing but his mouth.

A gasp, followed by a groan, sieves out of me as his tongue erases the drama of the last few days. I grip the sheets while rush after rush builds into an unbearable ache. It's right there, so close, and…

"Don't stop," I gasp out.

He intensifies the hot, wet pressure on my core. My toes curl. My body bucks against his mouth as he works me with frustrating patience that's so, so good.

And so close, so…

Searing streaks of pleasure drive me into the sheets. My body is lost to me for a few glorious seconds as it pulses to the rhythm of my pounding blood. My entire world is white light and consuming fire and… Nate Hanover.

His grin is almost too much when he looks up from between my legs. I release a long exhale, weak and content. No, not content. Sated, but not content. I couldn't be with him still down there.

I reach for him, and he climbs up my body to hover over me again. I pull his head down for a long, probing kiss. I can still feel his heat between my legs.

"You okay?" he asks, pulling back to search my face.

"More than okay," I say, tracing my finger along his jaw.

His smile is something I want on my phone lock screen. I brush my fingers over it now, imagining how it would brighten my day every time I looked at my display. People would see it and ask if that was my partner, and I'd enjoy the flash of appreciation mixed with jealousy when I said yes. *Yes, this incredible person is mine. So sorry. You'll have to find your own.*

A strange chill runs through me.

"What's wrong?" he says, the smile I so love tipping into a frown.

He adjusts to move off me, and I grab his arm to hold him in place.

"Nothing, just…"

I blink and look away, not sure how to express the sudden emotions swirling through me.

"Natalie?"

Tears burn behind my eyes, and I don't even know why. I'm not sad. I'm happy. Too happy, and maybe that's the problem. This is going to end. It's *supposed* to end. I should want that, right? This was just a conference hookup turned conference fling and Saturday we go back to our real lives.

The liquid must be more than I thought, though, because I feel a drop slide down the edge of my face to the pillow.

"Hey, what's wrong? You're scaring me," he says, searching my eyes.

"Nothing. It's… I'm… imagining you on my lock screen."

His concern shifts into amusement as he stares down at me. "You're crying because you're imagining me on your phone? Is the photo that bad?"

I choke on a laugh and swat at my eyes. "No, not that, it's just… a weird thought. Another thing real couples do that we won't ever do after this ends on Friday."

His smile fades, and I can't read his new expression.

"Is that what you want?" he asks after a long silence.

Is it? That was the plan but…

"It has to be, right?" I say quietly. "We both have our lives that won't work together outside of this one fantasy week where they intersect."

We're just a pretend conference couple…

I still can't guess what he's thinking when he rolls to the mattress beside me. He doesn't say anything as he slides an arm under his head and studies the ceiling. Something doesn't feel right, but I don't know what it is. Does he agree or disagree? Did I hurt him again or is he worried about hurting me? How can we fix a problem we don't understand?

"No, you're right," he says, but I don't like the edge in his tone.

"Nate, I—"

He cuts me off with a sad smile. "Really. I'm not upset. I get it and I don't disagree. This week has been a whirlwind. It's impossible to trust our feelings and know what's real and what's not."

He checks his phone, and I *really* don't like the impassive expression on his face. It's the same one I see in the seminars and when he's with everyone else. It's his world-famous mask, and it's the first time he's worn it for *me.*

"This was amazing. *You* are amazing," I say, examining him closely.

He shoots me a quick smile that I don't believe for a second. "So are you. Hey, I have to run. Message you later?"

He pushes up and swipes his clothing from the floor without even waiting for my response.

A small voice in my head is screaming for me to stop him. To fix whatever is breaking right now, but I still don't understand what it is. We're on the same page. We're doing exactly what we're supposed to be doing and reacting in the way we're supposed to be reacting. Everything is perfectly right, so why does it feel so wrong?

He's never going to be on your phone screen, Nat.

I watch in silence as he tucks in his shirt and buckles his belt. He turns to the mirror on the wall to check his appearance and fix his hair. I can't see his reflection well, but I observe enough in his tense shoulders and back to know he's not okay. I can also tell I'll have zero chance getting him to talk about it.

"Please, message me when you have time. I want to see you again," I say, fighting to keep the desperation from my voice.

"Of course." He twists back for a stiff smile before shoving his phone in his pocket. "And hey, good luck Friday. You deserve that contract. I'll be rooting for you."

He even adds a wink.

A wink?

The clatter of the door signals I'm alone, and honestly, I haven't felt this alone in a long, long time.

15—WEDNESDAY 3:12 PM

NATE

I'm not upset. This is fine. It's all fine.

So what if I got fired for doing my job?

So what if I lost Natalie for doing what she wanted?

I'm afraid to use the elevator properly as I step inside. It'll probably snap from its cables the second I push the correct button and stand at a respectable distance from the other passengers. I'm definitely not going near a set of stairs if there's a chance I might follow protocol and attempt to descend them safely.

Maybe next year I can run a seminar on *When Right is Wrong: Why Being a Responsible, Good Person Breaks Shit*. Oh wait, I won't be here next year, since I'm no longer employed.

My first few hours of unemployment have been turbulent, to say the least. I'm not sure where to go or what to do from here. Eon was "kind enough" to leave my room reservation open for tonight, so I'm not officially homeless until eleven tomorrow morning. They didn't cancel my return flight, either, so I still get to go home. So generous.

I haven't told the guys what happened yet. Marcos is presenting at four, and I didn't want to distract him. I don't even know where Nash is. Myra has sent me a dozen messages, but I stopped reading after the first two.

She wants to debrief and help me sort through what happened. She's worried about me. She *just has* to make sure I'm okay.

That's a hard pass on all those fronts. I don't need help sorting through what

159

happened. For once, it's *not* complicated. There wasn't a person in the room who didn't understand what happened when Eon Tech's top brass came down hard on Amit, who defended himself by saying it's my fault for botching three opportunities with Sandeke's contact. Myra remained silent until she was forced to weigh in and said she agreed I could have handled things better.

I have no doubt the "things" she's referring to were the make-out session in the workshop lab. The only silver lining in the entire parody was that Colin wasn't invited, so there were no offensive jokes. Funny how he not only has his job, but also my sales territory until they replace me.

By the time I even got the floor to speak, there was no point in defending myself. It was a sham trial from the start, and if they didn't drop the hammer then, it would have been soon anyway.

I thought Natalie would understand. I was lost and scared, and quite honestly, in shock when I showed up at her door. Not surprisingly, she reacted as beautifully as anyone could have. Her encouraging words are still echoing in my head. Her kisses and touches, still vibrating throughout my body. For a few fleeting moments, I felt like I could breathe again, like maybe I had a lifeline to cling to while my world was crashing down. But that was just another fantasy.

She did everything right and nothing wrong when she vocalized the understanding we both had. She didn't say or do a single thing that wasn't fair. In fact, she gave more than she had to, based on our agreement to be physical but not intimate. It's not her fault my shattered heart went rogue and rewrote the mess of this week into a tragic love story.

Romeo and Juliet. Everyone always focuses on the cheesy romance part. No one talks about the real point of the story: Love is poison. Literally. They both drank vials of deadly plant juice or whatever at the end, right?

One down, one to go. Natalie better be very careful what she imbibes over the next few days if Shakespeare gets his way.

My phone buzzes, and I reluctantly check the screen. Myra with more meaningless explanations? Natalie with a concerned check in? Nope, it's an explosion of emojis.

Roger: **Yo you finished with the telephone stuff yet? *telephone emoji* *thinking face emoji* *clock emoji* *alarm clock emoji* *timer emoji* *another clock emoji showing a time that's not this time* *another clock emoji showing a time that is closer to this time***

How long did this guy search for emojis?

Roger: **I know we said 6 but come early if you can. *heart eyes emoji***

Hope your ready to get your party on! *grin emoji* *martini emoji* *wine glass emoji* *cocktail emoji* *beer emoji* *champagne glass emoji* *champagne bottle emoji* *streamers emoji* *balloon emoji* *champagne bottle emoji again* (Guess that comes up twice in the search.)

A small part of my brain gets caught on the misspelling of "you're," but the rest reads this message very differently than it would have just a few hours ago. Honestly, there's nothing I'd rather do than "get my party on" and erase as much of this awful week as possible. Up until this morning, I didn't think I'd ever type the words I'm about to in response to a text like this, but here we are. Hey, if this is my last night, I might as well make it count.

Me: **On my way. Looking forward to it.** (No emojis because I couldn't come close to his standards.)

* * *

Not gonna lie, it feels damn good to have someone happy to see me for once. Not only happy, but uncomfortably excited. After being so thoroughly unwanted all day, the celebrity welcome I get when the door to P4 swings open is kind of epic.

"Nathan! My man!" Roger cries, throwing his arm around me. "Everyone, this is Nate. Nate, this is… eh, later. You want anything?"

Hell. Yes. I want all the things. Those emojis better not have been false advertising. I don't see any balloons and only one of the twelve clocks that were promised, but the bar appears to be keeping its word.

"This looks great, thanks," I say, grabbing a shot glass from the pile beside an impressive collection of liquor and drink options. It's a legit bar with legit glassware. This entire room is an escapist fantasy, actually. It turns out "P" stands for Penthouse so P4 is… Yeah, that math isn't hard.

Behind the standard hotel door, though, this "room" is really a suite, and a huge one at that. It looks like it has multiple bedrooms, a small kitchen, dining area, and a living space with giant couches and an enormous television. There even appears to be a hot tub or some kind of water feature on the balcony. It's hard to tell through the group of guys hanging out and looking… vaguely familiar.

I squint back at Roger who's grinning at me like I'm royalty and I should absolutely know why I'm here and be just as thrilled.

And then, I do.

Three years ago.

Miami.

Marcos and I made a fortune that weekend.

A snort-laugh escapes me as I fill a shot glass with whisky and throw it back. I fill it again, chuckling at an image of Fate in its prissy celestial theater laughing its ass off right now. This entire thing is too perfect and hilarious to be chance.

I get fired from one job and hired for another an hour later? In any other circumstance, I would have stalked right back to the door and issued Roger a Thanks-But-No-Thanks for his employment offer, but right now, this scenario is gold. I have nothing to lose and everything to gain at this point.

I swallow my third shot in three minutes.

"Whoa. Someone's ready to get their party on," Roger says, returning to my side.

"You could say that. So what's the gig?"

"That's my boy," he says, grinning as he flings his arm around me again and squeezes my shoulders. "No Marcos this time?"

"Nah. He's moved on. Great place," I say, waving around the room. "Business must be good."

"I know, right? Get this," he says, leaning close. "I live here now."

"You *live* here?"

"We all do."

"Like, as a house?"

"Well, it's a suite, but we get our mail here, if that's what you mean. Oh, except for Jordan who still has his sent to his mom's place and Toby who has a PO Box. Jordan's mom doesn't live far, though, so it's not as bad as it sounds. Who even gets mail anymore, right?"

"Right."

Yeah, I'm confused. To be fair, I've spent most of this week confused.

"We have our own show. Three nights a week and private events on top of that. Part of the contract is that we get this place all to ourselves!"

"Wow."

He nods and pops a handful of nuts in his mouth. "Dude, it's a dream."

It kind of is, actually.

His expression turns conspiratorial. "So listen. I wasn't entirely honest with you."

No shit. But I'm way past anger at being deceived at this point. I wouldn't have any human interaction at all if I cut lies and betrayal out of my life.

"Yeah, um, so hear me out. See Remy over there? Don't look!" he hisses when I do. Right. Sorry. "He's taking off to do the whole SUV-Suburban-McMansion-Dog thing."

Is that a thing?

"Congrats?"

The alcohol is already kicking in, so I probably shouldn't swallow the fourth shot in my hand. Of course I absolutely do.

"Which means…" He stops and waits… for something.

"He's getting married?"

"No, dude! We're gonna be down a guy!" I wince when he smacks my chest. "Tonight?"

"Tonight?" I ask.

It would be so much easier to communicate with this person if he used complete sentences.

"Supremely epic," he says.

More verbs and nouns would help too. We're fine on the adjective front.

"Tonight will be supremely epic?" I clarify.

"No. I mean, it will, but it's more than a gig." He glances at the group of guys, who are now staring openly at us. He could probably drop the wasted attempts to be discreet, but bends close anyway.

"It's an audition," he whispers.

"An audition?"

"Yeah, dude! The guys already love you. I can tell."

Really? They just look like they're wondering why we're still whispering about a topic they already know we're whispering about.

"If things go well tonight, you'll be getting an offer!"

Oh. Um.

"An offer?"

"An offer!" He hits me again. No surprise there. "We want you to join us, man! Our lucky number six!"

He throws his arm around my neck and pulls me in for what I'm guessing is an affectionate "we're about to be stripper colleagues!" dude hug.

In a million years, I wouldn't have guessed this would be my career trajectory when I boarded the plane at JFK on Sunday.

I really, really want another shot of… alcohol (doesn't matter which one), but I'm already past buzzed and firmly in "bad decision" territory. It's probably not a great place to be when you have an entire buffet of bad decisions coming your way tonight.

Roger's eager grin is inches from my face.

"Wow," I say finally. "That's, uh… a lot."

"I know! You're welcome, man. I knew you'd be thrilled. It was so hard not to say anything earlier, but I wanted to surprise you."

Surprise me with the opportunity to audition as a full-time stripper? Has that ever been on someone's wishlist?

After this shitty day and four shots, however, it's sounding pretty good. It's not like I have a better offer. I scan the opulent space. Expensive furnishings, daily housekeeping service, onsite pools, restaurants, and spas—it really is kind of like a fantasy. My gaze rests on the guys who are back to laughing and lounging with a camaraderie that sends a stab of envy through me. They have support, purpose, security, and friendship built right into a lifestyle and career.

Could I live like this? I used to have it with Marcos and Nash, but everything changed this year. They found their individual love and purpose. They're moving on, as they should. They're happy, and I'm happy they're happy, but where does that leave me? I know it's only a matter of time before their philosophical aban-donment becomes physical. We're not going to be roommates forever, and some-times I worry the only reason we still are is because they feel sorry for me. Who wants to be the pity boarder or the weird family friend who lives in the spare room down the hall?

"Thanks, man. I appreciate the opportunity," I say, forcing a smile.

I might even mean that. He's giving me a chance at a time when everyone else is stripping them away. I didn't even remember this person two days ago, and now he might be the only one who wants me.

Yeah. That dismal thought earned another shot.

Cheers.

"Whoa. Slow down, tiger," Roger says, extracting the bottle from my hand. "Bad day?"

"Something like that."

"Okay, well, grab a water and let me introduce you to the guys. You already know Ramón and Erik from Miami."

* * *

Two minutes until showtime. I gave Fate another salute when I learned tonight's "big event" isn't even a performance at all, but a *class.* I'm still not sure what that means, except that our "instructor" costumes are basically the business casual attire I've worn every day for the last six years. In fact, I literally just changed out of the light blue button-down I arrived in to don a dark blue one from Roger. I wasn't sure how to take this fun fact, but I guess I've been insulted in worse ways than learning I dressed like an "instructor" for half my life.

"You ready?" Roger asks, while—yep, you guessed it—smacking my chest.

Ow.

"Yeah. So how many people come to these things?"

I expected a stage or something. Or a ballroom. Or… well, really anything besides this empty room that's been converted into an empty room with several folding chairs and a buffet table of refreshments. How exactly are we supposed to "teach" anything here? *What* are we teaching?

"It depends on the thing," Roger explains.

That doesn't answer my question.

"Why here? Shouldn't you do this in a more formal environment?"

"It's vibe-y, right?"

Also doesn't answer my question.

"Hey, relax, man. You're gonna do great," Roger says with a wink.

It's hard to believe that when I'm half-drunk and still not entirely clear on what the thing I'm supposed to be doing is. Then again, those same facts are also why I'm not nervous about it. What could possibly go wrong?

Cheers and laughter erupt from the entrance, and I glance over to see one of the other guys leading a group of strangers into the room. Four women, two men, and… oh no.

I blink in disbelief at the last person to enter. This can't be happening. The person's eyes widen when they see me, and Roger must notice the moment our brains explode.

"Oh hey, do you two know each other?" he asks.

I have no idea what to say, but it doesn't matter when Chad grins and… sorta bounces?

"Nathan? No way! You registered too?" he cries.

Registered? What exactly is this again?

Roger claps a hand on Chad's shoulder and another on mine. "Nate, here, is one of our senior instructors," he lies.

"You are? No way!"

I swallow hard and force a smile. My stomach sinks further when I do the math. Seven of them, seven of us if we include Remy who's leaving the group to purchase an SUV.

Please don't let this be a partner thing.

"This is the coolest shit ever! I want Nathan," Chad tells Roger, who gives me a sly wink.

"Look at you already locking down clients," he says.

Clients? Well, *that's* not happening.

"I promise to listen very carefully," Chad tells me with a half-serious, half-joking expression. I'm actually not sure which of those I'm rooting for right now.

"He's with Sandeke Telecom," Roger whispers at my ear. "VIP. You lucky dog."

What?!

"Well, it seems like you two are already acquainted, so I'll leave you to it while I pair up the others. Grab a drink, get comfortable, and we'll begin in about fifteen minutes, sound good?"

Chad is still grinning when Roger slaps my arm and takes off. In fact, Chad hasn't stopped grinning since he recognized me.

"How long have you been doing this?" he asks, grabbing a glass from the bar.

He studies the bottles, probably to determine which is a banana-based liqueur.

"Four minutes," I say.

He laughs, thinking I'm joking.

"Sorry, I'm just in shock. You come across as so uptight and boring. I had no idea you were actually fun."

"Um, thanks?"

"When Mr. Reedweather suggested we sign up for this, I almost didn't. You know what convinced me?"

In twelve million guesses, I wouldn't guess right.

Unless it's mermaids.

"Cashews."

Oh well. It was worth a shot.

"Cashews?"

He nods, finally settling on…

I squint as I watch him fill his glass to the brim with cranberry juice. He knows that's just cranberry juice, right? I'm thinking not when he holds it up to toast another imaginary glass and says,

"Ready to get drunk and have some fun?"

I return a tight smile. "So, cashews?"

I shouldn't have asked, but how could I not?

"Oh! Right. So there's this girl." His grin turns almost shy as he scans the room like she might be here. I guarantee she's not. Well, unless she's one of the four who just came in.

"And… she likes cashews?"

"Yes! Kind of. I don't know. I've never seen her eat any. She owns an artisanal nut stand. They do the best candied walnuts, but don't try to get them near a holiday. It's ridiculous. Anywho, Reedweather and I watched this movie a few months ago and we had this idea where *we* could do that. Him with rummy, and me with, like, cashews."

I nod. What the hell are we talking about?

"I see."

"So yeah, when they gave us the list of optional activities this week, we were like, OMG, it's fate! So we signed up."

I'm not questioning Fate's role in this for a second.

Touché, Fate. You win.

"But Reedweather didn't come?" I ask, while he shudders through the burn of his cranberry juice.

"Ah, good stuff." He clears his throat. "No, unfortunately, he couldn't make it tonight, so Bill from Sales took his place."

He waves toward the middle-aged man who is laughing heartily with… damn, I already forgot their names. I hope that's not part of the audition process.

"Oh, that's too bad. Is Reedweather okay?"

"Yeah, he's fine. He had to watch something on TV."

"Like, a news thing?"

"Hmm, no. It's some show about a hospital in Cleveland that has all these doctors who sleep with each other but someone always dies and-or finds themself in immanent peril."

"Well, it *is* a hospital, I guess."

"Yeah, but not from hospital stuff. One guy had a snowboarding accident. One lady was hiking and she *might* have fallen off a cliff, or she was pushed by her twin so her twin could take her place and sleep with the doctor with the beard. We don't know yet."

Right.

"I see. It sounds like you'd rather be watching that than doing this."

Whatever *this* is.

"What? No way! And now that I get to learn from the best, I wouldn't dream of leaving. Like the brochure said, strip dancing is good for the body and good for the soul… mate."

Hang on.

My gaze shoots to Roger who's effortlessly schmoozing the guests.

Instructor.

Chad wants to learn from the best.

Cashews.

Okay, scratch that last one, but the rest… Am I… teaching Chad how to dance?

He takes another long swallow of his juice.

I'm gonna need one of those too.

"So does Eon Tech know about your side job?" Chad asks while I pour myself the reverse version of his drink. All vodka, no cranberry.

I take a sip. "I'm not employed there anymore so I guess this is my main job now."

"What?! Oh no! What happened?" he cries.

It's kind of sad that a person I barely know is more distraught about my abrupt dismissal than my own coworkers.

"It's not worth getting into. We're here to have fun, right?"

"Right." He holds up his glass, and I tap it with mine.

We're so ending up as besties by the end of the night. Assuming the artisanal nut romance doesn't work out, maybe I can move in with him when Marcos and Nash shack up with their significant others.

He leans in and lifts his brows. "I didn't have any of those tearaway pants you all use, but I wore my easy zipper pants. Hope that's cool."

I choke on my drink and force it down my throat.

"I'm sure what you're wearing will be fine," I manage finally.

"I figured the challenge added by my pants would be offset by the polo. No buttons." He fans his yellow polo shirt to demonstrate.

I mean, there *are* buttons on it, but I guess this isn't exactly a science.

"Good choice," I say with a quick smile.

"So between you and me, I'm a little nervous."

"I get that, but no one judges here. That's not what this is about."

Probably.

"Yeah, but you all are all muscle-y and shit." He waves over me.

I guess?

"I should have known when I saw you at the pool that you were a stripper," he says, shaking his head. "What with the abs and pecs and all that? Sorry, I missed it."

"Yeah, um, it's fine."

"One of my best friends used to be a stripper. Maybe you know him? His name is Marcos."

I have no idea how to respond as I stare at him. That might be the only time in history someone has said "Maybe you know him?" and the other person actually does. I also know that Marcos does *not* know Chad is his best friend.

"Okay, everyone! May I have your attention, please?" Roger shouts.

The din of conversation dies as we turn our attention to our host.

"First of all, on behalf of The Six of Us Undress, we'd like to thank you for trusting us with your bodies and your soul… mates."

Everyone applauds.

Okay, quick note. If I join "The Six of Us Undress," the first thing I'm doing is changing our tagline. Definitely the welcome speech. Hopefully, the name is negotiable as well.

"At this time, you should all have your partner for the evening and gotten comfortable with each other. Before we begin, does anyone have any questions?"

Chad does.

"Yes?" Roger says.

"Hi, everyone. Chad here. First time stripper. The brochure said to bring your positive mood, favorite grooves, and sexy moves. The first two are fine, but I only know about two moves. One and a half if you count the fact that the second move is the first move but with an extra half pivot. Is that going to be a problem for my routine?"

Roger returns a patient smile. "Not at all. That's what our expertly trained professional instructors are for! You just tell them your vision, and they will customize the perfect routine for you and your soul… mate!"

Huh. Wow. That's… kind of genius.

In fact, if you remove all the terrible aspects of this venture, it's actually not a bad business model. People have a variety of reasons for wanting to do something like this, and yet, many might be too shy for a formal class and/or not physically able to keep up. Customizing a routine and session to the individual in a small group setting maintains privacy, while also cutting some of the high overhead costs associated with private instruction. It's kind of the best of both worlds. Adding food and beverages to brand it as an "event" instead of a class drastically increases the perceived value, which boosts the overall sticker price, thus jacking up net profits.

I don't know what Roger is charging for this, but I bet they're each making more than they do for a traditional show, while working less. They're also leveraging skills they already have, which increases the ROI for any time and money invested in employee training and new routines.

The hotel wins too if it's an exclusive opportunity for their guests. Catch their interest at the public show and sign them up for a private lesson. The resort probably gets a cut, and in return supplies a steady stream of customers already primed for this type of activity, along with resources that would be debilitating overhead for a regular small business. The liability insurance alone would price some out of the market, but Roger probably pays almost nothing if he's able to latch onto the resort's policy.

Meanwhile, the guys get a royal lifestyle and who knows what other perks?

Roger, you little overly enthusiastic brilliant devil.

Is this the core of their business? If not, it should be. I'll be quizzing him hard on his financials and organizational structure later.

"So where do we start?" Chad asks, placing his glass on the floor. He shakes out his arms and does a few head rolls.

"I guess you should tell me more about the woman and the, uh, cashews. We can choreograph your routine from there."

Chad claps his hands. "Yes, perfect. So, she owns an artisanal nut stand at the mall. They have the best candied walnuts."

Yep. We established that. Still no cashews.

"So you said. Where do the cashews come in?"

"Right! Well, her name is Brooke but she's way out of my league, you know? She's so smart and funny and pretty and she knows basically everything there is to know about nuts."

I guess that makes sense if she owns an artisanal nut stand.

"She sounds great."

"She's my dream girl, *but…*"

She's out of his league.

"She's out of my league."

"So you said. Where do the cashews come in?"

"Right! Well, I was thinking it would be like a skit, you know? I'm the lowly walnut, and she's the high-end cashew!"

Of course there's a skit involved.

"Gotcha. So do you want a skit or a dance routine?"

"The skit would be the dance routine."

Oh, I see. This person doesn't understand what a skit is.

"Right, so you're the walnut and she's the cashew. How are you envisioning this *skit* going down? Where, when, that kind of thing?"

"Great question, Nathan!"

"Thanks."

"Here's my thought. The stand closes at seven. I show up at 6:55 and wow her with my sexy dance. She realizes walnuts and cashews can be happy together after all, and we go back to her place. Or my place. That part of the vision still needs work."

He wants to do this in a mall? He knows what kind of "dancing" this is, right?

I clear my throat.

"Um, well, while that sounds… like a plan, I wouldn't recommend taking your clothes off in public, depending on your municipality."

"Oh! No, of course not."

He lifts his shirt and shows me a very tight undershirt that might also be a misdemeanor in some municipalities.

"I'd leave this on," he explains. "And these."

He unbuttons his pants to show me his neon green biker shorts.

I'm not sure what argument to use against *this* plan except that maybe Brooke might prefer a different means of being wooed.

But I said there'd be no judging, so I settle on, "Ah. Good idea."

He nods with a grin and re-buttons his pants.

"I'm sure there's a special way to undo the button," he says.

"Not really."

"No? Not even like this?" He unbuttons them again, but adds a scrunchy face.

Definitely not that.

"That's my sexy face. I've been practicing. You need to work it to get it, you know?"

As long as he doesn't say that to her.

"I see."

I take another long swallow of my vodka.

"Okay, I think I've got the premise of what you want for your routine. Why don't you show me your 'moves' and we can work from there."

"Great idea!"

"Thanks."

"One sec."

He bends down for a quick sip of his juice, then bolts back to his feet. After a few more head rolls and limb shakes, he stills with a serious expression. It's way better than his sexy face, so I'll be encouraging that one.

"Ready?" he asks.

"Ready. Let's see it."

Chad nods and settles into ready-mode.

After a deep breath, he steps forward, spins, squats to touch the floor, straightens, spins again, and steps back.

His wide, killer clown grin resurfaces as he waits for feedback.

Huh.

"Yeah, so, that's… a start."

I scan him for a few seconds, trying to determine the most flattering features he'd want to showcase. It also has to be something he can do physically and in public.

"Okay, how about this? You be Brooke."

I put my glass on a nearby table and freeze when he holds up his hand.

"Great idea! One sec," he says.

I wait while he grabs a chair and plops onto it.

"Does she sit at the nut stand?"

"No. She stands. It's more of a counter-style nut stand. Not the typical ones you see everywhere."

"Right, so maybe you should be standing like she does."

"Don't I have to sit for the lap dance part?"

I stare at him. "You want to do a lap dance for her… at the mall?"

"Wait, you think we should do that?"

"No."

"Oh." He looks disappointed. "Well, maybe we can do that back at the apartment?"

"I mean, you can do whatever you want back at the apartment, but… Tell you what, how about we start with the *skit* and see where we're at?"

"Excellent idea, Nathan! I'm so glad we're partners."

"Thanks."

He claps once and settles into the chair.

I force away a sigh and motion to him. "So you need to be standing like Brooke will be."

"Oh! Right. Chair is later."

Let's hope not.

He pushes the chair to the side and shoves his hands in his pockets. "I won't see her hands," he explains. "They're behind the counter."

"Ah. Good call."

I really don't want to risk any more distractions, so I just start my routine. Walking and button-opening seem like skills he can handle, so I strut forward with a distant stare, while slowly unbuttoning my shirt.

His expression fills with wonder, and I'm concerned he might be taking his role as Brooke a little too seriously. When I get about halfway to where he's standing, I tug the open shirt off my shoulders and let it hang around my elbows.

"First part. What do you think?" I ask.

He applauds, then frowns. "That was amazing, except, I don't have buttons like that."

"Not now, but you will when you do the routine for her. Do you have a button-down shirt you can wear?"

He makes a face. "Yeah, but I'd rather wear something I'm comfortable with. For the confidence, you know?"

"But you're taking that thing off."

"Yes."

"So…"

"I'm thinking a light green polo. Does the color matter?"

I really don't want more things to argue about.

"Okay, fine. Is it like the one you're wearing now? And no, the color doesn't matter."

"Yes. Exactly the same, just green."

I nod and motion toward it. "Got it. Can you give me your shirt? I'll see what we can do."

He nods eagerly and tugs it over his head. I toss the button-down to my right and pull on the polo. It's an awkward fit, but I suppose that works for this scenario.

"Alright, let's try this again," I say, returning to the starting point. "So the trick is, you want to tease first, you know?" I move forward again and lift the hem to show my stomach. "Don't give them everything, just enough to make them want more."

His wide eyes are locked on me, and I find myself really hoping this Brooke woman is quirky enough to appreciate the attempt. The dude is willing to put in the effort, I'll give him that.

"So how many inches do you lift it? It looks like around four?"

He moves toward me and ducks to inspect my abs.

"Um, yeah, it doesn't really matter. It's not a science. Whatever you're feeling."

"So let's say three to six inches?"

"Sure," I mumble. "You good? Ready to move on?"

He nods and runs back to his place. Shoves his hands in his pockets.

And go.

I continue walking, adding a little more swagger this time. When I'm about five feet away, I rip the shirt over my head in one smooth motion.

"Damn," Chad whispers. "How'd you do that?"

"Take off a shirt?" I was really hoping that part would be an existing skill.

"Yeah, but like, all effortless and sexy. You were, like, *whoosh*."

He demonstrates.

"Like that," I say. "You do exactly that."

"Can I try?"

"Of course."

I hand him his shirt and stand where he was. "Okay, now *I'm* Brooke, and you try it."

"The shirt-off part or all of it?"

"All of it."

He shoots me a nervous smile and rubs his hands. "Okay. This is so… ah! Okay, here goes."

He takes a step forward. Stops. Another step. Stops. Lifts his shirt and holds it in place while he glances down to check the distance. Satisfied, he steps forward, spins, squats to touch the floor, straightens, spins again, and steps back.

I sigh and shake my head. "Did I do that?"

"Do what?"

"The spin thing."

"No. I added that for flavor."

What flavor, exactly? Oh wait, cashews, that's right.

"Okay, look. I love your enthusiasm but…" I stop as his wide, eager eyes fix on me. "You know what. Leave it in. Alright. Now, do the rest."

"The stripping part?"

"Yes."

He blows out a breath and shakes out his arms. "Oh my god. Okay. Here we go."

After another step forward, he pulls the shirt up his chest with both hands but it gets snagged on his necklace. He grunts in frustration while struggling to free himself, and I wait for the swearing, headless torso to solve the polo shirt.

"Maybe don't wear a necklace when you do this for real," I say.

"That's an excellent idea, Nathan."

"Thanks."

"Now what?"

I'm concerned we're already past his skill level, but the guy is paying (probably a small fortune) for this. Well, his company is. That thought also deserves a drink. I swallow more vodka only to see I'm halfway through the glass already. Guess that's why this is starting to get more fun.

"That's up to you," I say. "How far do you want to go?"

"All the way! Obviously."

"Um, I wouldn't recommend that at the… mall."

"This is for the later one."

"I thought that was going to be a lap dance?"

"Well, on the way to the lap dance. Like, she's sitting on the easy chair, and I'm in the kitchen and come out all sexy, like…"

He adds the scrunchy face to his strut.

"Don't do that," I say with a cringe. "Just keep a casual expression."

"But I want to look sexy, right?"

"Yes, but trying too hard is the opposite of sexy. You want to look like it's *not* hard."

"But it is."

"Maybe, but you want to make it look like it's not."

"How do I do that?"

"By not making that face."

"You mean, this one?"

"Yes. Don't do that."

"What about this?"

"That's the same face."

He curses, and I let out a long exhale.

"Okay, look. You're going to be fine. You just have to relax and have fun. If she's the right woman for you, she'll love it no matter how it goes. She'll accept you for who you are."

"Yeah? Thanks, Nathan. That's really beautiful."

I return a stiff smile and step back before he can hug me or something.

She'll accept you for who you are… like Natalie has since the moment we met.

Too bad that ended before it began.

"I'm going to do the whole thing again, but watch my face this time," I say.

Before I do that, however, I polish off my vodka. It's really taking a toll now, and the mind-numbing haze of this absurd situation is actually starting to wash away the horror of the day. I know my problems will be waiting for me tomorrow, but for now I don't have to worry about a single thing except teaching this guy how to make a face that doesn't look constipated.

When I woke up this morning, getting drunk with Chad Smith, while helping him take his clothes off would have been the last thing on my list of activities. Actually, it wouldn't have been on the list because that idea shouldn't exist.

"I'm so nervous about the pants part," he says with an anxious giggle. "Like, is it the button, then the zipper? Zipper first? All at once. So many questions. What if I can't do it?"

"I got you," I say with a genuine smile. "You'll do great. Brooke's heart won't stand a chance. Now, watch my face and pay attention to how I make it look like I'm *not* doing anything special. *That's* where the 'sexy' is."

As Chad gawks in awe at my ability to walk in a straight line, I feel like I accomplished something for the first time in a long time. It feels pretty damn good to be important to someone. To matter.

Maybe it's the alcohol speaking, but Roger's job offer is starting to look better and better.

16–THURSDAY 12:03 AM

NATALIE

I was just about to fall asleep when the knock on the door comes. Surprised, I roll out of bed, pull on a pair of shorts, and shuffle to the door. My heart rate picks up when I look through the peephole and see two men hovering outside. What the hell?

I yank open the door and meet a stranger's shocked expression.

"Sorry, um… You're not Marcos," he mumbles, then glares at the guy draped around his shoulders. "Dude, it's the wrong room."

"Nope. This is it," Nate slurs. "This is… where she is."

Yep, he's wasted. I guess I'm not surprised given the day he's had. In fact, the stranger holding him up is the only part of this scenario my brain is struggling with.

"Sorry for bothering you," the man says. "I'm trying to get him to his room. He said this was it."

"It's fine," I say. "We're friends. He can stay."

He shouldn't be alone tonight for a lot of reasons.

"Are you sure?" the stranger says. "We can keep trying to find his room. I would have let him stay with us, but we don't have the space. We already have six guys in a three-bed suite. Even the couches are full."

"Really, it's fine. Just put him on the bed. I'll take care of him."

I step back so they can enter.

"That's her," Nate says to the man. "The one I was telling you about? She's gorgeous, right? And so smart and sweet and she should hate me but she doesn't."

The man mouths an apology, while I bite back a smile.

"I'm Roger, by the way," he says.

"Natalie."

"Ah. So you're the one."

"The one?"

"He's talked about you nonstop this past hour. Once the clients left, he got plastered and told us all about the cashew to his walnut."

"The what?"

He shrugs. "No idea. He's a good dude, though. I think he had a bad day."

"I'm a… a… walnut, and she's a… cashew," Nate tells us as we help him onto my bed. His shirt is unbuttoned and his pants don't even look like the ones he was wearing earlier. Come to think of it, his shirt is a different color also.

"Yep," Roger says, patting his cheek. "You sure are. The best walnut I know."

Are the two of them close? Nate hasn't mentioned he was at the resort with anyone besides the roommates I met. "I'll text you tomorrow, man. Get some rest. Great job tonight. The client loved you."

"Really?" Nate says. "Someone actually liked me?"

The content smile that settles over his lips tugs at me.

"A client?" I ask. "Where were you?"

The man winces. "Oh, shit. You a girlfriend or something? He didn't make it sound like you were together, just that… fuck. I don't want to get in the middle of anything."

He holds up his hands and backs toward the door.

"We're not together. I was just curious."

"Oh, whew," the guy says, blowing out a breath. "Not that you can't have relationships in this biz, but it's a lot easier without them, you know? One day, you're movin' and groovin' with your boys, and the next you're buying an SUV and mailbox, you know?"

"Right. Um, and what *biz* is this?"

He cocks his head, looking concerned again. "You didn't know he…? Crap. Like I said, I don't want to get in the middle of anything. Well, I need to jet. Let me know if you need something."

He opens the door and slips out before I can respond. Hopefully, I don't *need something* because I'm not planning to knock on every door in the resort searching for "Roger."

I turn my attention back to Nate, who's drifting off with a peaceful look on his face. The pieces fall together as everything Roger just said sifts through my brain. Was he stripping tonight? It would explain the state of his clothing and weird direction of the conversation. It explains everything, actually, even his painful relief that someone "actually liked him."

I knew he was hurting when he left my room earlier. I wanted so badly to tell him the truth: That I didn't want him to leave at all. That I wanted him to stay and talk and figure out how we could make this last beyond Friday night. I wanted to ask him point blank if he'd be willing to break every rule we set because that's all I've wanted to do since that first incredible conversation. I wanted to tell him how special he is, and that the thought of never seeing him again makes my stomach ache.

I grab a bottle of water from the stash on the dresser and twist off the lid. He's already falling asleep when I get to him, so I brush his cheek to wake him.

"Here, drink some water before you pass out, okay?"

His glassy eyes meet mine and that silly smile returns. "I meant it," he says. "I meant it all."

"I know you did. Here, drink this."

He pushes up on his elbows but falls back, and I do my best to help him up enough to swallow the water.

"I'm serious. I… No one wants me, but he does. I'm good at something, I swear."

My chest tightens at the earnest expression on his face.

"Nate…" I say quietly.

He shakes his head and closes his eyes. "It's okay. Roger says I can stay. They don't have to worry about me anymore. They can move on. You can tell them someone actually wants me."

My heart cracks a little as he fades into sleep.

"So many people want you," I whisper, brushing my fingers through his hair. "*I* want you."

So much, and I hate that his brain is tearing him apart and telling him differently. I hate that he can't see who he really is through the blinders of an illness he doesn't recognize.

He stirs a little, and I reluctantly withdraw my hand. After pulling off his shoes and turning out the lights, I slide into the sheets on the other side of the bed. His back is to me, and I study the strong silhouette that's hiding so much pain.

I shift closer, craving his heat and the weight of his body next to me. I've slept alone my entire life, and suddenly it doesn't feel like enough.

"Natalie?" he says.

"I'm here."

I move closer until I can slip my arm around him from behind.

"Good," he says, capturing my hand in his.

Then, I settle into night four of our one-night stand.

* * *

I wake to the sound of running water and glance at my phone. 7:36 AM. A familiar scent drifts from the pillow beside me and my body warms as I breathe it in. Nate slept here again last night. He's in my shower now. Probably naked.

With a groan, I shove the heels of my palms against my eyes to center myself. Four nights in a row now I've shared a bed with Nate Hanover. Four nights in a row I woke with a rapid pulse and embers of desire simmering inside me. And now he's naked in my bathroom? He could have gone to his room but he didn't. Why? If I had to guess, he doesn't want to be alone with himself.

I roll out of bed and check the mirror on the wall to freshen up as much as possible. How long has he been up? What will his mental state be this morning? Yesterday was rough on so many levels. I'm sure a hangover won't help.

The water stops, and I'm moving toward my suitcase to grab an outfit for my own shower when my phone rings. Reece's smile lights up the screen.

"Hey, killer," he says when I answer the video chat. "How's the paid vacation going?"

"Not a vacation," I mumble for the hundredth time.

"Oh, right. The *conference*."

"It *is* a conference."

"Uh-huh. You know that New York also has plenty of facilities that can handle large groups of people who have to meet about boring shit, right? There's no reason you all have to fly across the country to talk about it under palm trees."

"First of all, the seminars are indoors and don't involve any kind of vegetation. Second, attendees come from all over the country, so we have to meet in a central location."

"I see. Which is why your conferences are all in South Dakota, right?"

"Don't be a smart-ass. You're just jealous."

"Of course I am, and you still haven't answered my question."

"Fine. The *conference* is going great."

My best friend is very skilled at demonstrating his skepticism.

"Clearly. I'm sure you have so many exciting things to tell me about networks and cell towers. That's why you texted me to call as soon as I could."

Yes, and I was hoping that would be last night. This whole thing with Nate, along with the high-stakes presentation, had me reeling. I needed to talk through what I thought was the end of the drama with the guy currently in my shower.

"Whoa," Reece says, his gaze focused on something behind me.

Or the guy *not* in my shower.

I turn, and yep. Whoa.

"Hey," Nate says, wearing nothing but his boxer-briefs.

"Oh, um, hey."

He sends me a weak smile, and I try to stay focused on his face. I try. So hard.

"Thanks for taking care of my drunk ass last night. Sorry that shit spilled onto you. I hope I wasn't too obnoxious."

"You weren't," I say with a reassuring smile.

Heartbreaking, but not obnoxious.

"Okay, good. And I used the hotel toothpaste and toothbrush. Hope that's okay. I can grab mine to replace it if you need it. I saw your toothbrush on the counter, so I thought you might be good."

"Yeah, no need. I brought mine from home. How do you feel?"

He shrugs, and his attention shifts to the awkward way I'm holding the phone.

"Shit. Are you on a call?"

"Yeah, but it's fine. It's my friend, Reece."

"Hey," Reece calls.

"Hey," Nate returns. "I'm Nate. Sorry to interrupt." He looks back at me, and I'm afraid the exhaustion on his face is more than just lack of sleep. "I'll get dressed and get out of your hair."

"No, you don't—"

But he's already in the bathroom, door closed.

"Huh," Reece says, drawing my attention back to the phone. "Is that why we needed to talk?"

"One of the reasons," I mutter.

"One?"

"The main reason."

"I'm thinking he's more than a *reason*. Just an FYI, that dude works out."

"Probably," I say, cracking a smile. "You're jealous of him too, huh?"

"A little. I've been trying for months to get abs like that."

"You know eating nachos isn't an approved abdominal workout, right?"

"Depends how big the plate is."

His gaze shifts again, and I turn to see Nate emerging from the bathroom, now in his pants from last night. The shirt is draped over his shoulder like he has no intention of putting it on, which makes sense if he's going back to his room to change anyway. Still, he needs to know what walking around like that does to people who have huge crushes on him. I get that he's not trying to be sexy right now, but *damn*.

"Thanks again," he says on his way toward the door.

"It was no problem. Really. I'm glad you came to my room. You shouldn't have been alone last night after everything."

He looks away, and it's obvious his critical brain is in hyperdrive right now. I can only imagine the level of self-recrimination going on in that complex head.

Then, he frowns.

"Shit. I didn't, um, say anything last night, did I? About where I was?"

I don't want to hurt him, but I can't lie, either. I'd want to know the truth if the roles were reversed.

"You didn't explicitly say anything, but it was kind of obvious what happened. Were you stripping last night?" I ask as casually as possible.

I feel Reece's stunned reaction through the phone. Yep, I have a lot of ground to cover with my bestie. He really should have called last night.

"No. I mean, sort of. Long story," he says.

"Was it the event Verna was talking about?"

"Hopefully not, because it would've been incredibly disappointing for all parties involved. Not to mention false advertising." He forces another quick smile I don't believe for a second and pulls open the door. "I'll text you later. Have a great day, Natalie. Thanks again."

And he's gone.

I stare at the door, my stomach in knots. He's obviously not okay, but what am I supposed to do?

"So that was fun," Reece says.

Crap. Forgot about him. "Yeah, um, we have a lot to discuss."

"Apparently. I'm not meeting Karin until nine for breakfast. Spill it, my friend."

* * *

I knock on Nate's door, not even sure he'll answer. It's almost nine, and technically I'm supposed to be on my way to *The Science of Power Harmonics and You* seminar.

Not surprisingly, Reece had a lot of thoughts on everything going on. The most annoying takeaway was that he and my dad must have a secret, two-person *Natalie Wants to Date But is Afraid* society of which I am not a member. Seriously, did they have a daily newsletter? He had way too many well-articulated opinions for that to have been the first time he discussed my dating life with someone.

Nate pulls open the door, now wearing gym shorts and that same tired look. He's clearly not going anywhere, which is a fresh slap in the face regarding his situation. What seminar was he supposed to attend this morning? Probably the same one I am since it's another Sandeke-sponsored lecture.

"Hi," he says. "Did I forget something in your room?"

"No. Can I come in?"

"Don't you have to go to the power harmonics session?"

"Yes. Can I come in?"

He hesitates, then steps back with a sigh. "Sure. What's up?"

I don't know what to say, so I do what I always do when words fail with him. I slide my arms around his waist and settle against his chest. Just touching him fixes things.

After a brief pause, his arms tighten around me and he rests his cheek against my hair.

"I really like you, Nate," I say.

"I really like you too," he says quietly.

My heart warms, relief flooding through me. Maybe he feels the same way? Only one way to find out. Direct has been our conversation style since the beginning. Here it goes.

"I know we said this was a fling, but I don't want a fling," I continue. "I want to try it for real. I want to eat meals together and hold hands everywhere we go. I want to save seats for you and text you throughout the day. I want to destroy

Rule Number Five and be the cheesiest of cheesy couples. I want to take this beyond Saturday and see how far it goes."

There I said it. *Please feel the same way.*

His body sags in a long exhale, but he doesn't say anything as my confession hangs in the air. With each passing second my hope sinks further. Was my read of the situation so far off? I thought… I mean, he just said he likes me too. But if he doesn't, why is he still holding onto me like he's afraid to let go?

There have been so many moments this week where I was sure he wanted the same thing. Where it felt like *I* was the one putting the brakes on whatever this is between us. My pulse is racing when I feel the heat of his kiss on my hair.

"I wanted that too, but…"

But? Oh no.

My stomach drops when I lean back to see his face.

"I'm not going back to New York," he says in an even tone. "Well, I'll return to get my stuff and close things out, but I'm not staying."

"What do you mean?" I try so hard to keep the growing panic out of my voice.

"There's nothing for me there anymore," he continues. His hard tone doesn't match the wounded look in his eyes. "My roommates are probably desperate to get rid of me so they can move on with their lives, and Roger offered me a dream job. He actually needs me. All the guys in the group do. I'm tired of being a burden and the weakest link, so I've decided to accept their offer. I'll tell Marcos and Nash tomorrow afternoon, once all of this *Tele-Con* drama is over."

I have no idea what to say. I can't even tell if the pinch in my chest is for him or me. Is this what he wants or just a livable Plan B in the wake of a graphic explosion of Plan A? He can't possibly want a career as a stripper. A job, sure. A career for someone like Roger, absolutely. But for Nate? He lives and breathes business. I know he's hurting and probably draped in self-doubt, but this can't be the only option for him.

"Are… are you sure this is what you want?" I ask, searching his face.

His gaze flickers just enough to tell the truth before his lie. "Yeah, of course. I mean, who wouldn't want to live the rockstar life at a world-class resort?"

Someone like Nate. Someone who *loves the security of complex problems that have finite solutions.* He craves stability and order, and the life he's choosing is the opposite of that. He didn't say what "job" Roger offered him, but I'm pretty sure it's not CFO of his stripping business.

Nate wasn't wired for "the rockstar life." I knew that after the first hour of our conversation. I also know the guy I'm falling for is lost and spiraling and reaching for anything to hold onto. Apparently, that's Roger and his magical thong.

I don't know what else to do as I take his hand.

This is goodbye. This might be the last time you see this person.

Our fingers lace together in an instinctive bond.

"I'm sorry for how this whole thing turned out," he says quietly. "We knew it wasn't real, but I didn't think it would end like this."

End.

Nothing about this feels right. It seemed like there was a reason our paths crossed the way they did. Every whacky coincidence became so much more than that. I met "the person no one knows" and that person is everything I didn't know I wanted. Whether he's a business executive or a full-time stripper, I just want to explore him inside and out. I think he wants that too but is too lost to see it.

Less than a week ago I didn't want any anchors in my life. Now I want to be one.

I swallow hard as I stare into his deep brown eyes. "Nate, no matter what happens after this week, please remember how special you are. You will find your way because you've always been 'the person no one knows.' You may be discovering a new side of that person or trying to figure out how he's evolving and adapting to new challenges, but it's still you. It will always be you."

His gaze softens as he cups my face. "Thank you for being here for me this week. It would have been unbearable without you and your support. You're an incredible woman, Natalie McAllister."

"And you're an incredible man, Nathan Hanover."

His thumb brushes over my cheek, and suddenly all I feel is the rapid pound of my pulse. The heat of his skin. His warm, hard chest when I slide my palm over him.

"I wish things were different," he says, his gaze dropping to my mouth.

They could be.

One thing that's *not* different? How much I still want him.

"Can we finally have that one-night stand?" I ask, searching his eyes.

"Definitely," he says with a grin as he leans in.

Previous heartache falls away when his lips brush mine. My insides clench with want, and I drag him into me to deepen the kiss. The taste of mint teases my tongue. The fresh scent of aftershave overwhelms my nose and spreads through me in a tantalizing warning that this moment will be a permanent memory.

I grip his hair to direct our kiss, angling and pulling in a vain attempt to satisfy the sudden craving. He tastes so good, feels even better. The ache in my soul spreads throughout my entire body, until I'm concerned about what will happen if I *don't* get to have him in the next few minutes.

"What about your seminar?" he murmurs against my lips.

"Don't care," I say, walking him toward the bed.

I yank the fabric of my top to untuck it, and he helps pull it over my head. Our kiss resumes with renewed desperation, and I follow him down to the sheets. I straddle his lap, inhaling him like I need it all in one breath. Maybe I do. Who knows if I'll ever get another chance to feel this kind of connection with a person?

With each kiss, I rock deep and slow until I feel every hard inch of him through his gym shorts. He groans and slides his hands up my thighs and over the curves of my behind. His bare back and chest are a paradise for my greedy fingers that trace each line and groove they can access.

He's still wearing too much clothing. We both are. He must be thinking the same when his hand brushes over my stomach to find the button on my dress pants.

"This okay?" he asks.

"Yes. I want yours off too."

His smile is criminal, and I draw it in to taste it as he skims the line of sensitive skin above my panties. I'm buzzing from his touch. Chills rake over and through me, and I moan when he slips his fingers beneath the fabric, instinctively moving against his hand for more direct pressure.

"Please tell me you fixed the problem from last time," I breathe out as his touch intensifies.

I let go of him long enough to squirm out of my pants, then adjust to drag him down on top of me as I fall to my back.

"Roger and the guys had a buffet at their place," he says with a sly grin. "I may have helped myself."

Despite the blazing tension, I can't help but laugh at the thought of Nate dipping into the "candy jar" of assorted condoms. Only in the bizarre saga of this week is that image not only plausible but expected.

"Good. I knew I liked Roger," I say, gasping when Nate presses his hips into mine. I feel him everywhere and it's still not enough. His hardness teases my entrance, making me grateful for that candy jar. I'm not sure my body would have accepted a substitute this time.

I slide my hands down his back and past the waistband of his shorts to find he's not wearing underwear. Of course he's not. It's like he studied a manual on how to turn me on, and I sink my fingertips into solid muscle. Our bodies grind together in simulated sex, the pressure between my legs building until I'm practically whimpering with need.

"Nate?"

"Yeah?" he says, dragging his lips down my neck to my collarbone. He tugs off the straps of my bra and kisses along the newly exposed skin.

My grip tightens on his hair, my body squirming with anticipation.

"You should get that condom," I whine.

"Is that so?" I can hear the smile in his voice.

"Yes. Maybe two."

His soft chuckle melts me as he presses a kiss to my shoulder and pushes up to follow orders.

He's a walking fantasy as he moves toward the dresser, his shorts barely on and hiding nothing. His powerful body is on full display from behind, and when he turns to come back, it's hard to believe he's real.

"Wait," I say.

His brow furrows as he stops.

"Sorry, I just want to look at you for a second."

His face relaxes into the beautiful smile that first drew me in.

"Ah. You know you have to tip me for this, right?" he teases.

"For what? Standing? What's the going rate for that?"

He laughs. "You'd be surprised. I made seven hundred bucks last night for two hours of work."

"What?!"

He shrugs. "And that was because I wasn't officially an employee, just trying it out."

"How?! I mean… no offense. If I was going to pay seven hundred dollars to watch anyone get naked, it would be you, but still…"

"No one got naked. Technically, I wasn't even performing."

I didn't realize how much the idea of sharing him bothered me until relief settles over me. I have no right to feel that way. I don't *want* to feel that way, but the thought of anyone looking at him the way I am now makes my fists clench.

He's mine.

He's not, though.

He should be.

That's not a legitimate relationship status.

"You didn't perform?"

He shakes his head. "No, it was some private instruction thing."

My jealous non-girlfriend heart also doesn't appreciate the word "private," apparently.

"How private?" it asks. Yep, *that* definitely had jealous non-girlfriend overtones.

He cocks his head. He heard it too.

"Not that kind of private. I taught Chad how to be a sexy walnut so he could seduce his cashew."

"Wait. Chad? *The* Chad?"

And yes, I realize how far I've fallen when the cashew-walnut aspect of that sentence isn't even on my radar of follow-up questions.

"Yeah. Long story. Is this really what you want to be discussing right now?"

"No. But I still have trouble believing that watching someone do a task we all do every day is worth seven hundred dollars."

His gaze turns mischievous, proving me wrong. That expression alone is worth seven hundred dollars. I am *not* telling him that.

"If I didn't know better, I'd say you're baiting me."

"Pssh." I wave my head. "Not at all. I have no interest in seeing what all the fuss is about."

"Really," he says in a skeptical tone.

I swallow hard. Yeah, I'm pretty sure my expression isn't cooperating as much as I'd like.

"So you have no interest in this."

He slides his hands beneath the waistband of his shorts on each side and pushes them slowly down his hips.

"No," I whimper, my gaze glued to him.

He smirks. "Okay. Fair enough."

He removes his hands, his shorts now dangerously low and showing off every perfect inch of his torso—the defined abdominals, the delicious ridges pointing south toward soft, tented fabric. There's definitely nothing there I want to lick or touch or explore. Certainly not the faint line of coarse hair or the hint of a tattoo peeking out.

"Unless, you, uh, *wanted* to prove me wrong," I say.

His knowing grin is almost too much, and my body erupts with lust.

He starts toward me, moving with a grace that's almost poetic.

"And what happens if I prove you wrong?" he asks, teasing me with a deeper plunge of his shorts. Ugh. He's painful to look at. Too soon, they're back where they were in an expert maneuver to leave me hot and covetous. I've never wanted to rip something off so much in my life.

"What do you want to happen?" I ask, wetting my lips.

He shrugs, his eyes dark with heat and hunger. "Maybe I get to give you a private lesson."

"Promise?" I ask as he closes the distance and crawls over me again.

"Whatever you want, babe," he says against my neck.

As he tickles the sensitive skin, I close my eyes and absorb everything I can. The feel of his weight on top of me, his scent, his taste. *Whatever I want?* I want it all.

"You," I whisper, threading my hands in his hair to hold him close. "I've always just wanted you exactly how you are."

He lifts his head to meet my eyes, and I see the pain and longing there.

"Thank you, Natalie. Really. You're such a beautiful person. I'm glad we had this time together."

He leans in to kiss me again, and suddenly, I forget all about primary and secondary careers. I don't care who wins the Sandeke account or what my tomorrow may bring. My plans and rules mean nothing in this moment. All I want is him, right here right now, just as he is.

And when he finally pushes inside me a few minutes later, I feel full with more than the thick heat of him. When my body ignites, my soul catches fire right along with it. My hips move in harmony with my heart, seeking all of him, every piece. I feel significant in this moment, wholly present in a way I've never experienced. Nothing matters except our connection and the way we get lost in each other. No rules, no plans, no fear of tomorrow. We still have now, and for once, that's enough.

I cling to him as he reads my desire and drives a harsher rhythm. It feels so good, each stroke another surge of pleasure that pushes me into an all-consuming blaze. My muscles tense. My toes curl. The room fades into nothing as the air siphons out and euphoria floods my entire body. This. Is. What. I. Want.

Always.

His intense expression morphs into a smile as we come down from the high. So beautiful. I reach up to draw him in for a soft, intimate kiss.

We break apart, and he rests his forehead against mine. I tighten my arms around his shoulders, and as the explosive sparks settle back into the warm glow of sated peace, I realize Nate isn't the only one who benefited from our short, unexpected love story. Yes, I helped him through a difficult time, but it also took this person, this *moment*, to learn a life-altering lesson of my own:

Living in the present is just as important as living for the future.

Nate thanked *me*, but as I close my eyes and draw him in for one last kiss, I'm silently doing the same.

* * *

It's an odd feeling regretting a memory you love. Nate and I probably shouldn't have had sex, but I'm glad we did. I hoped finally having him would purge him from my system, but all it did was embed him in my soul. I will never be able to forget the soft look in his eyes as I traced his cheek in the wake of passion, or the way it felt to burrow against him and have his strong arms wrap around me in a protective embrace. I still taste him, smell him, feel him with every fiber of my being, and I'm terrified those sensations won't fade as quickly as I need them to.

Because we decided not to be friends. It will be too hard on us emotionally to nurture a connection that can't go anywhere. It makes no sense to try to do the long-distance thing with no sustainable future and no past to hold onto. Why start something that shouldn't exist?

Also, these facts do *not* put me in a good state of mind for my meeting with Lanette and Theresa.

"You weren't at the harmonics presentation," Theresa says in a stiff tone.

"No, sorry. I wasn't feeling well. I'm really nervous about tomorrow."

I can't tell if she believes me.

"I see. Well, Sandeke's Senior Power Systems Analyst was the instructor. That would have been a great opportunity. Eon Tech thought so too, since all of them were there. Well, except your boy for some strange reason."

Because they fired that boy. Should I tell her what I know? It's a huge piece of very valuable information. I could easily say I found out through Chad or some other means. It wouldn't even hurt Nate to share it. I'm sure he doesn't care what happens to his former company, so why am I hesitating?

"Then, I guess it's good you were there as well," I say.

"That's not the point. Really, Natalie, I don't get what's wrong with you this week. You've seemed distracted and squandered multiple opportunities to nail down the Sandeke contract."

I glare at her, furious she could say that to me. How dare she criticize me after I'm the one who bore the brunt of this chaotic week? I'm the one who was asked to compromise my ethics and be someone I'm not. I'm the one who had to deal with Chad and Reedweather and mermaids and weird non-skits. I'm the one who fell for a guy I couldn't have and watched him get pummeled again and again, just to end up with nothing.

Honestly, I'm not sure I even care who wins the contract at this point.

"Well, we still have plenty of time to focus on our presentation for tomorrow," I say as evenly as possible. "What did you learn in the planning session with Barry yesterday?"

I can tell she has plenty more lambasting left in the tank, but I'm in no mood to deal with it. They've done nothing but make things harder for me.

Lanette has been noticeably silent, and I sense her cool demeanor. Does she suspect the truth? She knows I was interested in Nate, literally since day one. Oh, and she thinks he's married, which would put me even further up her hitlist. There's really no way to fix any of that, though. We just have to get through this week, land the Sandeke contract, and move on. I know if I can get them to sign, all will be forgiven and forgotten. Money heals most wounds and covers countless mistakes.

"They agree our advantage is our customizability," Theresa says. "Sandeke is a huge organization with facilities all over North America. They'll have a variety of needs, so we should focus on that. Eon is stuck with box solutions, whereas we can be flexible. Barry said we can go in low on the install, since we'll make it up in the service contract. Just make sure we get both. I'll email you the details so you can review the notes this afternoon. We'll meet for dinner to come up with the specific strategy."

"Just remember, we're presenting with Eon in the room," I say.

And heaven knows who else. I can't help but feel like this entire thing is a bloodlust event more than a sales presentation.

"Which is why we need to make sure they present *first*. We have to know their angle before we show our hand," Theresa says.

"They'll want the same. I doubt we'll have any control over that," I say.

"You're in with their man, right? What was his name, Chad?"

"Yeah, but so are they." Well, so *were* they.

"Why are you being so negative? Whose side are you on, anyway?" Theresa quips. "It's like you're fighting us as much as them."

"Maybe more than them," Lanette mutters, and I snap a look at her.

She returns a silent challenge, and a shiver runs through me.

She knows. She knows everything with Nate has been more than an act.

Shit.

Theresa seems too caught up in her own accusations to have noticed, though.

"I'm on our side, obviously, but part of my job is to read the competition and anticipate any potential barriers." I force down the resentment bubbling inside me. "Now, we can keep arguing about nothing, or we can start gearing up for tomorrow. I'd prefer to work."

Theresa studies me for another moment before shaking her head and pulling out her laptop.

"Let's start with the budget spreadsheet and see where we can pare it down," she says.

17—THURSDAY 6:27 PM

NATE

"Flamingos," Erik says.

"No," Ramón replies.

"Why not? It's Florida."

Erik has a point.

"Flamingos aren't sexy."

So does Ramón.

"What say you, *mi amigo*?" Roger asks me.

I was really hoping he wouldn't. I honestly have no opinion on which animal we should feature for our shows during "Zoolicious Month." I'm not a huge fan of dressing up like a flamingo, but I wasn't exactly doing cartwheels at the thought of being a panda, giraffe, or lemur either. (I'm positive Jordan didn't know what a lemur was when he suggested it because no one who's ever seen a lemur would do that.)

"Are we married to the animal theme?" I ask, trying to sound positive.

I've spent a lot of my first few hours as an official member of *The Six of Us Undress* trying to sound positive. Ever since I checked out of my room on the eighth floor and into my new home in the penthouses, what seemed like paradise last night is feeling less so by the second.

For the most part, I've been doing a decent job of playing along and smiling despite the deep fissures cracking open inside. I've spent most of this current conversation trying to sound the opposite of how I feel, but maybe my attempt wasn't successful when the guys frown at my latest objection. Who knew there were so many things I didn't want to emulate on a stage?

"November is always Zoolicious Month," Roger explains. "I guess it doesn't have to be a zoo animal if there's another one you like. It just can't be anything boring like a cat or a hamster."

"That's been done *so* many times," Toby says.

Has it, though? Neither animal was on my shortlist anyway.

"I just… Have you ever thought about focusing less on the costume theme and more on altering the experience for the audience?"

By their expressions, they have not.

"That doesn't make sense," Remy says. "How can you change the experience without changing the costumes?"

"Yes, exactly!" Erik agrees.

Ramón high fives him, which I'm guessing is also an agreement.

"I'm with Remy. The costumes *are* the experience," Roger says.

Ramón high fives Remy. So does Roger.

Okay, number one, Remy is leaving, so why does he even get a say? Number two, how are they so myopic? They really can't step outside of their tiny vision to see the massive potential of their business?

"I'm not saying what you wear doesn't matter. I'm saying there are other ways to create fresh experiences for the audience besides a different costume. I'm talking about value proposition."

Yeah, I'm already losing them. I take a deep breath and reset.

"Right now, you do the same show for a month, which means your customer pool only has access to one product in that period of time. Most of your customers stay for a week, correct? That's three opportunities to target them, but you're only taking advantage of one. Instead, you could offer three different experiences in that window and triple potential revenue. One customer, three shows."

They stare at me.

I stare back.

Did they get any of that? I'm not optimistic when they all turn to Roger for guidance.

Roger nods gravely as if he understands. "I see what you're saying. So we do the giraffe, flamingo, *and* lemur."

He doesn't.

Swallowing my frustration, I reach for the notepad and pen on the coffee table.

There is currently a list of twelve animals scratched onto the page—eleven if you count the fact that "orange tiger" and "white tiger" are listed as separate animals.

I flip to the next page and draw three X's.

"Tuesday's show, Friday's show, and Saturday's show," I say, pointing at each one. Beneath that I make a row of ten circles. "Your potential audience."

"We get way more circles than that each night," Toby says.

"I know. This is just an example," I say through a clenched jaw. "For the purposes of this example there are ten. In your present scenario, the most you would sell is ten tickets because each customer would only attend one show. Once they've seen it, they have little incentive to come back."

They nod. Then shake their heads.

Not sure what that means, so I ignore it and continue.

"Now, let's assume you did a different show each night. Tuesday was, say, *Eighties Night*. Friday was *Heaven and Hell Night*. Saturday could be, I don't know, *Tropical Paradise Night*. Each would have its own music, costumes, and vibe to create a completely different experience for the audience. If you—"

"What's *Heaven and Hell Night*?" Erik interrupts.

"Doesn't matter. The point is—"

"So how would we figure out the costumes and such?"

"In the real scenario we would have the theme clearly defined. I'm just using those as examples."

"Could we do an *Outer Space Night* instead?" Toby asks. "People love asteroids and shit."

"Or an *Extreme Weather Night*," Jordan suggests.

"Oh! Like tornados and those things with the ice balls?" Erik says.

"You mean, *your pants*?" Toby snickers.

"Fuck you."

"Pretty sure ice isn't caused by weather," Ramón says. "Asteroids are more science-y. I vote for *Outer Space Night,* too."

"Okay, fine! It's a space night. Whatever," I say, holding up my hand. "The actual theme isn't the point. The point is that by doing three completely different shows, you now give the same audience incentive to attend all three events while they're here for the week instead of one, thus turning these ten potential tickets—" I circle the circles,

"—into thirty potential tickets. You could keep the set design minimal and get your desired effect with lighting, costumes, and music, which would make it easy and cost effective to execute. You could even offer discount packages or other incentives to encourage the consumption of all three shows. Higher demand also means higher ticket prices. Your expenses would be the same so that's just extra net profit."

They're all nodding again, but I'm pretty sure most of them still don't get what I'm saying. That's okay. I've already learned I'll have an uphill battle with any improvement I try to make. Convincing all five guys (plus Remy who shouldn't have a vote) is never going to happen. The only one I need to sway is Roger.

He's squinting hard at my diagram and running something through his head.

Honestly, I don't even care what he decides as long as I've persuaded him not to do the irritating animal thing.

I feel some relief when a wide, enthusiastic Roger grin spreads over his face. Maybe this one small victory will soften the pang of regret that's been gnawing at me since I said yes and decided to give up my CFO dream for... lemur thongs.

"That's some good thinking there, Nate. Told you this kid was a regular Einstein," he says to the others.

I force a tight smile. "Thanks. If you want more details, I can put together a—"

"Nah," he says, swatting my arm. "No need, my man. Let's just stick with Zoolicious. We already have the confetti."

* * *

It's late, and I know Natalie has a big day tomorrow, but after the utter dejection of my first day at my new job, I need to escape the confusion for an oasis of calm. Marcos and Nash don't even know I've been fired and no longer have a place to sleep, so I didn't know where else to go.

I knock, wondering if she'll answer. I'm relieved when she does, and of course she looks perfect in her sleep shirt and shorts. Hair down, makeup off, she was clearly about to go to bed and probably isn't overly excited to be bothered by an outcast stripper.

"Nate, hi," she says in surprise. "Everything okay?"

"Yeah, um... Can I come in?"

"Of course."

She steps back, and I'm already breathing easier when her familiar scent fills my lungs.

"What's going on?" she asks.

Good question.

She slips her hand in mine, and I'm able to take another full breath when our fingers knit together.

"Nate? What is it?"

"Nothing, just…"

I swallow hard. How do I say, *my brilliant solution to everyone's problem is terrible for me?*

"Can I just stay here one more night?" I force out. "I'm sorry to ask, but Remy isn't leaving until Saturday, so I'd have to share a bed with Roger until then. I'd rather share with you."

"Sure, but…"

She studies me, and I look away. I don't want her to know anything's wrong. She needs to leave on Saturday thinking this is my HEA and everything will be fine. It *should* be my HEA, right?

"Are you ready for tomorrow?" I ask before she can.

"Yes," she says, but her tone is distracted, so I know I didn't deflect her concern. "Nate, what's wrong? I can see it in your face."

"Nothing," I say with a forced smile. "I'd offer to help you prepare for your presentation, but that feels unethical, even though Eon treated me like shit. I'm happy to listen, though, if you want to practice and get some general feedback about the non-technical components."

"Nate."

I pull in a deep breath. "Denver Sandeke is looking for blood, so this will be a survival-of-the-fittest scenario. Go in hard and don't back down. You're a killer, so—"

"Nate!" She tugs my hand, and I blink hard at the floor.

Emotion burns deep inside me. I fight to keep it down, but I'm so tired of fighting. It's all hitting me at once, and I don't know how to stop it. My dream, gone. My best friends, gone. My career, home, security, everything I've worked so hard for—all of it dissolved before I can even process what happened. Even Natalie is the picture of another good thing I can't have as she stands there staring at me with compassion I don't deserve. It's not her fault I'm not good enough. Not strong enough. That I'm just not enough, and I…

"Hey," she says gently as the tears break free from the blockade.

It's so freaking embarrassing, but of course she's nothing but kindness as she tucks her arms around me.

"You don't actually want this, do you?" she says softly.

No. But what choice do I have?

I don't respond. The truth won't help. What I want no longer exists. There is no future for me, so I might as well choose the one that's better for everyone else.

I bury my face in her hair, breathing her in while I still can.

"I'll be okay," I manage in a hoarse voice. "I just need to adjust."

I scrub at my eyes, furious at myself for breaking down. She pulls back and studies my face, her own eyes heavy with my pain. This is what I do to people. This is why I need to find a way to protect those I care about from myself.

"Actually, I should probably just go. Thanks for the hug. And listening. I meant what I said earlier. You're an amazing person," I say, brushing her cheek.

But she captures my hand against her face and doesn't let go. "So are you. You're lost, Nate, not broken. You need to tell Marcos and Nash what's going on. They love you so much. They won't let you wander alone."

Her words should warm me, but all they do is send a shudder through me. The last thing I want is for my messed-up path to drag them off theirs. They've suffered too. They've fought and lost. Struggled and won. They deserve to be happy.

"Okay," I lie.

She looks skeptical, and I force a brighter smile. I guess it's not really a lie. I'll be telling them the facts about the change in my circumstances. They don't have to know how much it hurts.

"You need to rest," I say. "You have a big day tomorrow."

Her eyes search my face for any hint of the heavy truth I'm *not* saying. She probably sees it. She's been an expert on me since the beginning. But instead of calling me out, she guides me toward the bed.

I drop the overnight bag I brought on the floor and climb under the comforter. She follows with an amused smile on her face.

"What?" I ask as she reaches for the light.

"You brought your stuff for a sleepover," she says.

"I didn't want to use your things again. It's easier if I just bring my own."

"It is." Her smile spreads into a grin. "It's just, that's another thing couples do."

I smirk and settle into the soft sheets. "True. So I guess I shouldn't ask if I can leave it here for tomorrow night?"

"Yes."

"Yes, I shouldn't ask?"

"Yes, you should leave it."

She shifts closer, and everything feels a little more right when she nestles against me. I put my arm around her, and she releases a content sigh.

"Want to know a secret?" she asks.

"Sure," I say, pressing a kiss to her hair.

"I kept the toothbrush you used this morning in case you needed it tonight."

* * *

I've just stepped into the shower when I feel a breeze from the open door. I squint through the glass to see Natalie approach with a tantalizing lack of clothing.

"You mind?" she asks, cracking open the stall door.

My gaze scours her body like I've never seen a naked woman before. I have. Plenty of them. Hell, I've seen *this* one a few times now, but in this moment, appreciating her beautiful form feels fresh and new. I should "mind" her invading my shower if I have any hope of staying focused enough to complete this daily ritual. But then, how can you properly appreciate a ritual if you don't break it from time to time?

"Not at all. It's your bathroom," I say, stepping back to give her space.

She scans me with a reciprocal hunger I feel in every part of my body. The warm water pelts my back. Steam drifts around us. It's a textbook scene from the cheesiest of cheesy couples movies, so I guess that makes it even more perfect for our story.

She reaches up to rest her finger at the base of my neck. Her gaze locks on its sultry path as it drifts down my chest, between my pecs, over the grooves in my abs. I can't even tell if the heat burning through me is from the hot water or the intensity of her stare. She spreads her palm and adds the other to push them back up my chest, sinking her fingertips into each muscle during the deep, slow pass. When her hands reach my neck, she tangles her fingers in my wet hair and presses close.

"I'm really tense," she says, her gaze locked on my mouth.

"Yeah?" I ask. "It's a big day for you. Makes sense."

"Right, so…"

Several droplets of water slide down her face, and she licks a few off her lips.

Her hips graze mine, sending a shiver of awareness through me. I'm already getting hard, and heat flares in her eyes when she notices.

"One last time?" she asks, imploring.

"*Another* 'one last time'?" I say with a grin.

"I mean, we're on day five of our one-night stand, so it's fitting, right?"

"Very."

I capture her head in my hands, and we come together with furious need. The heat of the water competes with the fire of her lips, running over us in slick encouragement. She melts into the kiss, moaning as her body molds to mine. Rubbing. Teasing. Torturing in an intoxicating invitation that has me stiff and aching. It feels so good to feel good, and she releases my hair to explore the rest of my body. Down my stomach, over my hip, and sliding up my inner thigh until she literally owns me in the palm of her hand. I groan at the mounting pressure as her gentle massages become more deliberate strokes. I kiss her again, our searching lips following the intensifying rhythm of our hips.

I grip her hair to lock her in place while my tongue plunges into her mouth to provoke her like she's teasing me. We're rigid with anticipation, already gasping for air we don't want. I back her into the wall, grinding against her with the pulse of our kisses. She reaches around to grip my ass and force our hips into harsher contact at each throbbing collision.

"You still have some of Roger's candy, right?" she gasps out, then moans again as I thrust against her and hold for a few glorious seconds.

"His candy? What, like drugs? We're not really into that."

She spreads her palms over my face to pull me in for another hard kiss. "Not that. The condoms from the condom candy jar."

I stiffen and pull back. Sorry, but…

Her eyes narrow at me as I laugh.

"The *what*?" I ask.

"The condom jar! You're the one who said you grabbed a handful of condoms from the candy jar."

I lift a brow. "I guarantee you, I did *not* say that."

"Yes, you did! You reached into the candy jar and…" She quiets, her earnest expression sinking into irritation. "Okay, fine, maybe that was the image in my head when you said you got some from Roger."

I can't help but laugh again. This woman. How is she so perfect for me?

With a sigh, I rest my forehead against hers and close my eyes. I can't believe that with everything I'll have to say goodbye to tomorrow, this person I didn't even know a few days ago will be one of the hardest.

"Yeah. I still have some," I say.

Her arms tighten around me, and honestly, as much as I'd love to have sex with her again, I'd be just as content standing here like this. She makes existing so easy. Just being around her helps me breathe. What am I supposed to do with that?

My body is still on fire for her.

My mind is still determined to let her go.

My heart is still breaking at the prospect of losing her.

But my soul… that's been forever altered by this truth.

* * *

I slide into the seat beside Marcos and his boss Martin Sandeke. I'm not surprised they're here. Everyone who's anyone in the industry has shown up for the climactic bloodbath sponsored by Sandeke Telecom. Marcos is clearly surprised I'm slipping into the back row with him rather than the front with one of the warring parties.

"You ready? You never responded to my text yesterday. I wanted to review your pitch with you," Marcos says. His eyes say a lot more as they search mine.

What's up with you?

Why are you here and not there?

What aren't you telling me?

Why do you look like you've just had sex?

I sense Natalie's attention and shoot her an encouraging smile. She seems to relax a little as she returns it. I still taste her and feel her everywhere. I've barely come down from the high of being with her, so I'm not surprised Marcos could tell something's up. Maybe it wasn't the wisest decision, but far be it from me not to help when the woman you're falling for asks for sex. I'm a giver, what can I say?

She might be thinking about that too when her face flushes and her teeth sink into her lip.

Later, I mouth to her, and her lips tip up in a grin.

I mean it too. We have one more day together, and I plan to make the most of it. All we have to do is get through her present nightmare and my upcoming one, then we're free to pretend tomorrow will never come.

I'm no longer worried about talking to my roommates. They'll be surprised, but probably relieved that I'll be "taken care of" and they can enjoy their own futures without the burden of dragging me along—not to mention the guilt for resenting every second of it.

"Dude, you're being obvious," Marcos mumbles, nudging my arm.

I grunt and force my attention to the front of the room. He's right. I have to lie low. My presence is going to cause enough drama as it is. I shouldn't be here, but I wanted to support Natalie, and fine… I also want to see my week-long nightmare play out live and in person. It's like having a chance to watch your own funeral.

Yep, I'm officially the first ghost ever to use its new powers to haunt a sales presentation.

Myra turns in her seat, and her eyes widen like she really is seeing a ghost. I hold her stare, refusing to back down. She wanted to meet this morning "to talk," and I finally gave her a firm no. I have nothing more to say to her. We're done and will always be done.

"What is going on?" Marcos hisses. "Why are you here? And dressed like you're going golfing, not about to give the presentation of your life?"

"Because I'm not," I say.

"What?"

"I'm not giving the presentation."

"Why not? This is your game."

"Not anymore. They fired me."

Martin, who couldn't have looked more bored scrolling on his phone the entire time we've been sitting here, suddenly seems much more interested in this event.

"*What?!*" Marcos whisper-shouts. "They fired you? *When?!*"

"Wednesday."

"Wednesday?! And you didn't tell me?!"

He really needs to take it down a notch. We're starting to get looks. Well, more looks.

I nod with a shrug.

"When were you going to tell me?"

"This afternoon. I'll give you the full version later."

"Nate, come on—"

"Welcome, everyone!" Denver Sandeke calls out, silencing the room.

Whew. Saved by the telecom Underlord.

Marcos looks pissed. So does Martin, although I'm guessing his look is due to the silent hatred he's exchanging with his father and not the fact that I didn't tell Marcos I got fired.

"We're so glad you could join us for this impromptu capstone session. What a perfect way to end an exciting, educational week of telecom. I'd like to give a special thanks to the wonderful resort staff who worked so hard to facilitate this last-minute demonstration. TPG, Eon Tech, we are all looking forward to a real-world masterclass in sales strategies."

I know from my discussion with Natalie that the two rival companies don't have any more information about what's supposed to go down than the audience. We're all collectively holding our breaths as we wait for Denver's next move. If I had to guess, it will involve unnecessary drama and perhaps a tiny bit of violence. It's been a while since I read Romeo and Juliet, but I'm pretty sure there's a climactic, blood-soaked power systems sales pitch scene toward the end.

"Eon Tech, why don't you start us off?" Denver says.

My former coworkers deflate at the same time the TPG employees stir in muted victory. Going second is a huge advantage. Natalie won't need it, but I'm glad she has it.

I sense Myra's ire as she stalks to the front of the room with her laptop and notes. Her gaze stalls on me as she scans the room, and I do my best to keep a neutral expression. I'm not exactly filled with goodwill for my ex-girlfriend, boss, and coworker, but I also don't want to be a factor in this confrontation. Natalie deserves the chance to win this on her own merit, so the best thing I can do for her is stay out of the way.

Once Myra finally starts speaking in a cool, straightforward tone, it doesn't take long for her to settle into the expert sales role and command the room. Her speech and body language are flawless. She's calm, confident, and comes across as knowledgeable and prepared. No surprise there. She's all of those things and deserves to be where she is, despite our interpersonal issues.

As the presentation builds, I sense the concern on the TPG side of the room. Myra not only does an excellent job of establishing her firm's position, she effortlessly addresses Sandeke's follow-up questions. We're all keeping silent scorecards, and with each new slide and successful exchange between vendor and potential customer, Eon's score steadily ticks up. Going second is usually an advantage, but it can also be a hindrance if the first presentation is so good it's a mic-drop game-ender.

I study Natalie with concern as Myra breezes through her conclusion with the poise of someone who knows she killed it.

Of course she did. There's a reason they fired me to pass the baton to her. I wouldn't have managed half of that.

By the time Denver Sandeke triggers a hearty applause at the end of her presentation, not one person in the room would want to be in Natalie's position. Anger simmers inside me when I catch the discreet glare Myra fires at her before landing a sharp look on me. I was hoping this wouldn't be personal, but I guess it is.

"Thank you, Eon Tech. You've given my team a lot to think about."

His "team" nods enthusiastically from their seats in the front row. Well, sort of. Chad was paying attention, but there's no way he understood any of that. Reedweather isn't even here. So by "team," Sandeke is referring to his Senior Power Systems Analyst and himself.

"Now we'll hear from Natalie McAllister of The Panther Group. Natalie, the floor is yours."

The icy grin on his face has my fists clenching in my lap. I was right. This guy is a bloodthirsty monster. He's loving this, probably *hoping* Natalie crashes and burns, not because he likes Myra and Eon Tech, but because he likes watching people implode. We all feel for her as she takes her place at the front of the room, but her steady composure gives nothing away. In fact, you'd never know this wasn't just another sales presentation to a bored manager in a stuffy conference room.

"Good morning. My Name is Natalie McAllister and I've been involved in power systems and UPS power interruption architecting for several years. I enjoy helping customers meet their needs with a customized solution for their unique situation."

Her warm smile for Denver draws a frown. He hates that he already doesn't hate her. I'm giving her five points for that.

"Power, as everyone knows, is directly tied to money. Not only does it keep your lights running, but it's an essential component of your data systems. And as you're well aware, keeping those systems running in the telecom industry is beyond critical—it's non-negotiable.

"My team and I have worked hard to compile a customized solution that includes the right mix of large generators and server room units, down to small control panels and individual computer UPS'. The key to the final design will be understanding your specific needs and providing a system that allows you the peace of mind that your system is stable and protected."

She clicks to the first slide.

"Why TPG? Because we offer solutions with one of the fastest reaction times in the industry, including performance clocked in at approximately five milliseconds. For those not familiar with backup systems, that's faster than you can blink your eyes. It only takes a split second for a power blip to take down your system or network infrastructure. Those microseconds could be the difference between an undetectable surge and a nightmare of costly downtime and system failures."

I start to relax the longer she talks. She's not saying anything revolutionary. In fact, I'm pretty sure even Chad is following this, and maybe that's where the genius lies. Unlike Myra who wowed with technical jargon, Natalie is giving the same information in a way even a guy who's obsessed with nuts and mermaids can understand. It's not what, but *how*, she's presenting that's giving her the edge. Myra dominated with confidence; Natalie is winning us over with what feels like a sincere desire to help. It's like she wants nothing more than to make sure Sandeke Telecom never has to suffer the pain of a power outage. She won't sleep until she can be sure their systems are secure.

By the time she gets to the details of their proposal, it's Eon Tech who's squirming in their seats. Natalie's solution is more targeted, more cost-effective, and more comprehensive than the generic proposal Myra presented. That's not surprising, considering neither company was given detailed design documents of the customer's systems to determine their specific needs. This means the TPG engineers did a much better job of extrapolating what they could from their research and general knowledge of the telecom industry. Judging by Denver Sandeke's approving nods and confirming responses, they guessed right on a lot of it.

I'm having a hard time keeping the grin from my face as Natalie finishes her presentation and opens the floor for questions. She nailed it. Against all odds, she's got this one in the bag.

"Yes, I have a question," Myra says.

My stomach drops as Natalie's pleasant smile wavers for a second. Where are the *emotional* backup systems when you need them?

"Yes?" Natalie says, voice even.

My attention snaps to Denver, but instead of preparing to intervene, he's settled back to enjoy the show. I already hated the guy, and now, I still hate the guy.

"You make some excellent points," Myra says. "But I'm struggling with one thing. Do you think it's a conflict of interest that you're having an affair with your counterpart at our firm? You know he was fired for his involvement with you, correct?"

Gasps litter the room. Is she for real? Rage burns inside me as she tosses me a triumphant look before focusing back on her competitor. Natalie has tensed amidst the shocked murmurs. It takes all of my willpower to remain seated and seethe quietly.

Denver looks damn near euphoric at this development.

"Wow," he says. "Interesting counterpoint."

"I knew it!" Lanette cries, an angry expression on her face. "You *were* into him for real!"

Natalie's boss looks ready to explode.

"I… It's not… I mean…" Natalie clearly has no idea what to say, and I'm furious that Myra threw mud like an immature preschooler. She knew she lost, so she resorted to playing dirty? This isn't even about Natalie. It's about me, and that's not okay.

"So, is it true?" Denver asks. "Do you have feelings for—what's his name —*Nathan*?" He knows my name. Asshole. "Do I need to disqualify both firms?"

"No!" they all cry in unison.

Natalie looks flustered as her gaze crosses between her boss and Denver.

"I just… I mean…"

"No," I say, pushing to my feet. "It's not a conflict of interest."

All eyes turn to me, including Natalie who looks crushed and on the verge of tears.

They want to play dirty? Fine. Let's play.

"The conflict of interest is that Eon Tech asked me to cheat and do something unethical, and I refused. The conflict of interest is that Myra is my ex-girlfriend and desperate to hurt me any way she can, including resorting to low, juvenile tactics. Mr. Sandeke, all of us in this room can see that, based on the two presentations, TPG is the better choice. I'm not saying that out of bitterness or bias. It's a simple fact. Personal feelings and vendettas have no bearing on the *facts* just presented by both firms."

My heart is racing beneath the collective attention. I hate drama. I hate being the reason for it even more. I sense their curiosity, their judgment. Most are hoping all of this is true so they have fun stories to gossip about later. The rest don't care if it's true as they plot their fun stories to gossip about later.

None of it matters. All that matters is making sure a beautiful person gets the respect and *contract* she deserves.

"Actually, I'm going to disagree with you on that point, Nathan," Denver says. "It seems that maybe *you* are the 'fact' that's most relevant to this conflict. Here we are discussing critical multimillion-dollar contracts, and the entire conversation has been dragged into the gutters because of a petty love triangle. I find it interesting that you're the focal point of an industry that kicked you out and forced you into a career as a stripper."

I flinch and stare at him in disbelief. How did he even know that? Who told him? Chad? Based on the baffled look on the younger guy's face, he didn't mean any harm if he did. Whatever. I couldn't care less at this point. The war is on.

Marcos bristles beside me, and I motion for him to stay out of it. There's nothing he can do to fix this, and throwing himself on his sword doesn't help anyone. (Even if Shakespeare would 100% approve.)

"And *I* find it interesting that you're the focal point of an industry that despises you and forced you to resort to personal attacks and name-calling like a five-year-old," I fire back.

A few snickers lift from around the room, including his estranged son, Martin. Denver reddens with fury.

"Brave words from a guy who makes a living taking off his clothes."

"*True* words, apparently. Thank you for supporting my point," I return, this time to a louder hum of amusement.

"Best. *Tele-Con.* Ever," someone says.

Marcos kicks my shoe, and I force away the rest of my venom. I want to tear this guy apart, but Marcos is right to stop me. What's my plan? Explode this into a straight-up brawl and get us all arrested?

"Technically, you shouldn't even be here," Denver says. "You're not employed by any of these firms, and therefore not invited. Unless you're here to perform for us today? Please, by all means."

He steps to the side and motions to the front of the room.

I glare at him, my fists clenched at my side. I don't give a fuck what he thinks, but I also don't know how to get out of this situation. What else is there to say? This petty skirmish is exactly what Denver wants. I'm only feeding his monster, not slaying it.

"Enough of this," Natalie barks.

The room stills.

"What are you doing?" her boss hisses, but Natalie waves her off.

"What's your choice, Mr. Sandeke?" she says, leveling a stare on him. "You said you'd be making the decision, so which is it? Eon Tech or TPG?"

My stomach drops at the serpentine expression slithering onto his face.

"Actually, I said I'd be *awarding the contract*. I never said it would be going to one of you."

Wait. Holy shit.

Natalie's gaze darkens, and I know she just came to the same conclusion. That slimy bastard!

"You were never even intending to choose one of us, were you? You already made your decision. This was all just a show, a sick game!"

"Natalie," Theresa snaps.

"What?!" she cries. "Am I wrong?"

"Sorry, Mr. Sandeke," Theresa rushes out, pushing up from her seat. "I assure you, Natalie will be removed from her position. We don't tolerate this kind of disrespect. If you allow us to—"

"No need. I'm quitting," Natalie says. "I'm better than this, and so is he!" She points at me.

"You fucked up when you let him go," she says to the Eon Tech employees. "He's one of the few things that's *right* about this industry."

She smacks the laptop shut, and we watch in stunned silence as she stalks to the door and slams it behind her.

Whoa.

What just happened?

"Like I said. Best. *Tele-Con*. Ever."

* * *

There's chaos, then there's a telecom conference that's gone awry. Within seconds of Natalie's departure, the room is buzzing with conversation and activity. A few attendees who probably didn't want to be here to begin with jump on the excuse to leave, but most cluster in small huddles around the room.

I ignore the cold looks generating from the Eon Tech and TPG groups, determined to go after Natalie. Except, I don't even get to my feet before Marcos is yanking me back by the shirt.

"Explain," he says.

"I will. Just let me find Natalie and make sure she's okay."

Marcos narrows his eyes at me, and I return a pleading look.

"Fine," he grunts. "But after that, we're having a long conversation."

"Deal."

I push up from my seat.

"Hang on," an unfamiliar voice says. I turn back to see Martin Sandeke also on his feet. "I'm coming with you."

Confused, I have no idea what to say as he starts toward the door. Even Marcos looks bewildered by his boss' strange announcement, but we're quickly following at his heels.

I'm glad I catch up in time to hear Denver say, "Of course you're teaming up with the strippers."

And Martin respond, "You're just jealous because not even a mortician would pay to see you naked."

Sadly, we don't get to enjoy Denver's flabbergasted reaction before we're pushing through the door into the quiet lobby of the conference wing.

"You see her?" Martin asks.

"No," I say. I pull out my phone and shoot her a text.

"Fuck. You have her number, I assume?" he asks me.

"Yeah. I just messaged her."

"Good."

Marcos is staring at his boss with a curious expression. I'm guessing this person isn't the type to be concerned about a stranger's mental health.

"Is it true? Did you two hook up? Is that why you were fired?" Martin asks.

"We hooked up," I say. "But that's not why I was fired."

He nods. "What about the rest? You a stripper now?"

Yeah, um, not sure how to answer that.

"Sort of? Does it matter?"

He shrugs. "Nah. That's just a really fun story." He turns to Marcos. "I have to run, but I want her. Whatever it takes."

Marcos looks even more confused. "Oh. Um…"

"That woman is a fucking badass, and I want her on my team. Make it happen."

And he's gone.

Marcos and I stare after him until he disappears down a neighboring corridor.

After a long pause, he clears his throat.

"Guess we'll be recruiting this afternoon," he mutters. "You hear from her yet?"

"No."

"Okay. Let me know when you do. For now, you're coming with me."

* * *

It's hard to have staring contests with two people at once, so I focus on my shoe instead. In my defense, the thing is making a very interesting pattern on the carpet of not-so-interesting patterns. I keep hoping Marcos and Nash will become just as interested in what my shoe is doing, but it doesn't seem to be going my way. Honestly, it's like they don't even care that I'm wearing shoes. Jerks.

"Talk," Marcos says. "You got *fired*? How could you not tell us that? Wait, where have you been staying? Were they still paying for your room?"

"You had enough going on. I didn't want to dump my shit on you. I'm fine."

They look pissed, so I return my attention to my much friendlier shoe.

"First of all, I guarantee you Nash didn't have anything going on," Marcos grumbles.

"Hey," Nash says, glaring at him.

"Am I wrong?"

"That's not the point."

Marcos rolls his eyes and focuses back on me. "Seriously, man. How could you think anything on our schedule is more important than you? That's huge, and I'm so sorry that happened. I can't believe you went through it alone. Are you okay?"

"I'm fine," I lie.

Even Nash rolls his eyes at that one. "Right. You're as fine as I am busy."

"Told you," Marcos quips.

Nash fires another glare at him.

Back to my shoe.

"Nate, come on. Level with us. You are not okay. You haven't been for a while. You think we haven't noticed? What is going on with you?"

I pull in a deep breath, not sure what choice I have. I don't want to unload on them, but they deserve the truth. I guess it's fine to tell them some of it now that I've solved the problem.

"Okay, fine. You're right. I haven't been good. These last few months have been rough, and..." I shake my head, trying to form the words. It's a little easier now that I've had the chance to sort through some of the mess with Natalie. Maybe there *is* something to talking about shit.

"My entire life I've overcome challenges," I continue. "But lately it feels like *I'm* the problem, and not just for my own life. My girlfriend didn't want me, my company didn't want me, *no one* fucking wants me. My entire existence has become nothing but an obstacle in other people's way. Even you guys. Admit it, it would be so much easier if I wasn't around."

"Nate—"

"Hold up—"

"No. You wanted the truth? It goes both ways, so let's just put it out there. I've looked out for you as best as I could since our Bellevue days. I love you like brothers and that will never change. You *are* my brothers, but it's time for me to accept the truth. You don't need me anymore. You both are successful and thriving, and I couldn't be happier about that. It's all I've ever wanted for you. But now, instead of holding you up, I'm just holding you back."

"What?!"

"You're not—"

"It's fine," I say, cutting them off again. "Really. I'm okay. The perfect solution fell into my lap yesterday. I was going to tell you this afternoon after the conference, but we might as well do it now. Just listen before you say anything."

I can't look at them as my chest constricts. Everything goes dark. This is supposed to be the triumphant reveal, the wave of the magical wand. So why does it hurt like hell?

But it doesn't matter. It's the right decision. It's the logical decision. I might need them, but they don't need me. The best thing—the *only* thing—is for me to let them go.

"What Denver said is true," I say quietly. "Roger offered me a job here at the resort, and I've decided to take it."

I swallow the block in my throat. The pain will fade. Once I settle into my new life, it won't hurt as much. I'll find something to love again. I have to believe that.

I force myself to continue. "I'll be heading back to New York tomorrow as planned to take care of a few things, but after that, I'll be moving down here to live with Roger and the guys. Hopefully, by the end of next week, you two will be free to move in with your girlfriends or whatever you want. You won't have to worry about what to do with me anymore. I'll be out of your way."

I'm not sure what to do as they stare at me in stunned silence. I can't tell what they're thinking. I'm not even sure what I was expecting. Relief maybe? Excitement for me and my new chapter? Not silence, though. I guess that was a lot to process at once. They'll need time to adjust as well.

I dig my fists into the comforter beneath me and study the absent movement of my shoe again.

It's okay.

I'm doing the right thing.

This is how it has to be.

"Hell no you're not," Marcos snaps.

I glance up in surprise. Wow, I've never seen him so pissed.

"Are you fucking serious?" Nash echoes.

My gaze crosses to him. I've never seen him so *anything*.

"You want to mess around with performing again, fine," Marcos spits out. "But you're not throwing away everything you care about to do it."

"I know, but—"

"No! You listen for once. Everything you just said is straight-up bullshit. You are *not* a burden. You are *not* 'in the way.' You are our brother, more important than anything, and I'll be damned if I'm letting you abandon us for some dude named Roger you met five minutes ago."

"Technically, it was three years ago," I mumble. "Miami, remember?"

He looks ready to punch me. He doesn't and takes a deep breath.

"You're going through hell," he continues in a softer tone. "You were already hurting and you got a shit-ton more dropped on you this week. We will sort through that, along with all the other stuff that's clearly been going on with you, but we're doing it in our shitty little apartment in Manhattan. We're doing it *together* like we've done since we were kids. Like we will always do until the day we die."

Speechless, I blink at him through the pound of my tattered heart. It's so full and broken at the same time. None of this makes sense. He can't mean that. They must not understand. Everything he's saying...

"But if I'm gone, you can move in with Eva and Paige and—"

Marcos holds up his hand. "I'm gonna stop you right there. I don't even want to know how long you've been marinating in that bullshit. Eva and I have no intention of moving in together any time soon. She loves her cat, and I'd literally die if I had to live with it. Until we figure that out, there's no long-term sleepovers happening."

"And Paige would never leave her brother," Nash says. "Not until he's got his own life sorted out. Besides, it makes no sense for me to have my own place when I'm bouncing around from city to city. I'm in LA as much as New York now. Why the hell would I pay for an apartment I'd never use?"

Oh. I hadn't thought of that. Either of those things, really. What else has my messed-up brain warped and overlooked in its bid to tear me down?

Marcos drops to the bed beside me. I'm prepared for an actual punch this time, but he pulls me in for a hug instead. Not even a half-assed symbolic one, but the real kind. The kind brothers exchange when one of their worlds implodes and their lives fall apart. I close my eyes, trying to breathe through the weight on my chest.

"We're not doing life without you," he says, tightening his hold. "We're fucking not, so call this Roger whoever and tell him you quit."

"I…" Don't know what to say. I'm shaking with emotion when he pulls back and searches my eyes. God, he's serious. He really cares about me that much. *Wants* me that much.

"Call him," he says in a firm voice. "You're going home with us, Nate. Where you belong."

"Oh, and call your other bosses and tell them to go fuck themselves," Nash adds.

I won't be doing that one.

"Better yet, I will."

Marcos smacks the phone out of his hand.

"Relax," he mutters to Nash.

Pretty sure Nash didn't have the numbers for my bosses anyway, except maybe Myra. Oh. Yeah. That would have been the call.

"Our point is, your brain is lying to you, dude," Marcos says, focusing back on me. "Just like it lies to me and to Nash and to everyone else at some point in their lives. Our brains lie all the time, and that's where the rest of us come in. You've held us up and pushed us forward so many times throughout our lives. Do you honestly think we're not jumping at the chance to do the same for you? We will always want to fight your battles with you. We will always want you around. Not out of guilt or obligation, but because we love you."

"Like, a disgusting amount," Nash grunts.

I can't help but smile. He really does seem disgusted by how much he loves me.

"The whole point of friendship and community is to fill in the gaps," Marcos says. "We're not supposed to do life alone, and the three of us chose each other to make sure we didn't have to."

Nash scoops my phone off the bed and flips it toward me. "Call Roger. Right here, right now, so we know you did it."

I take a deep breath. "It'll break his heart."

Marcos crosses his arms with a hard look. "It'll be a lot easier for him to replace you as a stripper than for us to replace you as a brother. Call him."

* * *

Roger *was* devastated, but I'm pretty sure the other guys were fine with it since I'd done nothing but challenge their status quo for the twelve seconds we worked together. I'm positive I heard one of them say "an *Outer Space Night* was a stupid idea, anyway."

I actually agree with that.

I'm way more concerned about Natalie as I wait for her in front of her room. In the selfish mist of my own drama, I'd forgotten she also must be going through hell after what happened. I don't like that she hasn't responded to my text. When she didn't answer my knock on her door either, I sank to the floor and leaned against it to wait. She must be wandering the resort to hide, an activity I know well.

I still have trouble believing what Marcos said. How can they care about me so much? I'm a failure on every level by objective definitions. It doesn't seem up for debate, but he thinks there's more going on with my head, so I'm not sure of anything anymore. He said we'll be finding a good therapist when we get back to New York, and maybe he's right. Natalie certainly agrees with him. What could it hurt to talk to someone and try to sort the lies from the truth? The fact that I can't accept what's right in front of me or trust any of my own thoughts and judgment means something isn't right.

I've only waited a few minutes before I sense Natalie turn the corner. It's a feeling more than anything. A fresh breeze for my soul.

She stops abruptly, her pretty eyes widening when she sees me.

"You didn't answer my text," I say, pushing to my feet.

She averts her gaze. "I know. Sorry. I just… needed some time. How long have you been waiting here?"

"Three hours."

"What?! Why the heck would you… Wait. The seminar wasn't even that long ago."

I shrug with a grin. "Okay, maybe I rounded up to make you feel bad. Did it work?"

"No." But her lips move in the slightest twist.

I'll take that as a win.

I step aside so she can insert her keycard and wait as she enters. When I don't follow, she turns back and lifts a brow.

"You coming in?" she asks.

"Depends. Am I invited?"

She shrugs. "Sure. Why not? We're both dead now, right? Shakespeare won."

I let the door clatter shut behind me as she drops her purse on the floor.

"I had to go back for it," she mumbles. "Not the laptop. That's TPG property."

"Hey, Natalie?"

Before she can respond, I move in and wrap my arms around her. After a few tense seconds, her rigid frame relaxes against me.

"That sucked," she breathes out in a shaky voice.

"Yeah. It was pretty brutal."

I kiss her hair and tighten my hold. The wet heat of her tears seeps into my shirt, and I hold tighter as her soft hiccups vibrate against my chest.

"I blew it," she whispers. "All of it was for nothing."

I snort a laugh. Sorry, can't help it.

"What's so funny?" she asks.

"You are. You blew it? Not even close. Pretty sure what you did was the opposite of 'blowing it.' Unless you count the fact that you kicked ass so hard, you *blew* up the industry."

"What are you talking about?"

She pulls back and swats at her cheeks.

"Okay, well, after we finish here, I'm supposed to set up a meeting with you and Martin Sandeke."

"The head of SAT Systems? Denver's son?"

"Yeah, but I wouldn't call him that if I were you. Pretty sure that's the worst insult you could pay him."

"Why does he want to talk to me?"

"Because he wants to hire you."

"No way. For *what*?"

I shrug. "From what I gathered, it appears you will be a Senior Fucking Badass."

She rolls her eyes. "Hilarious."

"No. Actually, I'm serious. He followed you out and was pissed he missed you."

Her eyes go wide as my words register. "Wait. He was there this morning? He saw the whole thing?"

"Yep. And he was so impressed he told Marcos to do whatever it takes to lock you down. And yes, he called you a 'fucking badass.' Maybe don't put that on your resume."

Her grin should be on there, though. Her eyes too. Her hair, her brain, her gorgeous heart.

"Told you. You're incredible," I say.

"Nate..." She falls back into my arms, but my smile fades when I feel the jerk of tears again.

"You okay? What is it?"

She shakes her head.

"I..."

She burrows into my chest, clinging hard.

"Nat, talk to me. What's going on?"

"I don't want to let you go," she whispers. She looks up, searching my face. "I *can't* let you go. I know you don't want to do the long-distance thing, but I'm not ready to give up. Maybe it doesn't make sense. Maybe it's a terrible plan, but I want you in it."

She cuddles close again, and I rest my lips against her hair.

"So I've been thinking about it too," I say. "I guess Greenwich Village isn't *that* far from the Lower East Side."

She stiffens. "What are you talking about?"

"I mean, it's a decent walk, but barely anything by subway, right?"

"Wait. Are you saying...? I thought..."

I crack a smile.

"But... What about Roger?!"

I clear my throat. "Yeah, uh, about that. My roommates refused to sign off on that transfer, so they're making me go back to New York. It's too bad because I was really looking forward to the lemur thong."

She squints at me. "What now?"

"It's exactly what it sounds like. The point is, I'm going back to New York. I have no plan, no prospects, and no idea what I'll be doing there, but weirdly, I'll be returning in a better place than when I left."

"Nate! Ahh!"

She squeals and throws her arms around my neck.

Laughing, I hug her to me. "Kind of funny that we lived minutes away but it took a trip across the country to find each other."

"It's not funny. It's serendipitous, and I, for one, am grateful your life blew up."

My smile fades at the strange comment. What? She can't mean that.

She reaches up and tugs the ends of my hair while she thinks.

"I know this week has been really hard for you. It's been hard for both of us. It hurt so much to see you in pain, but I won't lie and say I'm not grateful for every shitty thing that happened."

"I don't… How can you say that?"

Her expression softens as she studies me. "Don't you see what also happened this week? We arrived on Sunday with our lives so figured out, we almost missed the point of the journey. We almost missed *each other*."

"We almost missed this connection," I say quietly.

She nods with a wistful expression, and as twisted as it sounds, maybe she's right.

I was so caught up in what I lost, I couldn't see what I'd found. I almost left here not knowing this amazing person existed. We would have gone back to New York on the same flight, still being strangers, still chasing after a HEA that doesn't exist.

That would have been the real tragic ending to this star-crossed love story.

And maybe that's the point. Maybe life is about the journey, not the destination. It's about the people you can't live without who make it worth living in the first place. Marcos, Nash, Natalie… *They* are my plan. My present and my future. Maybe it's okay to wander, as long as we're doing it together.

Natalie pulls my head down for a gentle kiss I feel in the recesses of my soul. A kiss that only could have happened in the vacuum of an exploded life.

"So yes. I'm *grateful* Myra dumped you," she says, searching my eyes. "I'm *grateful* the assholes at your company demoted you and forced you into a job you hated. I'm so incredibly grateful your path got knocked off course, Nathan Hanover, because it placed you firmly into mine."

18—SATURDAY 8:48 AM

NATALIE

The elevator is already packed with bodies and luggage when it stops at the fifth floor. A silent groan lifts from the existing crowd as two men make the inexplicable decision to force their way inside anyway. Nate and I get shoved further into the corner, and I manage deep breaths to keep my claustrophobia under control. Why wouldn't they wait for the next car?

"Well, isn't this an excellent example *Collective Encroachment*?" a familiar voice booms out.

Oh.

That's why.

Nate shoots me a look, and I bite back a smile.

"It sure is, sir. I'll get the crystals ready."

They laugh.

Nate furrows his brow.

I know from experience the unknown story behind those enigmatic wheat crystals keeps him up at night. If we can convince a passenger to switch seats so we're together on the flight back to JFK, maybe we can debrief and sort through it.

Wait. What if that passenger is Reedweather or Chad? Or Marcos or his girlfriend? Or… Geez. I'll probably know half the travelers on the plane at this point. It's amazing how different my return trip to New York will be than the trip here.

I slip my hand in Nate's and give it a reassuring tug.

"How was your first *Tele-Con*, my boy?" Reedweather says.

"Fantastic!" Chad replies. "I learned so much, sir. Did you know the purpose of fountains is to recycle shower water?"

No way that's true.

"Sure did, son. Most are also certified organic."

Definitely not true.

"That's so cool. They probably use them to water plants and stuff. That's why you usually see buckets nearby."

Nope. I feel Nate's irritation beside me. It's probably killing him to keep quiet. I'm glad he does, though, because this is amazing.

"I'm sad we didn't get to spend more time together, though," Chad sighs out.

"Ah. 'Tis regrettable, indeed. I'm sure you can understand the challenges of such a hectic week," Reedweather says with an admirable level of regret.

"Totally. I know how busy you were," Chad replies. "It's too bad you weren't able to make any of the extra seminars, company dinners, events, or team-building excursions. Maybe next year!"

"Yes, yes, perhaps. One must be covetous of one's time, my dear boy. *Antecedental Scheduling* they call it. You will develop this skill in time with some practice. It's about understanding what's important and knowing when to say *no*."

Well, from what Nate and I gathered this week, it's not so much about *when* to say no, as much as always saying no so you can watch TV and get massages.

"Are we still on for pre-flight cocktails?" Chad asks.

"Absolutely, son."

And drink scotch.

EPILOGUE

NATE

I massage my temples, grateful this isn't a video call. Arguing audibly with Roger about the feasibility of purchasing a company horse is bad enough. If I had to watch it too?

"But I just saw the bank balance. We have, like, five million dollars," Roger whines.

"No, you have fifty thousand dollars."

Zeroes can be very important. We've been working on that. We've been working on a lot of things since Roger hired me as a consultant to help him grow and manage his business.

"Fine, that's still enough for a horse."

"First of all, just because you *can* purchase something, doesn't mean you should. Second, remember what we talked about. That account is your operating account. That's the money you need to run your business. Capital purchases like a… horse… have to be considered carefully, particularly relative to ROI and cashflow. You have three large expenses coming up: your quarterly income tax prepayments, payroll, and that large bill from Dangerous Dungeons and Designs for the new Zoolicious costumes."

I've won a lot of arguments with Roger over the last couple of months, but not that one.

"But you said we should create a memorable experience for the audience," he says.

"I said nothing about a horse."

"You said lots of stuff about investments."

"A horse is not an investment."

"It is if you breed it."

Oh my god.

I blow out a breath. "Roger, I'm going to strongly advise against this. Not only are the ethics of using a horse for—*whatever it is you're planning to use it for*—questionable, it's a huge risk and liability for literally no reward."

"But we already have a name picked out."

"Can you use the name for something else? Didn't Remy just bring home that giant stuffed elephant his ex-boyfriend left him when they split? That should have a new name, right?"

He quiets. *Please be considering it.*

As his business consultant, I can't force him not to do something stupid. I *would* be responsible for cleaning up the mess when he did it, though.

"What about a pony?" he says finally.

I close my eyes and pull in a deep breath. "Okay, look. You're still coming up here to look at the club and meet with Kyle in a couple weeks, right?"

He better be because I've got all the contracts and paperwork ready to officially open a Stripply Business School of Sexy here in New York. I even found the perfect venue: a club in Midtown East owned by Eva's ex-stepbrother. I loved the concept so much that I worked out a deal with Roger to open and operate the first franchise here in Manhattan.

"Yeah, I'll be there," he sighs out.

"Okay, great. So how about we discuss your idea in person when you're here? We can talk through your objectives, look at the numbers, and find a solution that we both like. Sound good?"

"Fine," he huffs out. Then, "What's the point of even owning a business if you can't buy a horse for it?" he mumbles to himself.

I shake my head and check the time. Shit, it's later than I thought. "Look, I have to go. Remember to log into the accounting site I sent you and get familiar with it. You need to be able to do all of this stuff too, okay? At the very least, you need to understand what I'm doing so you can manage the business yourself."

"Wait. Why? Where are you going?" he asks, panic in his voice.

"Nowhere, but my job isn't just to run things for you. I want to teach you how to run this business yourself. That's the long-term goal. We'll review the chart of accounts together later this week. Don't worry about the reports section for now."

Explaining a P&L and balance sheet is an entire day in itself. I just need him to learn how to enter transactions in a way that doesn't involve shoving receipts in a tissue box. (He couldn't even use a shoebox like everyone else who doesn't know what they're doing.)

"Oh wait! One more thing," Roger says. "My friend Darius wants to start a business. I gave him your number."

"Oh yeah? That's great. What kind of business?"

"I'm not sure. He's a chef, so maybe, write a cookbook?"

Write a cookbook?

"Or start a restaurant. Could be that too."

Probably that.

"Sounds good. Tell him to call me, and I'll see how I can help."

"Awesome-sauce. You're the best. I told him that, too. I said, 'I got a guy. He's the best.'"

"I appreciate it. Good talking to you, Roger."

"Well, I'll let you go. Love you."

"Please stop saying that. Have a good night, Roger."

I hang up and stare at Natalie's gorgeous smile on my lock screen as I breathe a sigh of relief. I love the challenge of working with Roger and growing his business, but he's... a lot. Of all my clients, he's definitely the most, shall we say, high maintenance? He also pays me well to do what I love, so it works out for both of us.

In fact, my new business venture is going well all around. I never intended to start my own consulting firm. It just kind of happened. Shortly after I began helping Roger with his ventures, Eva and Paige asked for assistance getting their Evolve Agency up and running. Both women are incredibly skilled in advertising and marketing, but don't have much experience setting up the administrative backbone of a company. I've learned over the last few months that there are a lot of passionate, capable entrepreneurs who start a business in their area of expertise, only to learn the mechanics of actually running it is more complicated than they thought—especially as they grow and face additional challenges. Just because you make a fantastic Bundt cake, doesn't mean you're an expert at monetizing it and turning it into a thriving Bundt cake empire.

That's where I come in. What started as a few hourly consulting fees has become several monthly retainers and a legit full-time job. I can barely keep up with the clients I already have, and it seems like new ones are being referred to me every week.

And I love it. Each new client is a new challenge and a new problem I get to solve. I'm learning so much about a variety of fields and industries. But while their needs and goals may be unique, all of them require intimate knowledge of the same basic financial and organizational principles I know and love. Even better, as a consultant, I get to make my own hours, decisions, and recommendations. I can follow my heart and conscience and say *hell no,* if someone asks me to do something I'm not comfortable with. Best of all, I get to do it from my very own shitty apartment I share with my two best friends.

"Oh good, you're off the phone," Natalie says, poking her head in my room.

Did I mention my girlfriend lives just a few blocks away? She's also "blowing up" the sales department at SAT Systems, just like we knew she would. Apparently, Martin likes what she's done with the Manhattan office so much, he's planning to fly her to the other branch locations to shake things up across the board. Her official title is Director of Business Development but Marcos says their boss refers to her as the Director of Ass-Kicking. I won't sleep soundly until she gets that on a business card.

"Yeah, sorry. That took longer than I thought. Roger wants to buy a horse."

She tilts her head. "Is that... I don't... What does that mean?"

"It means he wants to buy a horse."

"An actual horse? Like, as a pet?"

"Yes. A *gray* horse, to be specific."

"He lives in a hotel."

"Correct."

She stares at me, and I shrug.

"Right. Well, when you're done... horse shopping... we need to go if we're going to get to Hoboken in time for Chad's thing. I still don't understand what it is."

"It's better that way, trust me."

I close my laptop and grab my coat from the back of the chair.

"Marcos is coming too, right?" I ask.

"Yeah. They're besties, remember? He's already in the living room."

"What about Nash?"

"No. He has... a... thing. He and Paige will meet us at the house later."

Nash always "has a thing" when he doesn't want to do something.

To be fair, none of us wants to do this, but Chad has been working up the courage to approach Brooke since the telecom conference three months ago. He texted us last week to say he's finally going to do it. Tonight. At 6:55.

In Hoboken. Grr. At least it's kind of on the way.

Natalie pulls me in for a kiss, which quickly escalates into more. I groan and sink my fingers into her hair to steal as much as possible. We've been so busy with life that our together time has been scarce and, according to my body, very insufficient. We were supposed to have a date night yesterday, but Marcos kept her late at the office, and I had to leave for my counseling session when she finally got out. Marcos received a very nasty look from me when I got back.

"Please tell me we'll have time alone this weekend," I say at her ear.

The slow, suggestive slide of her palm over my ass is a good sign. "Yes. I told the others we can do group stuff tomorrow. Tonight is couples only. And I even have a surprise for you."

"Really…" I draw out. "What kind of surprise?"

"It will be worth the wait," she says, adding a firm squeeze.

Hell. Yes.

With another quick kiss, she takes my hand and drags me down the hall toward our looming Nut Romance Adventure.

* * *

"You're gonna do great," I tell Chad.

He glances to his left. I'm assuming in the direction of the nut stand? I haven't seen it yet because he said to meet him by the juice stand, not to be confused with the *frozen* juice stand which is a different stand. To his credit, there are way more stands than I thought once you pay attention. Maybe stand-stripping really should be a thing.

"What if her contact lens gets messed up right as I'm about to do the hard part? Or what if she has a customer and can't watch?"

"Um, well… I'd probably only worry about the second scenario. If she's busy, just stand at a respectful distance and wait until she's not. Worst case, you do it *after* she shuts down for the night, not right before."

"But… ah!" He shakes out his arms and legs. "Guess what. I have a surprise."

Uh-oh.

"What kind of surprise?" I say hesitantly.

"Can't tell you. Okay, fine. I drew something on my shirt."

That's not good.

"I see. And, uh, what did you draw?"

I really don't want to go to prison today.

"It's a surprise!"

I press my lips together. "Are you sure about this? Maybe it's enough without 'the surprise.'"

"You said to go big or go home, right?"

"I didn't say that."

There's no way I said that to a person who thinks life-sized Mer-Nuts are an essential marketing strategy. In some cases, "going home" is the better choice.

"Hmm... Maybe it was Mr. Reedweather. Either way, aim for the stars, right?"

"Chad, just—"

"Relax, Nathan. It's gonna be great. And believe me, I'll be giving you all the credit."

"You don't have to do that."

Please don't do that.

"Thanks for being here," he continues. "I couldn't have done it without you. If Brooke and I end up having a kid one day, I'm making its middle name Nathan."

"Oh. You *really* don't have to do that."

"No, I will! You'd be the reason we even had a kid. We have to honor you. That's the blood code."

I blink at him. "Right, well, how about we discuss that part later? For now, you need to focus."

"Yes!"

"Oh, hey." I tug an imaginary necklace at my collar, and he cringes.

"Shit! It's good you're here. That would have been embarrassing." He removes the necklace and holds it out to me.

"Why don't you just put it in your pocket? That way you don't have to find me to get it back."

"No, no. I want you to have it."

He takes my hand and drops the gold chain into my palm. With a grave look, he closes my fingers around it and squeezes tight.

"You really don't—"

"No, Nathan. This is yours," he says in a low voice. "I will never forget what you've done for me. Never. Blood brothers."

I taught you to take your shirt off while walking.

He gives me a hard look. "I won't take no for an answer."

"Okay. Well, thanks," I say, holding up my closed fist before shoving the necklace in my pocket. I'll give it back another time. "I'm gonna join the others now. Just remember to relax and have fun."

He takes a deep breath. "I'll do my best. If I go down, you jump in and take over, okay?"

"No, I won't be doing that, but you'll be fine. You got this."

I slap his arm and leave before he can stop me again. Really, I just want to get this over with so we can continue our journey to Stone Harbor for a couples weekend getaway. Eva is already there, having opted to stock the house we rented, rather than watch Chad's performance. She called it a conflict of interest since they're technically coworkers. None of us challenged her convenient crisis of conscience. Not even her boyfriend who manages a rival firm.

Marcos and Natalie are seated on a bench within view of the nut stand, and I drop down beside Natalie.

"Is he ready?" she asks.

"I honestly can't tell. But he gave me this."

I open my hand, and Marcos snickers.

"Wow. You want me to help you put it on?" he asks. "Does it have a half-heart pendant for BFFs?"

"Shut up," I mumble, shoving it back in my pocket.

"Hey, look," Natalie says, bumping my arm.

I follow her gaze, and sure enough, Chad's secret crush comes into view. It looks like she's starting to pack up the vast quantity of nut containers.

"She's really cute," Natalie whispers. "Go Chad."

She is cute, and when we see Chad approach in his green polo and easy zipper pants, my pulse picks up. Why am I so nervous for him? It's not like there's any hope this goes well.

"Come on, man. You got this," I say under my breath.

I sense my companions' amusement beside me, but whatever. My knee bounces, and Natalie reaches over to settle her hand on my leg.

"He's gonna do great," she says.

I'm not even sure what the "great" version of this is.

I nod and focus back on the action. Too late to go back now.

Chad starts stretching. Full-on about-to-run-a-marathon body stretching. What the heck is he doing?

Brooke notices the movement and stares at him with a confused look. Pretty sure everyone in a fifty-foot radius is doing that now.

He finishes, and she stiffens as her attention locks on the newly limber potential stalker.

Oh no. What if…? I just assumed they knew each other and this was a fun little gesture. If this is his first approach to this woman…

Shit.

But before I can intervene, Chad begins "the strut." And he's doing it with his "sexy face."

"Nooo," I groan, running a hand through my hair. "What are you doing?" I mutter to myself.

"Is he okay?" Natalie whispers. "What's wrong with his face?"

I shake my head.

Maybe Brooke will be distracted by the strange walk he's suddenly adopted. He stops abruptly. Spins. Touches the ground. Spins. And steps back. She's definitely going to be distracted by that.

Everyone in the atrium is riveted to the scene as he grips the hem of his shirt and lifts, stopping somewhere between three and six inches.

Shit shit shit. She's gonna call the cops.

I can't look and silently groan into my hands at my miscalculation. Why didn't I ask more questions?!

Natalie kicks my shoe, forcing me back to the action. I thought she loved me.

But I'm shocked to see not a look of horror on Brooke's face, but shy amusement. She even releases a distinct giggle that actually makes the moment cute in a reality TV trainwreck kind of way. Maybe she does know him? *Please let her know him.* Would I be prosecuted as an accomplice if Chad gets arrested?

Brooke's reaction must give him more confidence because the killer clown grin breaks out on his face as he takes another few steps. Then stops. Then tries to shrug out of his shirt. But his polo *does* have buttons like I warned, and he didn't unbutton them. He tugs hard, twisting and jerking until at least one snaps off and he's able to clear the way for his head. Told you.

With the offending shirt in one hand, he flattens out his hair with the other. It's then that I realize the random black lines etched onto his undershirt are actually letters. This must be "the surprise."

He yanks the bottom of the undershirt to flatten out the writing to make it readable. Brooke leans forward and squints.

We do the same and probably look as confused as she does when we make out the word, *"Brooke."*

So the surprise was writing her name. Interesting approach.

"Brooke!" he belts out, then bows.

She bites her lip.

"Though I'm just a lowly walnut.
And you're an angelic cashew.
Would you please do me the honor,
Of letting me finally date you?"

Also interesting that the *poem* wasn't "the surprise."

"Aww," Natalie whispers. "This is actually kind of sweet. A little creepy, but also sweet."

Chad stands at attention, eyes bulging with his (also creepy) grin frozen on the lower half of his face.

Brooke covers hers with her hands and giggles again.

Please say yes. Please say yes.

"Um…" She peeks through her fingers. "Okay, sure. You want to get some coffee when I'm done packing up?"

The entire atrium bursts into cheers and applause as Chad yelps, "Woohoo!" and does a jumping half-spin in the air. What did we say about playing it cool?

He shoots me two thumbs up, and I return a congratulatory nod.

Well, that could have gone way worse. Actually, that might have been the best case scenario.

"Thank god," Marcos mumbles. "Can we go now?"

After Chad's earlier display, I'm a little skeptical of "surprises," but I try to keep an open mind as my girlfriend prepares hers in the bathroom attached to our bedroom. Marcos and Eva are enjoying their own romantic evening together in another part of the rented house.

"You ready?" Natalie calls through a crack in the door.

"Yep," I reply from the bed where she told me to wait. I'm hoping this "surprise" involves lingerie or… Actually, I'll take anything that isn't my name scribbled on her shirt.

She steps out of the bathroom, and whoa.

I will *definitely* take that.

She looks incredible in a silk robe and headband with black cat ears. Her long, blond hair hangs in soft waves I can't wait to run my fingers through. When she grips the edge of the door frame above her head, the robe falls open to reveal a hint of the skimpy outfit underneath. Her expression alone has me heating up as she pauses in that position like she's expecting to be admired.

Mission accomplished. Now *that's* a sexy face. Chad should take note. Wait, no. I don't want Chad seeing my girlfriend like this.

Smoldering gaze locked on me, she pushes away from the doorframe and sashays toward me with a runway-ready strut.

"First step: make them want it," she says in a low, sultry tone.

Gripping the edges of her robe, she yanks it open and flashes just enough skin to get my heart rate up before closing it again.

"Next step. Shoulder." She tugs the robe to show off her right shoulder, totally bare except for a thin strap. "Other shoulder."

Now I see both arms exposed with the robe still frustratingly intact over everything else.

I. Want. It. Off!

My blood is pounding. My dick is already two steps ahead.

Until…

Wait a second.

Her swagger.

Her tone.

Her instructions.

"Is this a stripping lesson?" I laugh out.

She breaks character with a quick grin before returning to a stern demeanor.

"Silence. Your job is to watch and learn," she commands.

As Roger would say, *Abso-fucking-lutely.*

Her gaze sinks to my mouth, then lands back on my eyes.

Damn. How is she so good at this?

"Next step."

She lets the robe drop, and my mouth goes dry. The green silk puddles around her feet as she shows off a barely there costume that displays every mouth-watering line and curve of her form. She's just started her seduction, and I'm already at her mercy. How long is this lesson? My entire body is throbbing.

Hang on. Is that a tail?

She turns and juts her amazing ass in my direction, swaying it in slow, seductive arcs.

The tail itself is long and striped, though. Nothing like a cat tail. It's some other animal, and I realize the cat ears on her head are something else as well. They almost look like… No. Can't be.

I snort a laugh, and she turns to face me again. This time, the sexy act is gone, replaced by a wry smile that is just as much of a turn on.

"Are you…? Am I being seduced by a lemur?"

She grins as she closes the distance between us and sinks onto my lap. She starts unbuttoning my shirt, and I run my hands along the smooth skin of her thighs toward her sexy… tail.

"I know how much you love lemurs," she murmurs against my lips. "Surprise, baby."

She shoves the shirt over my shoulders, and I shrug out of it. Her palms slide up my chest and curve around the back of my neck to draw me in.

Our lips crash together, searching and desperate. Her hips drive against my straining zipper as she pulses on my lap. A groan escapes me as she opens the button on my pants and reaches in.

"I looked it up," she murmurs against my lips. One hand continues to rub and tease. The other grips the back of my neck to drag me in for a hard kiss.

"Looked what up?" I say, inhaling sharply when she adjusts to sink onto me.

Holy. Zoologists. Damn, that feels good.

"Lemurs. Know what I learned?"

She begins a slow deep roll of her hips. I lean back to brace my arms against the bed. My head tips up, and I close my eyes as waves of fire surge through me with every buck of her hips. I push up to match her rhythm, burning with each explosive thrust.

She clamps her hands on my shoulders for more leverage.

Oh shit.

Harder. Faster. Deeper. I'm already so far gone. It takes almost nothing for her to own me now. She moans and launches into a more frenzied pace. Her fingers sink into my shoulders. So close. Just…

Her body tenses. Her entire being becomes an artistic representation of her climax. So beautiful. I tilt my head back and let myself follow shortly after. Worth the wait? Hell. Yes.

This woman is seriously incredible. How do I deserve her?

Her breathing is shallow as she runs her hands over my shoulders.

"What did you learn?" I rasp out, shuddering through the aftershocks of my own release.

She leans in and presses her lips to my neck, her words vibrating over my skin. "Based on the top searches, a shocking number of people think lemurs are cats and-or lay eggs."

I tilt my head front to stare at her. She maintains an even expression for two seconds before freeing an adorable grin.

I burst out laughing and rest my forehead on her shoulder.

"Yeah?" I say, kissing her collarbone.

"People also seem to really want them as pets. What's the thought process there?"

I can't stop another laugh.

"God, I love you," I mumble against her.

She forces my head up and cups my face with a serious expression.

"Even more than lemurs?" she asks, searching my eyes.

"That's not fair," I reply with a frown.

She sighs. "Damn. Maybe one day."

ABOUT THE AUTHOR

Thank you for taking this journey with me. I would love to hear from you! For updates, reveals, and more subscribe to my newsletter and join my fun, laidback reader group on Facebook: Aly's Breakfast Club.

You can also follow Aly's original music wherever you stream music:
Spotify
Apple Music
Amazon Music

Find Aly here:
Facebook Reader Group – Aly's Breakfast Club
Newsletter
BookBub
Spotify
Apple Music
Facebook Page – Author Aly Stiles
Goodreads
Website
Instagram
YouTube
Blogger sign-up for notifications about future releases, ARC reviews, and cover reveals
Pinterest

Aly Stiles
PO Box 577
Trexlertown, PA 18087-0577

Find Smartypants Romance online:

Website: www.smartypantsromance.com

Facebook: https://www.facebook.com/smartypantsromance

Twitter: @smartypantsrom

Instagram: @smartypantsromance

Newsletter: https://smartypantsromance.com/newsletter/

PARANORMAL/SUSPENSE

GIFTED (Gifted, Vol 1)

CURSED (Gifted, Vol 2)

SÖREN (Gifted, Vol 3)

HAUNTED MELODY

TRAITOR

ALSO BY SMARTYPANTS ROMANCE

<u>Green Valley Chronicles</u>

<u>The Love at First Sight Series</u>

<u>Baking Me Crazy by Karla Sorensen (#1)</u>

<u>Batter of Wits by Karla Sorensen (#2)</u>

<u>Steal My Magnolia by Karla Sorensen (#3)</u>

<u>Worth the Wait by Karla Sorensen (#4)</u>

<u>Fighting For Love Series</u>

<u>Stud Muffin by Jiffy Kate (#1)</u>

<u>Beef Cake by Jiffy Kate (#2)</u>

<u>Eye Candy by Jiffy Kate (#3)</u>

<u>Knock Out by Jiffy Kate (#4)</u>

<u>The Donner Bakery Series</u>

<u>No Whisk, No Reward by Ellie Kay (#1)</u>

<u>Dough You Love Me? By Stacy Travis (#2)</u>

<u>Tough Cookie by Talia Hunter (#3)</u>

<u>The Green Valley Library Series</u>

<u>Love in Due Time by L.B. Dunbar (#1)</u>

<u>Crime and Periodicals by Nora Everly (#2)</u>

<u>Prose Before Bros by Cathy Yardley (#3)</u>

<u>Shelf Awareness by Katie Ashley (#4)</u>

<u>Carpentry and Cocktails by Nora Everly (#5)</u>

<u>Love in Deed by L.B. Dunbar (#6)</u>

Dewey Belong Together by Ann Whynot (#7)

Hotshot and Hospitality by Nora Everly (#8)

Love in a Pickle by L.B. Dunbar (#9)

Code of Matrimony by April White (#2.5)

Code of Ethics by April White (#3)

Cipher Office Series

Weight Expectations by M.E. Carter (#1)

Sticking to the Script by Stella Weaver (#2)

Cutie and the Beast by M.E. Carter (#3)

Weights of Wrath by M.E. Carter (#4)

Common Threads Series

Mad About Ewe by Susannah Nix (#1)

Give Love a Chai by Nanxi Wen (#2)

Key Change by Heidi Hutchinson (#3)

Not Since Ewe by Susannah Nix (#4)

Lost Track by Heidi Hutchinson (#5)

Educated Romance

Work For It Series

Street Smart by Aly Stiles (#1)

Heart Smart by Emma Lee Jayne (#2)

Book Smart by Amanda Pennington (#3)

Smart Mouth by Emma Lee Jayne (#4)

Play Smart by Aly Stiles (#5)

Look Smart by Aly Stiles (#6)

Smart Move by Amanda Pennington (#7)

Lessons Learned Series

Under Pressure by Allie Winters (#1)

Not Fooling Anyone by Allie Winters (#2)

Can't Fight It by Allie Winters (#3)

The Vinyl Frontier by Lola West (#4)

Out of this World